CO[illegible]ME ARTHUR

THE TRUE STORY OF THE ANTI-FASCIST SPY WHO IDENTIFIED THE LONDON NAILBOMBER

NICK LOWLES

PARTISAN BOOKS

www.partisanbooks.com

This is a Partisan Books publication, first published in the UK in 2021

ISBN 978-1-9196065-0-7

Edited by Nick Ryan

PARTISAN BOOKS

www.partisanbooks.com

CONTENTS

ACKNOWLEDGEMENTS

For Arthur, a man of great humility and courage. You join an illustrious group of anti-fascist moles inside far-right groups in Britain. We salute you.

Nick Lowles is chief executive of anti-fascist campaign HOPE not hate. He is author of *White Riot: The Violent Story of Combat 18, Hooligans: The A-Z of Britain's Football Hooligan Gangs,* and co-author of *Mr Evil: The Secret Life of Pub Bomber and Killer David Copeland* | www.hopenothate.org.uk

WARNING
There is a lot of racism and bad language in this book. We have not censured the words of people and their writings because we believe it is important for the reader to understand the true nature of the British far right and the people within it.

We hope no-one is offended and you understand why we have not redacted offensive and abusive terms and words.

INTRODUCTION

Twenty-seven years ago this summer, a young man approached me with a quite extraordinary request. Simply put, he wanted to join the British National Party (BNP), then the UK's most prominent far-right movement, as a spy. He was a committed anti-fascist and had been active on demos and protests, but felt the best way he could fight the threat was from the inside.

Over the next decade this young man, who I'm going to call "Arthur", operated at the heart of Britain's far-right movements. He attended over 400 meetings, rallies and leafleting sessions, and gave us detailed reports of everyone he met, everything he saw and everything that was being planned.

This is his story.

***

Back in 1994, I was working for the anti-fascist organisation *Searchlight*. This would later would morph into HOPE not hate, the organisation I now lead. At *Searchlight* we specialised in running 'sources' inside fascist groups, with the aim of disrupting them, but most of the people we dealt with were those who had 'turned' – that is, they had started off as fascists and nazis but over time, and for a variety of different reasons, decided that what they were doing was wrong and came over to us.

What Arthur did was rare: very rare. There were others who went to the occasional far-right meeting or joined a group for a few weeks or even a few months, but to go inside for 10 years was quite remarkable. He never asked for money and was never interested in fame. In fact, one of the main reasons he doesn't want his full name used is that he doesn't want the embarrassment of work colleagues finding out and having to explain himself.

Arthur was in the far right during a particularly violent period. The nazi-terror group Combat 18 (C18), which took its name from the first and eighth letter of the alphabet, "AH" – to signify "Adolf Hitler" – was at its peak and the BNP was taking its "Rights for Whites" campaign to the doorsteps of the rapidly-changing East End of London. Almost every time Arthur went out with his new nazi 'friends', the discussion would soon turn to talk of the racist violence they had committed, and the violence they wanted to commit.

Arthur travelled in cars with nazi thugs when they screamed racist abuse at Muslim or black women walking down the street. He attended house parties where his host would bring out papier-mâché moulds, made up to look like the faces of black people and filled with red paint, and then encourage his guests to stab them repeatedly. He attended Holocaust denial events, as well as skinhead gigs that erupted in violence, and meetings where C18 leaders would urge the audience to kill their opponents.

But Arthur was not a passive observer. He was an anti-fascist on a mission. He reported back everything he saw and armed with that information we set about undermining, destabilising and disrupting the far right. We would write up his information in the pages of *Searchlight* magazine, which in pre-internet days was compulsory reading for every BNP member. Arthur would deliberately spread gossip, telling one person or group what another was saying in order to set off their paranoia and foment dissent. Just as importantly, he gave us a unique insight into the workings of the BNP and the types of people it attracted – something that is impossible to glean simply from reading their publications or academic articles.

There were times when we passed details of BNP meetings and activities over to anti-fascists, and their mobilisations would be cut short. Bookings would end up cancelled and fascists would literally be chased off the streets. On one occasion Arthur got caught up in these clashes and was struck on the head with a hammer by an anti-fascist. On another occasion he was confronted with being "the mole", but stood his ground and nothing could be proved. Despite all this, and despite the real dangers he put himself in, Arthur carried on. He knew the risks, but he understood they were worth taking.

It is not an exaggeration to say that Arthur greatly contributed to the failure of East London BNP to capitalise on its breakthrough council victory in Millwall, in September 1993. For the next few years many of the BNP's attempts to organise were disrupted. Leafleting sessions were cut short, if they happened at all, for fear of anti-fascist resistance, and the drip-drip of information that appeared in the pages of *Searchlight* so undermined the BNP and created such a deep sense of paranoia that organisers came and went and entire branches collapsed.

But all that was about to be thrown into sharp relief one horrendous moment in spring 1999.

***

On Saturday 17 April 1999 a bomb exploded close to the tube station in Brixton, south London, injuring several people, including a young baby who had a three-inch nail embedded in her skull. A week later, another bomb exploded just off Brick Lane, in the heart of the East End and London's Bangladeshi community.

Fear gripped the capital and many of London's diverse communities were worried they would be next. Arthur, like many of us, suspected that the bomber was motivated by far-right ideology and helped us draw up lists of potential suspects. One of the names he jotted down was David Copeland, a young man he had met at several BNP events a couple of years before.

On the morning of Friday 30 April, the police issued a CCTV image of the man they believed was responsible for what were being called "the London nailbombings".

Arthur was at work when he saw the front page of the *Evening Standard*, which carried the image of a short man with a white baseball cap carrying a sports bag. Arthur looked, and then looked again.

"David Copeland," he said to himself.

Unfortunately, this identification could not stop the third – and most deadly – bomb, which went off a few hours later at the Admiral Duncan pub in Soho, long-recognised as heart of the capital's gay community. Three died, including a pregnant woman, and dozens were injured.

The following day, after Copeland had finally been arrested, Arthur attended a party at the home of one of his fellow east London BNP activists. "There was an excitement in the air," he was to later recall. "Some of the people there openly supporting the bombings and believing whoever had been arrested was only one member of a terrorist cell, and hoped that his comrades would attack another target that night."

During the course of the evening there was intense speculation as to who would be targeted next, with people throwing out the names of the minorities they despised most. As the party came to close, one woman remarked sadly: "Well I'm sorry there were no more bombs tonight."

This was the world that Arthur occupied for 10 years. A world where people uttered the most appalling racist bile and dreamed the most dreadful and violent things.

Arthur understandably grew tired of this work and eventually called it a day, to get on with his life. Years later, and a long time after we had lost touch, he reached out to me after I referenced him on a podcast about Robbie Mullen, a HOPE not hate informant within the proscribed terror group National Action; Robbie had bravely helped expose a plot by National Action's former spokesperson to kill a Labour MP. While Arthur was grateful for the mention, he wanted to tell me that I was wrong to compare him to Robbie, feeling what Robbie had done was so much more courageous than anything he had attempted.

Twenty-seven years after Arthur walked into the coffee lounge at the Sherlock Holmes Hotel, in London's Baker Street, he remains as humble as ever. He is featuring in a new Netflix documentary detailing the hunt for the London nailbomber. He is also finally emerging from the shadows to tell his story.

In preparation for the airing of the Netflix show, Arthur was interviewed by a national newspaper. Asked whether he considered himself a hero, he replied:

> "I would like to describe myself as an anti-fascist, I started out as an activist with the Anti-Nazi League leafletting and canvassing against the British National Party and the National Front. Briefly I was involved with Anti-Fascist Action, who were a more militant group. Then it all turned 'secret squirrel' with me joining the BNP and pretending to hate black and Asian people and to believe that the Zionists ruled the World, so that I could gain the trust of these men and women and obtain information. But at the end of the day, I see myself as being an anti-fascist.

> "As it happens, I've known nurses who helped care for the victims of both the Admiral Duncan bombing and the Manchester Arena bombing. I would say that they and their colleagues are the heroes and heroines, men and women dealing with the consequence of stupid, futile violence every day. Also, the people who were left injured or traumatised by David's bomb in Soho or by the other idiot at the Ariana Grande concert, who have refused to let what happened destroy them, they are heroes too."

Codename Arthur is a reminder of the dangers of the far right, the violence they enact, the world they would like to create and - given half a chance - the mayhem and terrorism many would like to cause. Just as importantly though, it is a tribute to Arthur and everything he accomplished over so many years for the cause of anti-fascism.

There is a lot of hate in this book, but there is also an underlying message of hope. Despite their vile racism and sometimes extreme violence, the far right failed to create the society they dreamed of and most of the people Arthur knew dropped out of activity and faded away. London stood tall against the politics of hate during the 1990s and 2000s and remains one of the most diverse, tolerant and multiracial cities in the world. Even in Barking & Dagenham, where the BNP was the official opposition on the council between 2006 and 2010, they were driven out by people power and a total rejection at the ballot box.

By going undercover inside the BNP, Arthur helped disrupt them and by doing so set them back many years. And, throughout it all, his bravery, humour and humility shone through.

To everyone at HOPE not hate, Arthur is a total anti-fascist hero.

CHAPTER ONE: GOING IN

It's hard to explain the feeling. There I was, sitting in the coffee area of the Sherlock Holmes Hotel in Baker Street, waiting for a young man who was offering to help. Was it a trap? Was he for real? I had no idea.

In any other situation I would have had other people there, watching to ensure he was alone, maybe even to search him before he reached me. But it was the middle of the summer holidays, people were off and I was fairly new to this game. Above all though, amidst the nervousness and apprehension, I had a good feeling about this meeting.

It was July 1994 and *Searchlight*, the anti-fascist organisation I was part of at the time, which specialised in running a network of informers inside far-right groups, had received a call from a young man offering his services. More specifically, he was offering to "go inside" – by which he meant infiltrate a far-right group.

I had a host of questions for him, and most involved me asking him to tell me about himself. Arthur told me that he had considered himself a socialist for quite some time, but he was not really political active. He had grown up in a political household and remembered going round to a house of a family friend as a teenager and meeting a veteran of the Spanish Civil War who had actually met George Orwell on the ship to Spain.

He said that he felt compelled to get active after the far right became active in his local area, so, together with a friend called Richard, set up a local anti-fascist group, which was essentially a branch of the Anti-Nazi League (ANL). "There were a mix of people, men and women of all ages, mostly white but some Asian people too," he recalled. "Some of us very politically involved, others less so."

The group leafleted locally and attended demonstrations across London in the early 1990s, including one against the British National Party (BNP) bookshop in Welling and the TUC Unity march in the east end. He was even a delegate from his local group to the ANL national conference. It was at one of the Welling demos that Arthur first saw Gerry Gable, the founder of *Searchlight* and the man who brought me into anti-fascism five years before. After his speech, Gerry moved around the crowd selling the *Searchlight* magazine, so Arthur headed off after him and bought one. The very next day sent off a cheque to subscribe.

While Arthur's group was closely linked to the ANL, he would often go to other anti-fascist activities in London on his own. He attended a protest against the National Front's Remembrance Sunday march to the cenotaph, a counter-demonstration against the BNP's annual rally and joined others totally completely out-manoeuvring nazi skinheads attending a Blood & Honour concert on the

Becontree estate in Dagenham. Not for the last time he got a whack around his head, though this time from a policeman.

His last open anti-fascist activity was with Anti-Fascist Action (AFA), the militant anti-fascist group which had a strong and well-earned reputation for violence, in Dagenham against the BNP. Later that day, after AFA had regrouped in Carnaby Street, they attacked a smaller group of nazi skinheads, leaving several badly injured. Arthur felt uneasy about the violence, given the unfair odds, but obviously he kept his views to himself. Later, in the pub, one of the main AFA lads handed him a drink and commented: "You're looking nervous". Arthur was. The next time he saw London AFA, he was, as far as they were concerned, a fascist and so a legitimate target.

Arthur's growing involvement in anti-fascism saw him read extensively, but one book more than any other caught his interest. *The Other Face of Terror* was an account of Ray Hill, a former leading nazi turned anti-fascist mole and co-written by Andy Bell. For four years in the late 1970s and early 1980s Hill operated at the top of the British fascist scene, including a two-year stint as the deputy leader of the British Movement, but all the time he was passing information over to his *Searchlight* handlers. The book was a racy read, and Arthur was hooked. "I read Ray Hill's book from the 1980s when the British National Party was newly formed, and it seemed like a really worthwhile thing what he had done," Arthur was to later recall. "And," he added with a long, slightly sheepish pause, "to be honest, interesting."

Arthur was clearly nervous as he sat there in front of me. He knew what he wanted to do, but he wasn't clear whether we would accept him. "I wasn't sure that time whether *Searchlight* just recruited people like Ray Hill, who realised that National Socialism was not for them, or whether they took people who were anti-fascist to start with."

As he was mulling over his initial approach to us, he attended a protest in central London to counter the National Front's annual demonstration at the Remembrance Sunday parade. As he was leaving the event he was confronted by some members of Youth Against Racism (run by the left-wing group, Militant) who mistook him for a nazi and began threatening him. "They searched me for incriminating evidence and found a book by Graham Greene in my carrier bag. For some reason they decided that nazis wouldn't read Graham Greene, so they let me go."

Bolstered by this experience, Arthur was now convinced that if could fool them, then he could fool the nazis themselves.

Arthur left our hotel meeting with an instruction to write off to a British National Party address and request the information pack that their newspaper promoted. This was before the internet took off, of course, and before social media provided instant connections. It was to be the start of a 10-year journey, and descent, into British fascism.

***

Arthur's first instruction from the BNP was to make his way to Stepney Green tube station in London's East End, where he was to meet others and head to a party meeting. With great trepidation, he exited the tube and looked around. A group was gathering

BNP National Organiser Richard Edmonds

outside the entrance, among them a few faces he recognised.

Standing a few inches taller than the others was Richard Edmonds, the BNP's National Organiser and an infamous Holocaust denier. Also there was the much shorter Derek Beackon, who had been in the national spotlight almost a year before when he'd won a council by-election in the local borough of Tower Hamlets. Accompanying Beackon was BNP party leader John Tyndall, a veteran of the British fascist scene. Short and squat, Arthur would have recognised him anywhere.

While Tyndall conferred with Edmonds, before departing with Beackon in a car, Arthur began introducing himself to the others. There was Arthur Flinders, a large-framed party stalwart who was known simply as 'Arf' (or 'Big Arthur'). Alongside him was Ian Dell, who had recently been appointed the party's Chief Steward, and his wife Gabriella, who was to turn out to be quite eccentric. Then there was Colin Smith, seemingly in his mid-30s, dressed in a brown suit with a BNP patch sewn onto it.

Another new recruit was Alex, an 18-year-old skinhead who until recently had sported a swastika tattoo. He was happy to tell people that he'd felt forced to scratch it off with a razor while in prison to prevent himself getting a hard time from the black lads in there. Alex told Edmonds that his grandfather was Jewish, to which the BNP elder replied: "Best if you don't tell too many people about that."

Ian Dell (centre) joins Richard Edomnds (right) at a BNP papersale on Brick Lane

As they boarded a van together, Gabriella Dell began a long conversation with Edmonds about the racial eugenics of cats, before announcing to everyone that she had got involved in nationalist politics at the age of 14 because she'd been attacked by a six-year-old Jewish boy with a recorder. As the van moved off, she expressed her sorrow for a mixed-race kid standing with his mum on the pavement, claiming that he was "a victim of his parents' betrayal of races".

Arthur looked around at the others and took some comfort in seeing that he was not the only person to consider her completely mad.

As they made their way up the M1 motorway, Edmonds recounted his recent trip to Germany, where he took part in the Hess Memorial, an annual far-right march to commemorate Hitler's former deputy who had died in a German prison seven years before. Gabriella's husband Ian, a longstanding party member and close to Edmonds, piped up that he thought that the Secret Intelligence Service, MI6, had in fact murdered Hess. In jovial mood, Edmonds began singing German nationalist songs.

Keen to be accepted into the group, Arthur remarked about a black British athlete who had recently been exposed as a drug cheat. Edmonds laughed loudly. "Did you hear what Arthur said?" he shouted to others. "He said that they are all a bunch of niggers and cheats!" That, of course, was not what Arthur had said, but in order to fit in he let it slide.

In that moment, Arthur knew he could blend in with this group. "I'm embarrassed to say now, but it felt good."

With several of the passengers in need of a comfort break, the BNP van stopped at a motorway service station, parking up alongside a coach packed with black people. Quickly, everyone hid their party badges and covered copies of the *British Nationalist* newspaper, which many had been reading on the journey, with jackets or pushed them to the floor. Colin Smith even took off his jacket so as to hide his BNP patch.

***

Arthur was surprised how full on it all was, right from the start. He had read a lot about the BNP, and nazism in general, and had expected the casual racism but not the overt and continual proper nazism. "I felt properly sickened," he would later recall. "They might be talking about a particular Jewish woman and say that they could 'make a good lampshade out of her'. I could never work out whether that was some sort of twisted satire where they were essentially saying that all the stories of Nazi atrocities were all so ludicrous, that the whole Holocaust must be made up, or if they genuinely liked the idea of turning a Jewish woman into a lampshade.

"My first day with them was especially difficult. I was trying really hard not to look shocked but I thought it must be so obvious from my body language and everything. They didn't say anything though, so either they were oblivious to my discomfort because their views were so normalised to them, or I hid my feelings well."

Arthur, of course, got used to their vile remarks. "I very quickly became immune to those comments and jokes. It became normal to me. Also, constantly hearing about the inferiority of people of African origin became very normal to me too. This was just the world I was in.

"I recently re-watched *Schlinder's List* and I had forgotten how much many of them adored that film. They loved to quote the line, 'Shoot her!' or they would impersonate Amon Goethe taking pot-shots at Jews or anybody else they fantasised about murdering. So, watching the film, I was quite shocked that once all those things were quite normal to me."

***

Eventually, they arrived at a pub on the outskirts of Nottingham where they waited for details of the rally venue. The pub was close to where the rally was supposed to be held, but the landlord got wind of what was to happen and cancelled the booking at the last minute. After a few frantic phone calls they were on their way again, this time to the nearby former mining town of Mansfield, where local organiser Steve Belshaw had booked a church hall in the name of the Ramblers Association.

The hall was quickly filling up as Arthur and the London contingent arrived. By the time the meeting started there were as many as 100 people inside, primarily made up of people from across the Midlands, but with small contingents from the south and north of the country. At the back of the hall was a book stall, where party literature was sold. Arriving suitably late was party leader John Tyndall.

After initial introductions from the chairman, who Arthur was to later learn was the East Midlands BNP leader John Peacock, the floor was given over to Richard Edmonds. The party's National Organiser spoke admiringly of the collapse of the Berlin Wall, telling the audience that when faced with a great edifice, people had pushed hard and eventually brought it down. He was convinced that if they did the same in the UK, "the system" would collapse and the BNP would be swept to power.

The next speaker was Mike Newland, a mild-manner and softly-spoken individual who was the party's press officer. He upset many in the crowd when he told them that they should not attack "Reds" (a widely-used term for political opponents). These attacks were, he said, a sign of living in the past and an acceptance that those gathered had no belief that they could win power. While no-one said anything directly to Newland, several grumbled about his speech and about him more generally in the break that soon followed. Unbeknown to Arthur at the time, Newland was particularly unpopular among the party's rank and file, largely because of his aversion to violence and (relative) political moderation.

Newland was followed by Ian Dell, who called for volunteers to offer their time to protect meetings and other party events. Next up was Eddy Butler, a tall, dark-haired man who, as the party's election organiser, had masterminded their council victory in Tower Hamlets the previous year. He explained the party's focus on contesting elections and urged people to come forward as candidates as soon as possible, so they could begin working in the chosen council wards well in advance with warm-up leaflets, before switching to door-to-door canvassing.

Those who were hostile on the doorstep were to be quickly ignored, so as not to reinforce their opposition to the BNP. Arthur would soon discover that some party activists in London would take a quite different approach, marking down anti-BNP households in order to give them a mouthful of abuse or some party literature to wind them up.

The keynote speaker was John Tyndall himself, a man who Arthur had read much about, both in Ray Hill's book but also through the pages of *Searchlight* magazine. A pompous man with a bombastic delivery style, Tyndall was a veteran of the British fascist scene, having been active since the late 1950s. He railed against the recently announced IRA ceasefire in Northern Ireland, which he viewed as a sell-out by the British authorities and then reminisced about a time when the Government would supposedly respond to a single hair being harmed on a British citizen's head by sending in warships and troops around the world. The audience clapped enthusiastically. Reclaiming a lost past – one where Britain ruled the waves – was far more enjoyable then talking of elections and canvassing sheets.

Tyndall ended his speech by complaining that some in the movement were so impressed – or even obsessed – by "a certain country in the 1930s" that they wanted to copy it. But, he told the audience, what was really great about this "certain country" – by which of course he was referring to Nazi Germany – was that it had applied itself to its own time and it was important for British nationalists to do the same here and now.

Tyndall's speech was met with a standing ovation, though there were also more than a few rumblings of discontent and even mockery. Even Richard Edmonds, who remained Tyndall's loyal sidekick to the end, put on a Colonel Blimp style voice, pompous and jingoistic, to copy Tyndall voice in the van to the laughter of others.

The journey back to London was uneventful and generally quiet. A brief discussion about Hari Krishna followers was punctured by Ian Dell saying that "we have plenty of space in the camps for those bastards." Arthur rested his head against the window and reflected on the day. He was in the BNP and seemingly accepted. Not bad for the first day.

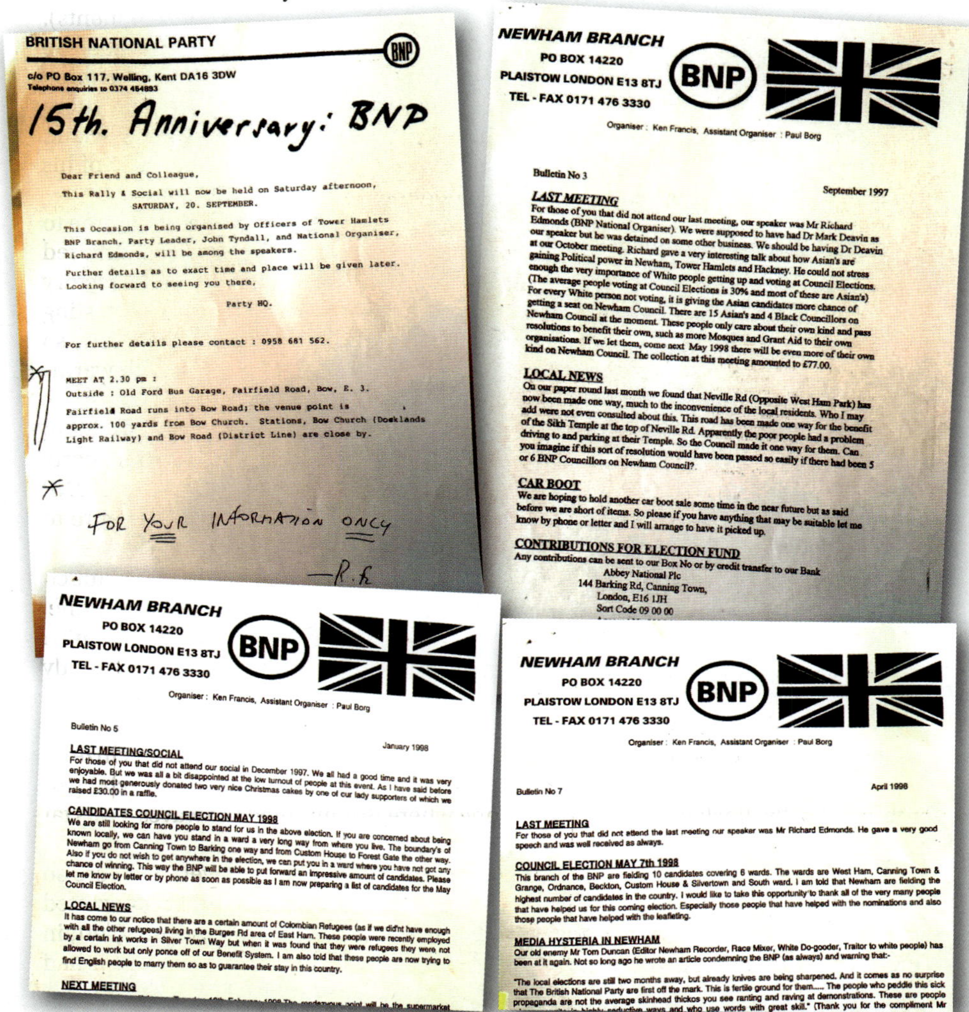

BRITISH NATIONAL PARTY

c/o PO Box 117, Welling, Kent DA16 3DW
Telephone enquiries to 0374 464893

15th. Anniversary: BNP

Dear Friend and Colleague,

This Rally & Social will now be held on Saturday afternoon, SATURDAY, 20. SEPTEMBER.

This Occasion is being organised by Officers of Tower Hamlets BNP Branch. Party Leader, John Tyndall, and National Organiser, Richard Edmonds, will be among the speakers.

Further details as to exact time and place will be given later.
Looking forward to seeing you there,

Party HQ.

For further details please contact : 0958 681 562.

MEET AT 2.30 pm :
Outside : Old Ford Bus Garage, Fairfield Road, Bow, E. 3.
Fairfield Road runs into Bow Road; the venue point is approx. 100 yards from Bow Church. Stations, Bow Church (Docklands Light Railway) and Bow Road (District Line) are close by.

FOR YOUR INFORMATION ONLY

—R.E.

NEWHAM BRANCH
PO BOX 14220
PLAISTOW LONDON E13 8TJ
TEL - FAX 0171 476 3330

Organiser : Ken Francis, Assistant Organiser : Paul Borg

Bulletin No 3

September 1997

LAST MEETING

For those of you that did not attend our last meeting, our speaker was Mr Richard Edmonds (BNP National Organiser). We were supposed to have had Dr Mark Deavin as our speaker but he was detained on some other business. We should be having Dr Deavin at our October meeting. Richard gave a very interesting talk about how Asian's are gaining Political power in Newham, Tower Hamlets and Hackney. He could not stress enough the very importance of White people getting up and voting at Council Elections. (The average people voting at Council Elections is 30% and most of these are Asian's) For every White person not voting, it is giving the Asian candidates more chance of getting a seat on Newham Council. There are 15 Asian's and 4 Black Councillors on Newham Council at the moment. These people only care about their own kind and pass resolutions to benefit their own, such as more Mosques and Grant Aid to their own organisations. If we let them, come next May 1998 there will be even more of their own kind on Newham Council. The collection at this meeting amounted to £77.00.

LOCAL NEWS

On our paper round last month we found that Neville Rd (Opposite West Ham Park) has now been made one way, much to the inconvenience of the local residents. Who I may add were not even consulted about this. This road has been made one way for the benefit of the Sikh Temple at the top of Neville Rd. Apparently the poor people had a problem driving to and parking at their Temple. So the Council made it one way for them. Can you imagine if this sort of resolution would have been passed so easily if there had been 5 or 6 BNP Councillors on Newham Council?.

CAR BOOT

We are hoping to hold another car boot sale some time in the near future but as said before we are short of items. So please if you have anything that may be suitable let me know by phone or letter and I will arrange to have it picked up.

CONTRIBUTIONS FOR ELECTION FUND

Any contributions can be sent to our Box No or by credit transfer to our Bank
Abbey National Plc
144 Barking Rd, Canning Town,
London, E16 1JH
Sort Code 09 00 00

NEWHAM BRANCH
PO BOX 14220
PLAISTOW LONDON E13 8TJ
TEL - FAX 0171 476 3330

Organiser : Ken Francis, Assistant Organiser : Paul Borg

Bulletin No 5

January 1998

LAST MEETING/SOCIAL

For those of you that did not attend our social in December 1997. We all had a good time and it was very enjoyable. But we was all a bit disappointed at the low turnout of people at this event. As I have said before we had most generously donated two very nice Christmas cakes by one of our lady supporters of which we raised £30.00 in a raffle.

CANDIDATES COUNCIL ELECTION MAY 1998

We are still looking for more people to stand for us in the above election. If you are concerned about being known locally, we can have you stand in a ward a very long way from where you live. The boundary's of Newham go from Canning Town to Barking one way and from Custom House to Forest Gate the other way. Also if you do not wish to get anywhere in the election, we can put you in a ward where you have not got any chance of winning. This way the BNP will be able to put forward an impressive amount of candidates. Please let me know by letter or by phone as soon as possible as I am now preparing a list of candidates for the May Council Election.

LOCAL NEWS

It has come to our notice that there are a certain amount of Colombian Refugees (as if we did'nt have enough with all the other refugees) living in the Burges Rd area of East Ham. These people were recently employed by a certain ink works in Silver Town Way but when it was found that they were refugees they were not allowed to work but only ponce off of our Benefit System. I am also told that these people are now trying to find English people to marry them so as to guarantee their stay in this country.

NEXT MEETING

NEWHAM BRANCH
PO BOX 14220
PLAISTOW LONDON E13 8TJ
TEL - FAX 0171 476 3330

Organiser : Ken Francis, Assistant Organiser : Paul Borg

Bulletin No 7

April 1998

LAST MEETING

For those of you that did not attend the last meeting our speaker was Mr Richard Edmonds. He gave a very good speech and was well received as always.

COUNCIL ELECTION MAY 7th 1998

This branch of the BNP are fielding 10 candidates covering 6 wards. The wards are West Ham, Canning Town & Grange, Ordnance, Beckton, Custom House & Silvertown and South ward. I am told that Newham are fielding the highest number of candidates in the country. I would like to take this opportunity to thank all of the very many people that have helped us for this coming election. Especially those people that have helped with the nominations and also those people that have helped with the leafleting.

MEDIA HYSTERIA IN NEWHAM

Our old enemy Mr Tom Duncan (Editor Newham Recorder, Race Mixer, White Do-gooder, Traitor to white people) has been at it again. Not so long ago he wrote an article condemning the BNP (as always) and warning that:-

"The local elections are still two months away, but already knives are being sharpened. And it comes as no surprise that The British National Party are first off the mark. This is fertile ground for them..... The people who peddle this sick propaganda are not the average skinhead thickos you see ranting and raving at demonstrations. These are people ... and who use words with great skill." (Thank you for the compliment Mr

CHAPTER TWO: RIGHTS FOR WHITES

Two weeks later Arthur found himself inside the BNP bookshop, which was in Welling, south-east London, and also doubled up as the party's headquarters. The building was opened for business in 1989 and had long been a focus of anti-fascist opposition, which had only increased after several racist murders in the area in the early 1990s. In October 1993, a few weeks after the BNP had won a council seat in Tower Hamlets, a protest against the building attracted as many as 40,000 people. Unfortunately the day was marred with violence, and 72 people were injured in clashes between protesters and the police.

"Two at a time," barked an incredibly grumpy Jim White, a Scot who worked in the shop. "JT rules," he added (referring to the leader, John Tyndall). "And only 10 minutes in the office." Inside the office, between the bundles of party newspapers and shelves stuffed with books, was a skinhead drinking coffee. He told Arthur that he was in the process of being evicted by his local council, after two Asian families complained that he was harassing and victimising them. Looking at a tattoo spelling "hate" on his fist and a spider web on his neck, Arthur could fully understand how he might be considered intimidating.

Back outside, Jim White was having a massive row with Simon Chadwick, a party activist who had recently moved down to London from his home in Chesterfield. Turning to Peter Illing, a BNP activist from Watford who was also heavily involved in the nazi music scene and who had brought Chadwick to the bookshop, White shouted: "You ought to have known better than bring him here – you know he is going to get expelled from the party?"

"You are a member of Combat 18, you scum!" White then screamed at Chadwick.

Arthur watched Chadwick as he left the shop and wandered down the street. He made monkey noises at any black people he came across. Arthur was to later learn that the 'abuse runs' were a regular practice for Chadwick.

***

I would meet Arthur every week during the initial months of his infiltration. We met in a series of hotels across London, alternating from time to time. Hotels were chosen as they provided quiet places to talk and the chances of either of us bumping into anyone we knew was small.

Over coffee or a beer, Arthur would tell me everything he could remember from his outings with the BNP. He got into a pattern of listing out everyone who was present, and would often come to our meetings with notes he had written up immediately after his trips out with the far right.

Security was always an issue for us and when he first went 'in' he didn't have a mobile phone. Meetings would have to be planned in advance and they were difficult to change at very short notice. For his safety and mine, I or a colleague would sometimes watch him arrive or scout the area first to ensure he was alone and not being followed. Obviously the trust between us grew rapidly and in a way that's sometimes hard to explain to those who have never found themselves in this situation. Arthur was quite literally putting his life on the line for the cause of anti-fascism and I had a duty to do whatever I could to protect him. Just as significantly though, we shared secrets that only a handful of others knew. Even within *Searchlight*, only Gerry Gable knew Arthur's identity.

We operated on a need to know basis: and no-one else needed to know.

***

Formed in 1982, after a split in the-then preeminent far-right party, the National Front (NF), the British National Party (BNP) had emerged as Britain's leading far-right political movement by 1990. The BNP was founded and led by John Tyndall: a tall, chinless figure with a slightly disengaged air. A poor man's Colonel Blimp, if you

BNP leader John Tyndall addressing a party rally in Milton Keynes

will. He was a fiery orator, however, who would work himself and his audience into frenzy in the manner of his hero, Oswald Mosley, the pre- and post-war leader of the British Union of Fascists and then the Union Movement.

Tyndall had first joined a nazi organisation in 1959 and went on to be a leading member of various fringe extremist movements, such as the White Defence League, the National Socialist Movement and the Greater Britain Movement. He had also acquired several criminal convictions, including possession of a gun and organising a paramilitary group. In 1967, he joined the recently launched National Front and within a short time became its Chairman.

Yet while the NF was to become the most successful post-war fascist group in Britain (at one stage reaching 17,500 members), Tyndall was constantly attacked for his authoritarian leadership style. By 1980, the NF was in decline. Tyndall left, claiming that the party had been taken over by "gays and skinheads". He formed the New National Front and then, two years later, the British National Party.

Joining Tyndall in the move from the NF was Richard Edmonds, a former teacher who was to become the BNP's National Organiser. A tall, gangly man, Edmonds was a committed national socialist and was instrumental in ensuring production of a second edition of *Holocaust News*, a newspaper which denounced the Holocaust as a Jewish and American lie. Edmonds was also popular among the BNP rank and file.

While Tyndall rarely ventured out from his Sussex seaside base of Hove, Edmonds attended every BNP activity he could, and this earnt him respect from party activists. His long-time ambition was for a party headquarters and bookshop, representing (in his view) respectability and progress. His dream was fulfilled when he accepted redundancy from his employers, Cable and Wireless, and used his payoff to purchase a shop and flat in Welling, thus providing the BNP with a base.

Under Tyndall and Edmonds, the BNP courted controversy through a series of highly provocative marches and rallies in areas with large ethnic minority populations. In 1989, a static BNP rally in the West Yorkshire town of Dewsbury attracted several hundred local white youths who went on to run riot, attacking Asian shops and passers-by. In 1991, the party marched through Thamesmead in south-east London, passing within yards of the spot where the black teenager Rolan Adams had been killed only weeks before. Unsurprisingly, this confrontational stance attracted recruits to its cause: not only many disillusioned NF and British Movement (a hardline and openly nazi group) supporters, but also the skinheads of Blood & Honour (an umbrella group for the white power music scene) and football hooligans who had previously been unaligned to any political group.

Much of the BNP activity during this time was concentrated on east London where, in 1990, it launched its "Rights for Whites" campaign, hoping to capitalise on the perceived injustices felt by many local white people. The stabbing of a 15-year old white boy in a Tower Hamlets school was used for maximum political advantage: the BNP galvanised support with a 400-strong march and rally addressed by the dead boy's stepfather. In an area of high unemployment, bad housing and underfunded public amenities, the BNP's propaganda pinned the blame, regardless of the true causes, on the shoulders of ethnic minority

BNP supporters holding a rally in Sunderland in 1992

communities and, more generally, on "Britain's multi-racial experiment".

The BNP rallied the disenchanted and within two months its policy was paying dividends: it obtained 9.7% of the vote in one local election. This was to be the beginning of two years of rolling successes for the party, which culminated in a successful by-election victory in the (later abolished) Tower Hamlets ward of Millwall in September 1993. While this result surprised and shocked the political establishment, for the small group of BNP activists it was the product of months of hard work in the area, as for the first time they adopted political organising techniques such as canvassing and specifically targeting a by-election (which generally attracted lower turnouts). Complacency and division between Labour and the Liberal Democrats meant the BNP squeezed through the middle.

While the BNP's man Dereck Beackon went on to lose his seat again in May 1994, the party increased its vote considerably when the whole council was up for election. Combined with the growing interest and experience of electoral politics, this convinced the BNP's leadership that it needed to move away from its violent past. However, it was the BNP's growing electoral threat, and especially its win in Millwall, that convinced Arthur of the need to defeat them from within.

***

A few days after the visit to the bookshop, Arthur was out campaigning ahead of yet another by-election in Tower Hamlets, this time in Shadwell ward. Their candidate was Gordon Callow, a party veteran with a long and violent past. Callow began his political life as a violent thug in Oswald Mosley's Union Movement in the 1950s, before switching allegiance to Colin Jordan's National Socialist Movement in 1962 and then to the National Front in the 1970s. His predilection for wolves over people could have been considered quaint had it not been for his violent side. Among his favourite pastimes was spitting on Jewish women in the street and attacking the Lord Mayor's parade in London in a year when the position was held by a Jewish man.

Arthur was one of nine BNP activists out campaigning that evening. Richard Edmonds and Dereck Beackon had been expected to make an appearance, but neither showed up. They put out a general recruitment leaflet on one of the main estates in the ward, but after only an hour retired to a local pub. A hot topic of conversation was the expulsion of Phil Maxwell, whose crime had been to stand up at a recent BNP meeting and announce that he was Jewish by birth, but later had become a Christian. His Jewish ancestry appeared reason enough for his expulsion.

The BNP was out again the weekend before polling day and this time there were 25 of them. However, leafleting was again limited as the first sight of anti-fascists led to a retreat to the pub for the rest of the day. The pub became a regular feature of Arthur's activities over the years.

Anti-fascists demonstrating against the BNP bookshop in Welling, in October 1993

Their presence in the ward had stirred local tensions, though. Over that weekend a 36 year-old local man, Chandon Miah, was attacked from behind by a white man and had his throat slashed. Miah required several stitches to close up the wound.

On election night, a group of 30 BNP and Combat 18 supporters took up base in a pub near the count. Fortunately there was no trouble as police surrounded the building and would not let the group leave.

While London BNP was split into several branches, it was common for party activists to attend each other's branch meetings and activities, something we exploited to the full. We had another source in London BNP at the time but Arthur was younger, newer and far keener to travel.

In late September 1994 Arthur travelled over from east London to a north London branch meeting in a pub in Camden, where the landlord was a party member. About 20 people were there and Richard Edmonds was the keynote speaker. He spoke about how "the white race" would be a minority in the UK within 20 years, and how Asians were becoming more "arrogant" each day and that crime was soaring. He reminisced about travelling to New York as a young engineer, but how that the city had been "ruined" by immigration - a fate he argued was befalling London. The Camden meeting took place just as an outbreak of bubonic and pneumonic plague was ripping through south-central and western India, a fact that Edmonds lost no time in racialising.

"The plague provides a perfect reason for all those Indian doctors in the UK to return home where they would be more needed," he said, to a mixture of applause and laughter.

Another by-election in east London saw Arthur regularly going out with his new BNP friends two or three times a week. Leafleting was not too bad, but canvassing proved more of a challenge. Of course he hated it when people abused him for being in the BNP, but it was actually worse when they were in total agreement.

On one occasion, Arthur was paired with Richard Edmonds on a canvassing round in Weavers Field ward, in Tower Hamlets. The election had not yet been formerly called but Edmonds claimed he had it on good authority that it was only going to be a matter of time before it was.

Depressingly for Arthur, the reaction to the BNP's message on the doorstep was positive and their canvass returns suggested that they had the support of 50% of all white voters spoken to. The rest were either hostile or apathetic. One of the other BNP teams claimed to have knocked on the door of a policeman, who happily told them that the whole Metropolitan Police force was behind them "except for those bastards at the top".

The mood in the pub afterwards was quite euphoric and they were all excited at the potential in the ward. It wasn't long though before the conversation turned to their arch enemy: *Searchlight*. Gordon Callow announced that he was planning to sue the anti-fascist group for saying that he was a certified lunatic. He said that he had already paid out £800 in legal costs, but that that was a small investment given that he was going to get at least £115,000 in damages. Linda Miller added that *Searchlight* had "no right" in bringing up people's spent convictions.

Miller played an interesting dynamic within the group, especially being the only woman to regularly come out campaigning. She was loved and feared in equal measure by her fellow BNP members. She lived in a flat in Tower Hamlets, which she adorned with nazi and racist regalia. Her kitchen was covered in BNP, Blood & Honour and Combat 18 material. There was also a sticker of a black man with three eggs stuffed into his mouth, featuring the caption: "I've had a mouthful being black."

On her sitting room wall was a massive club, with a detachable handle producing a steel spike.

Miller particularly hated Tony Lecomber, the party's East London election coordinator, and clearly the feelings were mutual. During the Dagenham parliamentary by-election in June 1994, which saw John Tyndall pick up 9% of the vote, Lecomber said to Miller: "Are you endeavouring to deliver as few leaflets as possible?"

Later in the campaign she told Lecomber that she was unable to attend a leafleting session because she had a doctor's appointment, to which he replied: "What you're basically saying is that you are too old and pathetic."

But Miller could give as good as she got, and would incessantly tell other party members of her long-running vendetta against an Anti-Nazi League (ANL) organiser who worked on the local market. She was often overheard describing what she wanted to do to her, and much of it involved violence.

She could also sometimes be a dangerous person to be around. After retiring to the pub after one leafleting session, she began encouraging the others with her to attack some men in the pub who she claimed were giving her dirty looks. Fortunately for Arthur, there were no takers.

Arthur knew that he could never get involved in violence, but that was easier said than done when there were violent people all around him. However, we were also conscious that he could run away at the whiff of trouble as that would risk blowing his cover. We discussed it early on in the infiltration and agreed the best – and probably only – strategy was to move himself to the back of the group in the hope of avoiding trouble. Depending on what happened, we would then discuss if any action was needed when we next met or spoke.

In preparation for the election push, the party put on an activist training event in a pub in West Ham, in east London. Of the 20 to 25 or so in attendance, about half were east London activists well known to Arthur. But then there was a smattering from across the capital and a few from further afield. The largest contingent from outside east London was a group from Croydon, led by veteran nationalists Paul Ballard and John Merritt. With them was a man who introduced himself as 'Baz,' again from Croydon, who was well-known for his racist and antisemitic cartoons. Baz's real name was actually Mike Barnes.

Also in attendance was Paul Henderson, from Woking in Surrey, who was later to boast about his collection of Nazi uniforms he kept at home in his bedroom. As the meeting was about to begin, news spread that Steve O'Connell was stepping down as East London organiser as his wife was pregnant and he didn't want his political involvement bringing trouble home.

With John Tyndall running late, Edmonds opened the meeting by praising the

London BNP and comparing them to the "lazy branches" in the north of England. Just to drive the point home, he told the audience he would say the same even if Tyndall had been present or he was being recorded. Of course, when he delivered his main speech later during the training, when he was being recorded and Tyndall was in the room, Edmonds did not repeat his disparaging comments about the northern membership.

Tyndall finally arrived and went straight into his speech, which at one-and-a-half hours was long and tedious even by his standards. But even this was just touching the surface of what he wanted to say, telling the gathered audience that he was avoiding talking about BNP policy as that would have taken all week.

As usual, Tyndall mixed his British nationalism with his national socialist beliefs. He spoke admiringly of Dunkirk and the British spirit it demonstrated, before checking himself and saying that he was against the war in the first place. He praised the hierarchical structure of Japanese society, and then remarked on a great book written by a great leader in Germany in the 1930s. While he did not mention Hitler's name directly, he did reference him later.

In the Q&A session afterwards, someone asked Tyndall his views on the Holocaust - or "Holohoax" as he referred to it. Tyndall agreed that it was an important subject to discuss and debunk within party circles, but while out canvassing they should leave the issue alone. Eddy Butler, by contrast, said he thought it wasn't an issue, but Mike Barnes, who drew deeply offensive antisemitic cartoonist under the name Baz, believed passionately that they should dispel the "lies" of the Holocaust to the general public.

Tyndall was then asked his views on green politics, to which he answered that it was "an issue that the BNP should not dwell on too deeply".

After the meeting they retired to the bar. For some reason Tyndall went into the ladies toilet, where he remained for a good five minutes. Everyone was laughing at this, but as soon as he re-entered the bar there was embarrassed silence. Arthur was to learn that Tyndall would regularly use the women's toilets in pub, and he himself witnessed it on several occasions. To this day, Arthur never quite understood why.

***

Arthur was surprised how easy he found it playing the part of a far-right activist. Sometimes he would reflect on his conflicted emotions. Before joining he had presumed that fascists were violence-obsessed extremists who used foul and racist language and were always on the look out for trouble. They were indeed all these things and, especially in the early years of his infiltration, there was rarely an outing where one or more were not talking about the racist violence they had, or would like to become, involved in. There were even occasions when Arthur feared that some of them would commit acts of violence in his presence.

However, Arthur also found friendship, which was perhaps unsurprising given the amount of time he was spending with them. He laughed at their jokes, heard about their families and shared intimate and quite personal thoughts. Sometimes

Arthur struggled to divorce the political from the private, and this could make him feel guilty. He was an anti-fascist with fascist mates.

Richard Edmonds was a case in point. He was one of the most extreme national socialists that Arthur met, obsessed with denying the Holocaust and regularly using foul racist language, but at the same time was endearing and friendly. Arthur knew he should hate him, and he did politically, but at the same time he genuinely liked him and considered him a friend.

That said, there were also some people that Arthur found it quite difficult to be around. One of these people was Simon Chadwick, the ex-C18 heavy who was involved in the BNP for the first year of Arthur's infiltration. Every time Chadwick was in his presence, he would be talking about violence or shouting racist abuse at someone. And of course, like any bully, his targets were primarily women, children or men walking on their own.

I was of course quite pleased that Arthur took a dislike to Chadwick, as I had my own history with him. Before moving to London, Chadwick had lived with his grandmother in Chesterfield and worked for the Department of Employment in Sheffield. I was studying in Sheffield at the time. In July 1991 I photographed a BNP demonstration in Walsall, where Chadwick was marching along with a video camera, in an attempt to record anyone opposing them. He was enthusiastic supporter of the recently formed Combat 18, and, in keeping with the group's early activities, had been involved in many violent attacks against left-wing and anti-fascist opponents.

While researching anti-fascists in Sheffield, he was given my name after he turned up at the university one day and spun a yarn about his sister wanting to get involved in anti-fascism. Using his access to the national computer at work, he set about trying to find my home address with a view to attacking me. Unfortunately for him, one of his fellow BNP activists who he told of his plans was someone I and my close mate Paul had put inside the BNP in South Yorkshire. We set about getting our revenge. We learnt everything we could about Chadwick and eventually built up a dossier that helped get him sacked from his job. We reported his involvement in a serious and unprovoked street assault on an Anti-Nazi League activist in Mansfield, for which he was arrested and later convicted.

I had largely forgotten about Chadwick until Arthur started reporting on him. Chadwick had moved to London after being thrown out by his Labour-supporting grandmother and had clearly not changed his politics. He remained the violent bully he always was. We began spreading rumours that he was a police informer, having "sung like a canary" after being arrested for the street attack in Mansfield, which led him to be ostracized from C18. I later heard he had received at least one beating. We also reported him to the DHSS (as it was known in those days) for selling the *Evening Standard* while also claiming benefits.

Six months into Arthur's infiltration, he reported back that Chadwick had decided to move back to Sheffield and leave the far right behind. He hadn't changed his views, but as "*Searchlight* had destroyed his life" he had had enough. Result, I thought!

***

The Annual Rally was the highlight of the BNP's political year. In 1994 it was held in the luxurious Hatfield House, set in the sprawling Hertfordshire countryside. Unsurprisingly, given the salubrious nature of the location, the event was booked in a false name - in this case as the Pro-Market Foundation. Arthur travelled there on a coach from east London with many regular faces, including Gordon Callow, Linda Miller, East London organiser Steve O'Connell and party press officer Mike Newland. It was here where he also met a trio from Watford, Pat Garratt, Trevor and a C18 supporter, introduced only by his nickname 'Jaffa'. Trevor told Arthur that on the way into London Jaffa had to be restrained from attacking a black woman in a petrol station.

"You can get them later," Trevor had told a pumped-up Jaffa.

Sitting in the pub and waiting for the coach to arrive, there was a discussion about the American black nationalist and Nation of Islam leader, Louis Farrakhan. There was general agreement that he was a "good bloke", though only because he wanted the separation of races and was strongly antisemitic. Someone had got hold of a video featuring Farrakhan and thought it was brilliant, saying that he was calling the Holocaust a fraud and that Jews were behind the slave trade.

They were met by Hatfield House security as they arrived at the front gates. Despite saying they were there for the Pro-Market Foundation meeting, the security quickly realised who they were, but let them through anyway. Richard Edmonds later said that he made them an offer they could not refuse: namely if they allowed the meeting to go ahead he promised never to return again.

Arthur went off with a few others to get coffee in the restaurant. In the queue ahead of him was the party's press officer Mike Newland, who was loudly protesting that many people were wearing Combat 18, [nazi band] Skrewdriver and even swastika t-shirts. To make matters worse, 'Geordie Paul', originally from Newcastle but now residing in London, came over with an armful of food he had just stolen from the counter.

"You thieving northern bastard!" shouted Jaffa, angrily.

By the time the rally started there were between 400-500 people present, which Arthur thought was impressive but was told it was smaller than the previous year. Aside from the coach from London, the other big contingents were from the West Midlands, where the Black Country organiser boasted of bringing 38 from his area alone. There were also sizeable contingents from the East Midlands, where regional organiser John Peacock was marshalling the troops, and West Yorkshire.

The event was opened by David Bruce, the BNP organiser for nearby Cheshunt and close aide to Tyndall, who boasted that the elaborate security precautions and redirection points were testament to the opposition's fear. While Arthur was still trying to figure out the logic of that comment, Bruce went on to say that the opulent surroundings befitted the party's new image and recent successes. Consciously or unconsciously, Bruce was clearly deciding to overlook the sea of nazi regalia and t-shirts in front of him.

Richard Edmonds continued the theme of the party going from strength-to-strength. While he admitted that Dereck Beackon's loss of his seat so soon after winning in the East End was a setback, he called on local branches to step up efforts to find candidates and get to work early. He then called Michael Davidson, the east London candidate who had recently been attacked with a hammer, to accept the gratitude of the audience. To his embarrassment the east London activist had slipped out the marquee to take up a seat in the bar.

If there remained any illusion about the true nature of the event, it was punctured by the next speaker, Günter Deckert, leader of the neo-nazi National Democratic Party (NPD) in Germany. In a hardline antisemitic speech, he repeatedly called the Holocaust a "hoax" and at one point talked about "a certain species who put nothing into society but would take plenty out".

Deckert was far more militant and extreme than any of the other speakers. He clearly enjoyed being able to say things he couldn't in Germany. On several occasions he drew parallels between the situations in Britain and his home country, riling against their immigration policies and the supposed power of the Jews over the political establishment.

There were repeated cheers from the crowd when he kept raising his right hand in a Hitler salute, joined of course by a small team of armband-wearing nazis he'd brought with him.

Claude Cornilleau was next up: he was leader of the French and European Nationalist Party (PNFE), a French nazi group even more extreme than the Front National. He too focused heavily on the power of Jews in France. In what was a long and boring speech, he only caught the interest of the audience when he said that his organisation took down names of collaborators, by which he meant politicians and journalists, who came out with anti-French or anti-nationalist sentiments. When the time was right they would pay, he added, to great applause.

The longer the Frenchmen went on, the more empty chairs appeared, to the point that Steve O'Connell had to go outside and tell the heavy-drinking BNP supporters to quieten down.

Party leader John Tyndall gave the keynote speech, but by this time it was 5pm and everyone was clearly bored and frustrated. Tyndall attacked Channel Four's investigative series, Dispatches, which had recently aired a programme highlighting the links between the BNP and C18. He claimed it was a political hatchet job and said it was up there with (comedy show) the Two Ronnies as a comedy great.

Almost as soon as he condemned the media for trying to portray the BNP as extremist, he then turned his attention to the Second World War. This was a "suicidal war started by the Jews", he told the crowd. While several people were heard laughing during his speech, no-one left the hall and he received a decent standing ovation at the end.

The post-conference social was held back in central London. Arthur boarded the coach in the company of Daniel Jacks, who was soon to become the lead singer for the notoriously racist C18-linked band, No Remorse. The trip was largely uneventful, except for an almost universal burst of laughter at a man who was apparently talking to the window. No-one had any idea who he was, and it later transpired that he had boarded the coach in the morning and had simply been wandering around Hatfield House all day. The social was held in a pub in Holborn and attended by 60-70 people. There was general euphoria that the day had passed without any anti-fascist interruption. Both Richard Edmonds and Ian Dell said that this proved that there were no *Searchlight* spies in the BNP. Arthur smiled, nodded in agreement, and caught the tube home.

***

Arthur was pumped up after the Annual Rally, telling me everything that had happened in great detail. While he had begun to get used to the casual racism of BNP activists and their thirst for violence, the presence of the German and French speakers at the rally reminded him of the fascist nature of the party.

But Arthur was also impatient and he wanted us to do more with the information he gave us. I would explain that it was pointless to expose him by giving out too much information too quickly and that the longer he remained in the better the access to information he would get. He understood that, but there was a tension there that ebbed and flowed over the years.

While Arthur was motivated by a desire to do as much damage as possible, he loved the sense of adventure, too. Danger can be frightening and it can also be exhilarating. Arthur was quite open about this element of his motivation from the beginning and we factored that in to how he was run – sometimes to his annoyance. He would often dismiss concerns about being exposed and there were times when he clearly felt we could have done more with the information he gave us. Perhaps we could, it's easy to take a view in hindsight, but we were motivated by our own agenda as much as his. We wanted him in for the long-term and that meant not taking unnecessary risks.

***

Edmonds was correct in thinking there was going to be a council by-election in Tower Hamlets, but it was in Lansbury ward and not Weavers Field as he thought. Derek Beackon was the party's candidate, which split opinion among party activists. While Beackon had the name from his Millwall victory, he was a less than inspiring candidate. He was lazy, poor with the media and did not have a good rapport on the doorstep. But reservations aside, Beackon was their candidate and the party threw everything at the election.

Leafleting and canvassing teams were out every day, early evenings during the week and late mornings on the weekend. It was debatable how much each team would actually accomplish, with the time spent in the pub far exceeding the time on the doorstep. Their efforts were hampered by deep divisions within the East London BNP branch, both over the poor organisation but also bitter personal differences which saw two distinct factions emerging.

Alex Cooper and Linda Miller making their voices heard outside an election count in east London in 1994

Arthur went out as often as he could, which generally meant three or four times a week. Aside from the regulars, he met several new interesting people during these campaign sessions. There was Trevor Malcolm Smith, a former bank manager who was once National Front Treasurer in the late 1970s. He was vitriolic in his antisemitism and was an incessant letter writer. He told Arthur about the time he had come across a letter in the street, written by a rabbi, about three young boys who had been abused. Smith ran off 1,000 copies and distributed them door-todoor in the heavily Jewish area of Stanmore. He also boasted how his handiwork got a mention on the magazine-style television series 'That's Life', when it ran a segment about people complaining about abusive and offensive letters they had received.

Malcolm Smith was not alone in letter writing campaigns. A close friend of his was Jim Blake, a housing worker, who was up to similar tricks. To get revenge on a Jewish work colleague who had complained about his poor performance, Blake wrote a letter to the local paper claiming to be a Jewish Holocaust survivor who had finally managed to settle down in London thanks in no small part to the excellent assistance from a certain Jim Blake. The management at work were so pleased with the letter that they gave Blake a special award and his career never looked back.

Another offensive move was when Blake wrote a letter to his local paper in the name of Julius Streicher, the editor of the deeply antisemitic nazi publication *Der Stürmer*, pretending to be a Jew attacking non-Jews. There was, understandably, a local uproar, and a couple of weeks later the editor printed an apology for the distress caused. Directly under the apology was a letter signed by Arnold Leese, the leader of the virulent antisemite Imperial Fascist League, who had died several decades before.

Malcolm-Smith took great delight recounting his exploits. He even told Arthur that his next plan to was send out a thousand cards to people across Lincoln inviting them to a service to commemorate the alleged ritual killing of a nine-year-old boy by Jews in 1255. At the bottom of the letter he intended to add an extract from, so he claimed, the Talmud, the Jewish religious book, saying that all gentiles (non-Jews) should be tortured to death. The letter was to be signed off in the name of the Bishop of Lincoln.

Another interesting group Arthur met on these campaign sessions was a trio from Coventry, who appeared to be friends with Watford activists Peter Illing and Pat Garratt. They proudly bragged about how they'd threatened a leading female Anti-Nazi League activist on her doorstep with a machete. However, it did not quite go according to plan, as they were spooked by a neighbour and ran off, dropping the machete as they fled. One of them had only recently come out of prison for assault.

There were not the only ones involved in bother. Arthur Flinders had been recently charged for assaulting a black man, while Colin Smith was arrested during the campaign for pulling a hammer out on two people he thought were anti-fascists, only to discover they were really plainclothes police officers. Alex, the young skinhead from south London (whose father was an officer in the Merchant Navy), was growing his hair in advance of a trial for yet another violent incident. Meanwhile, Linda Miller continued her plans to attack the east London Anti-Nazi League (ANL) activist, but when another BNP member told her it was wrong to hit a woman, he was told that the ANL activist wasn't a woman but "an animal". On another occasion, BNP leafleters came across a group of ANL activists who were also campaigning in the ward. Attempts by Miller to encourage an attack on the group were only headed off after Richard Edmonds came rushing over to calm things down.

As the campaign wore on, the attitude on the doorstep began to change. Many white households started to publicly voice their irritation at the attention they were given by the BNP. Meanwhile, black and Asian households were becoming increasingly vocal in their opposition too, so much so that the BNP asked the police for protection on one particular leafleting session. This proved to be costly for Michael Davidson, as he was driving around in a car without insurance and was promptly arrested.

Despite the party's optimism, the BNP would eventually come third in the byelection, a long way off from both Labour and the Liberal Democrats. While the party leadership tried to present its 20% vote-share as a triumph, there were growing grumbles of discontent from party activists. Derek Beackon's 1993 council victory seemed a distant memory.

CHAPTER THREE: WARRING FACTIONS

Tension between the British National Party (BNP) and the nazi-terror group Combat 18 (C18) had been obvious since Arthur joined the BNP in the summer of 1994. As time went on this friction would develop into open warfare. And Arthur had a ringside view of it all.

C18, as most tended to call it, had originally been set up by the BNP in 1991 as its stewarding group, in response to growing opposition the far right was experiencing at the hands of anti-fascists over the previous few years. Every time the far right tried to operate openly in London they were challenged, and more often than not very successfully. In 1989, 1,000 nazi skinheads were run ragged through central London as they tried to gather for a gig dubbed The Main Event and two years later there were more serious clashes around Waterloo station at another skinhead gig. In 1991, the openly nazi League of St George group tried to hold a meeting in Kensington Library, but this had to be abandoned after 200 anti-fascists arrived early, locked the fascist security in a downstairs room and took over the venue. Of course, there was a lot of fascist violence as well, most notably a horrendous incident in Bermondsey, when hundreds of fascists, football hooligans and locals attacked an Anti-Racist Alliance demonstration.

It was in response to this growing escalation of violence that the BNP created a stewarding group to protect its meetings and campaign sessions. The stewarding group was initially led by Eddy Butler, and attracted burly party members and others who were up for trouble. Before long the group began to operate more independently, both to offer protection to other far-right groups, but also to go on the offensive against its political opponents.

From a stewarding group, it became Combat 18. The "Combat" was a reflection of their desire for confrontation, the "1" and "8" represented the first and eighth letter of the alphabet - "AH" - Adolf Hitler.

After years of seemingly being on the backfoot, the British far right - through C18 - was going on the offensive. They sought physical confrontation with their opponents and through *Redwatch*, a tatty photocopied newsletter, drew hitlists of people to harass and attack.

However, the group remained loyal to the BNP. "We support John Tyndall and Richard Edmonds 100%...The BNP is growing and anybody who would try and split the movement will be dealt with by us," wrote Charlie Sargent in an early issue of *The Order*, a C18 magazine that first appeared in 1992.

The BNP and C18 honeymoon could not last. Obvious contradictions existed between a political party seeking respectability and a street force hell-bent on confrontation. In January 1993, a BBC television crew was allowed in to a BNP meeting in east London as part of a documentary on the British far right. John Tyndall and Richard Edmonds were keen to impress, packing their meeting with supporters from across the south-east region while telling the presenter, Sarah Spiller, that it was just another local branch meeting. But when the camera swept around the room, it revealed that some in the audience were less than happy.

A small team from the East End Barmy Army, a mob of young and violent far-right activists who became the core of C18, began barracking the TV crew. Outside the hall, the sound recordist was struck on the head with a bottle, an incident that embarrassed Tyndall, undermining the respectable image he sought. A week later, Spiller interviewed Tyndall and brought up the attack, pressing him to condemn it. Increasingly irritated with the line of questioning, Tyndall snapped, ordering the crew and Spiller out of his house. Then, unaware that the camera was still rolling, he told Spiller that the film crew had got what they deserved.

The resulting programme was a public relations disaster. C18 was equally annoyed, though for different reasons. It had protested about the presence of the film crew but its objections had been over-ridden by David Bruce, the BNP's Deputy Organiser. In criticising the BNP's handling of the incident, C18 was also attacking the party's general approach. Paul David 'Charlie' Sargent, writing before the BNP's Tower Hamlets victory in issue two of *The Order*, made plain his growing contempt for the party.

"The struggle in the '90s has evolved to a new level and our present leaders have failed to respond. The Nationalists are still using the failed tactics of the 1970's – rally's [sic] and elections – to win support."

In turn, an April 1993 World In Action TV documentary about C18 compounded the BNP's growing unease at the thuggery of its stewarding force. The programme detailed the group's violence, identified its leaders and revealed its close relationship to the Loyalist paramilitaries of the Ulster Defence Association (UDA) in Northern Ireland. Many in the BNP were horrified, none more so than David Bruce, who had long called for a separation of the two groups. His voice struggled to be heard, though. Despite his long service to British nationalism and his strong support for party leader John Tyndall, he was widely disliked by the party's rank and file; his slightly dark complexion and his occupation as a taxi driver gave rise (bizarrely) to allegations that he was Jewish: perhaps the worst offence that BNP members could imagine.

"We do believe that Dave Bruce is a half-Jew and has no place in the leadership of a nationalist movement," declared C18, even while it claimed to still be fully behind the BNP. The World In Action programme was to be a turning point in the relationship between the two groups.

Charlie Sargent was irritated by what he perceived as the diluting of the BNP's politics in a bid to become more electorally respectable. C18's initial leader, Sargent had a history in the far right stretching back to the hardline nazi British Movement in the late 1970s. He began publicly criticising the party and even

Charlie Sargent walking with John Tyndall in Walsall in 1991

discussing alternatives.

"*The Order* magazine will be sponsoring a national socialist rally in London, in October," he announced in a direct challenge to the BNP. "This will be the first major NS rally held in London for ten years."

In fact, with the encouragement of John Cato, Sargent had planned such a meeting six months earlier, but his inability to get a big-name foreign speaker, and the fallout from the World In Action programme, had caused him to temporarily shelve the plan.

It soon became clear that the two groups were heading their separate ways. Bruce felt confident enough to address a BNP meeting in London and declare that the party should rid itself of C18. Even Eddy Butler, the man who had established the stewards group in the first place, was thinking along the same lines: he had created a monster he couldn't control. Sargent soon learned what was going on through his friends in the party rank and file.

"People like Butler and Bruce are total Tory's [sic] and view most working class people as scum to be used," he wrote in *The Order*. "Such people can have no place in a National Socialist movement who must be seen to protect and help the White working class of Britain."

As the BNP pounded the streets and walkways of Millwall in the run-up to the council election in September 1993, C18 conducted its own activities, including sending a 20-strong mob running down Brick Lane in the heart of what would become 'Banglatown,' smashing windows in response to a protests by local British-Bangladeshis after a vicious racist attack on 17-year-old Quddus Ali a few days before the vote, which had left the young man on life support.

Meanwhile, C18 was advancing its own agenda. "The October meeting will start the ball rolling, followed by meetings in Scotland, Yorkshire, and in the Midlands, over the next year," Charlie Sargent reported in the autumn issue of *The Order*. "At these meetings, a National Socialist manifesto will be drawn up that suits every group...As the Movement evolves so a natural leader will emerge." He made it clear that the BNP did not feature in his future plans.

"Should We Split From The BNP?" Sargent quizzed his readers. "My own view is yes! The BNP is riddled with cranks and informers. Recent history shows that a man with a middle class accent and college tie, who is a member only five minutes, will always be pushed and promoted over a working class lad who has put in years of hard work. However, many may wish to stay inside the BNP, and if that is the case, we propose those cells inside the BNP must work with the aim of taking over the BNP from within, in all forms of power, at every Branch level i.e. the funds and membership must be controlled by National Socialists, and promote our manifesto."

That manifesto, such as it was, clearly favoured the boot over the ballot box. Sargent had no time for people prancing around pretending to be politicians. He wanted action. In this, as in his ideology, he drew inspiration not from the UK but from across the Atlantic in America, particularly from people like Robert Jay Mathews, a neo-nazi legend who in the mid-1980s led a small group of racist followers in declaring war on the United States government.

In the space of 18 months, Mathews' group, known variously as "The Silent Brotherhood" or "The Order", conducted a campaign of killings, financed by robberies and counterfeiting operations, which they hoped would ignite a race war. In 1984 they assassinated Alan Berg, a Jewish radio talk-show host, outside his house, after he had made a number of disparaging comments about the white supremacist movement.

They also murdered a fellow extremist, Walter West, who they feared would expose their plans to the police. A security guard was killed during one of their robberies, too.

"By ones and by twos, by scores and by legions we will drive the enemy into the sea. Through our blood and God's will, the land promised to our fathers of old will become the land of our children to be," Mathews announced in a written *Declaration of War*.

To finance its operations, The Order carried out a series of armed raids, beginning with the theft of just $369 from a pornographic store in Spokane, Washington, and then working its way up to what was then the largest-ever seizure from a US armoured truck when, in July 1984, a dozen armed members stole $3.8 million. Of the $4.3 million in total the group obtained from robberies, only $600,000 was ever recovered. To compliment its heists, The Order also established a major counterfeiting operation which it hoped would eventually undermine the financial stability of the US economy.

The group came to an abrupt end with the arrest of Tom Martinez for possession of counterfeit money. Though on the fringes of the group, Martinez was a trusted friend of Mathews and, despite warnings from those around the leader, had been allowed to know too much. Fearing prison, he struck a deal with the authorities, telling them all about the group, its leaders and plans. The FBI, which had had few previous leads, began making arrests.

Mathews made a last stand, single-handedly occupying a building on Whidbey Island in Washington state and holding off the police. A 12-hour stand-off ensued. Rather than surrender to face possible life imprisonment, Mathews died under a hail of bullets and a fire that ripped through the building. The demise of The Order had come just in time: the group had intended to disrupt the 1984 Los Angeles Olympics and had even devised a plan to poison the water supply of three major cities.

Mathews instantly became a white supremacist martyr. His defiant stand and his uncompromising belief in direct action enticed thousands of other right-wing extremists disillusioned with the political process. He was (mis-)presented by them as an ordinary American aggrieved with society. His death also did much to publicise the novel that had been his inspiration: *The Turner Diaries*, a fictional account of one man's fight against the American system.

Set in the late 1990s, *The Turner Diaries* depicted a national socialist underground army taking up the battle with the American government, which it claimed was under Jewish control. A race war developed after the government outlawed the right to bear arms and attempted to enforce racial integration. Leading the revolt was a white underground movement called The Organization, with a secret leadership known as 'The Order'. Members conducted a terrorist campaign, from the blowing up of FBI buildings to a rocket attack on Congress. Supply lines were cut as the economic infrastructure of America was slowly destroyed. Finally the white population was victorious, but only after Israel was destroyed by nuclear weapons.

Described by some as a modern-day *Mein Kampf*, *The Turner Diaries* became a core text for thousands of neo-nazis throughout the world after it was published. It introduced the term ZOG – the Zionist Occupation Government – to describe a conspiracy theory of a Jewish-run society, a myth adopted by neo-nazi movements in several countries. While the notion that Jews controlled society has long been a central plank of far-right thinking, *The Turner Diaries* provided it with a demonic catchphrase, and the acronym ZOG became ubiquitous among far-right extremists.

Written in 1978 by Andrew Macdonald, a pen name for former Physics professor William Pierce, *The Turner Diaries* is arguably America's most important white supremacist novel. Pierce began his political involvement with the John Birch Society, before moving over to the American Nazi Party under the leadership of Lincoln Rockwell. Shortly after a fellow Nazi Party member assassinated Rockwell, Pierce left to join the National Youth Alliance, with its mottos "Free Men Are

Not Equal" and "Equal Men Are Not Free". In 1974, Pierce founded the National Alliance, through which he built up arguably the most important and well-funded nazi organisation in America, controlling a compound in West Virginia, as well as publishing and music businesses. It is hard to overstate the impact of Pierce's book on the violent extremes of the right, even to this day, nearly 20 years after he died.

One of the most devastating examples of Pierce's influence occurred in April 1995, when former Gulf War veteran Timothy McVeigh planted a bomb which devastated a federal building in Oklahoma City, killing at least 168 people, including 19 children, with more than 680 others injured. It was the single most destructive act of domestic terrorism in US history. McVeigh too had taken inspiration from *The Turner Diaries*.

In late 1993, C18 published a glossy black and white magazine, called simply *Combat 18*. 'The Black Mag,' as it became known, was over 50 pages of pure hate. It contained death threats, bomb manuals and the most offensive cartoons and pictures imaginable. It mocked the Holocaust, abused opponents and called for murder and terrorism. It proved to be the final straw for the BNP, and a month later John Tyndall proscribed membership of Combat 18 in a special bulletin to members.

"Things have now reached a pitch at which the BNP is no longer prepared to tolerate this divisive behaviour, and it is hereby issuing a notice of complete

C18's Will Browning confronting a World in Action camera crew

repudiation of Combat 18 and declaring that group to be a hostile organisation. All BNP members who have hitherto maintained links with both sides should be informed that henceforth and with effect from now they must decide where their loyalties lie. If they wish to remain in the BNP they must sever all connections with Combat18. If they wish to remain with Combat they must consider themselves no longer members of the BNP."

C18 had been ostracised by its founders, but responded with suitable outrage. "Those involved in the struggle now have a straight choice," Charlie Sargent wrote, "between the failed policies of Tory nationalism or the ideology of Adolf Hitler. The two groups cannot work together, one must be crushed." His brother Steve responded in his own style, using the pages of C18 magazines *Putsch* and *Thor Would* to ridicule the BNP leader, calling him "Tinpot" or "Tindole".

The combination of vitriol and ridicule got the message across. Will Browning, C18's hardman and the most prominent figure in most of its violent attacks, was more direct. His first victim was Tony Lecomber, the BNP London organiser who had little time for C18. Lecomber had tried to establish a stewarding group in 1989, shortly after being released from a three-year sentence for attempting to bomb the headquarters of a left-wing organisation, and firmly believed any such group should be under strict BNP control.

Lecomber had been in prison again when C18 was launched, serving a three-year sentence for attacking a Jewish teacher caught peeling off a BNP sticker. He became an outspoken critic of the gang when he was released in late 1993. He was keen to reassert his authority over the London membership and, as a close ally of the BNP's election coordinator Eddy Butler, was a supporter of the community politics that saw the party win in Millwall.

On a personal level, Lecomber had little time for Will Browning, remembering an incident in 1990 in east London when he'd received a nasty beating at the hands of anti-fascists while Browning had wandered off to get a burger. On hearing Browning was now C18's supposed hardman, Lecomber simply laughed: "The man's a coward." What Lecomber failed to realise was that Browning was now quite different from that day in 1990: he was four years older, considerably broader and as fit as an athlete. This, Lecomber discovered to his cost in January 1994 when, on his way to a leadership meeting at BNP headquarters, he bumped into Browning. Despite putting up brave resistance, Lecomber was badly beaten, falling down a manhole in the process.

While Lecomber was to put on a brave face, claiming to people that it was an accidental slip that saw him fall, it clearly made him a worried man. A year later, Arthur noticed a machete in Richard Edmonds's van. He was told it belonged to Lecomber and was there for self-defence in case he ever bumped into Browning again.

A similar fate befell Eddy Butler, the architect of the stewards group and the Millwall by-election victory, whose private condemnation of C18 had earned him the nickname "Snake Lips". Soon after beating up Lecomber, Browning was collecting a C18 magazine from the printers when he learned that Butler was due there the same day. He waited for him and sliced him across the face with a knife; according to C18 literature, it was an attempt to cut out Butler's tongue.

***

Attitudes within London BNP towards C18 were mixed when Arthur joined the party. Perhaps understandably the East and North London BNP branches, heavily under the influence of Lecomber, Eddy Butler, Mike Newland and David Bruce, were generally wary if not strongly opposed to any links to C18. South and West London BNP were far more open to a twin track approach that saw a role for an electoral force and a street army.

In early March 1995, Arthur was out campaigning in Tower Hamlets when the conversation once again turned to C18. Dave King, a prominent east London party activist, summed up the views of many who had remained with the BNP after its split, when he said that C18 was originally a good thing, but since it spent more time fighting fellow nationalists rather than its political opponents it had lost his respect. However, he also felt that the BNP was wrong in proscribing the group, unnecessarily antagonising people, and a better course of action would be to separate but remain respectful. He also agreed with the C18 claim that Tyndall's behaviour had helped encourage state action against the group.

Croydon BNP epitomised the conflicting allegiances of many BNP branches at the time. Unarguably the largest and most active branch within the party in the mid-1990s, it was run by hardline and unashamedly open national socialists. Leading the branch was Paul Ballard, who like many others had a long history in the far right, stretching back several decades. Supporting Ballard was John Merritt, who had previously been in the National Front and part of Nick Griffin's (former NF leader and the future BNP leader) 'political soldiers' faction. In the early 1990s, the Croydon branch established *The Rune*, a hardline antisemitic magazine which denounced the Holocaust as a lie and glorified Hitler's Nazi regime.

In west London's Hounslow branch, local BNP organiser Warren Glass was actually active within C18. The same could be said of most of the activists there, and in fact there was an additional overlap with the Chelsea Headhunters, one of the most infamous football gangs of the 1980s and 1990s. One of the most prominent figures in the Headhunters was Warren's older brother Stuart, who was also active in C18.

Arthur had no intention of being involved in attacking anyone and also had no real desire to get arrested. However, that did not mean that he avoided C18 altogether. In late April 1995, Arthur attended a C18 drinking session in The Sun pub, in Bethnal Green. There were about 50 people there, including C18 leaders Charlie Sargent and Will Browning, with the latter selling him a C18 poster of a masked man holding an M16 assault, with the words: *"Combat 18 - The Voice of Britain"*. There were also a few people with Ulster accents and, most surprising of all to Arthur, about 10 women present. What amused Arthur most was to see several fellow East London BNP members there, including some like Dave King who publicly distanced themselves from C18 while in BNP circles.

A week later, Arthur was out with C18 again, this time joining them on the Derry Apprentice Boys march through central London. It was an impressive turnout, with 40-50 marching as a group. Several he recognised from BNP events, including Edinburgh BNP activist Warren Bennett and London activists Paul Ballard, Mike Barnes, Cameron Law, Keith Hope and Jim Samways. As the march approached Trafalgar Square, a group of C18 thugs broke off and tried to attack an elderly woman photographer who they knew worked for *Searchlight*. Despite being verbally abused and spat on, the photographer stood her ground and carried on taking pictures throughout.

Eddie Whicker, a long time member of the National Front who became involved in C18 at its outset and who had been implicated in a UDA gun exchange a couple of years before, was particularly irate at having his photograph taken, and responded by trying to strangle the woman with her own camera strap.

As the demonstration passed a Labour Party event that was happening in central London at the same time, someone spotted some left-wing newspaper sellers outside. C18 boss Charlie Sargent shouted: "Let's get the cunts!" and as a single group, they all moved forward to attack. Arthur very nervously tagged along. Placards were thrown, but little else had happened by the time the police arrived. Rumours spread that Sargent and a few others were arrested, but even if the C18 leader was, he was out and at a white power gig later that evening.

***

One of the most strident critics of Combat 18 was the BNP's press officer Mike Newland, who rarely lost an opportunity to complain about them and about Nazism in general. But this of course made him even more disliked by the rank and file, especially in the party's Croydon branch, which by the summer of 1995 was probably the largest and most active in the country. It was also one of the most hardline.

Newland was particularly upset by *The Rune*, the magazine produced and distributed by prominent figures within the Croydon branch. At one point he complained to senior members of the party, including John Tyndall, that the antisemitism and continual references to the German SS was incompatible with the new BNP and the party should ban the magazine from being sold at meetings. This of course quickly got back to Croydon members and only made them dislike Newland more.

At one leafleting session Newland was challenged by Croydon members over his comments, with one individual pointing out the hardline and violent histories of many of the BNP leadership. Newland shot back, saying that people like Tyndall and Lecomber had renounced their hardline views and respectability was the other way forward for the party. As Croydon activists literally laughed in his face, Newland shot back: "The trouble with people like you is that you want a nazi saluting club."

With senior Croydon figures watching on amused, Mike Barnes then chipped in, saying that many members were complaining about the quality of the *British Nationalist*, the newspaper that Newland edited. Newland snapped: "The fucking bastards, the cunts. I'm going to resign, the fucking cunts. After all I've done for this party, and I've been beaten up by the reds, they say that. I've had enough. The fucking cunts." The Croydon team went about their campaigning feeling quite satisfied with themselves.

A fortnight later, Arthur and several other London BNP members were among 40 people who attended a Loyalist social event in east London. C18 and UDA man Eddie Whicker was organising, which pleased Arthur as they got on well and he felt a sense of security in his presence. Arthur had by now become used to being in the company of these people and (to an extent) became increasingly immune to their extremism and casual talk and use of violence. That said, there were still times when he felt nervous or even scared. Being in the company of C18 members, with whom he had had no relationship and who would have had no hesitation in giving him a severe beating or worse if he was ever exposed as a mole, ranked among these.

Croydon BNP activist Adrian Woods was also present and excitingly telling people about his new group, the Surrey Border Front (SBF), which Arthur saw as an attempt to play part-time nazis while remaining in the BNP at the same time. Woods had long wanted to get a drum band together to perform at nationalist events in the UK and across Europe. As the drink flowed people lost their inhibitions and during one rowdy song most of the audience, including the BNP contingent, began giving nazi salutes.

News of Newland's threat to resign swept through London BNP, helped in part by Arthur who never lost an opportunity to stir the pot. He wasn't a natural gossiper, but he knew that in the febrile and paranoid atmosphere of the BNP a small story told here or there could cause untold damage. Hearing that Newland might resign, Croydon activist Steve Wheeden stuck the knife in more, referring to the press officer as 'Kike Newland'. He even inferred that Newland might be a spy:

"He comes out of the blue, what's he been doing all these years? Do we know anything about him?"

On another leafleting session, another Croydon activist John Merritt said that he had heard a rumour that Newland had a financial share in a brothel in Bognor Regis. While no-one really believed this, and there was certainly not a shred of evidence to back this claim up, they all thought it was highly amusing and worth spreading.

Newland gave as good as he got. On another leafleting session shortly after this, he was having a conversation with Colin Smith, a veteran far-right activist from south London. They discussed the Croydon branch. Arthur, who was paired with them, overheard the entire conversation. Smith told the party press officer that his girlfriend had offered to stand for the party in Croydon in the following year's local elections, but the local branch seemed uninterested in standing anyone. While Smith recognised the size and activism of the Croydon branch, he also said: "If you don't stand in elections then what's the point?"

Newland was not so generous: "I used to go down there but I can't be bothered anymore," he responded. "They're just a club. All they do is stay at home sharpening their weapons for the race war."

Arthur lost no time in relaying the story to the Croydon activists. Ballard appeared amused by Newland's comments, but Merritt and Barnes were furious.

Merritt called Newland the troublemaker, while Barnes said that he would love to do him over. Ballards' sanguine response might have been because he had other party targets higher in his sights. He remembered a call he'd recently received from Tony Lecomber, where the east Londoner had told that while he liked *The Rune* magazine, Ballard should in future "get rid of the National Socialist rubbish." Ballard told the others that he planned to add the words "the voice of National Socialism" to *The Rune* masthead.

***

Finally, after 18 months of timidity during which time the leadership lost much credibility and the party haemorrhaged members and even entire branches, it seemed as though the BNP had agreed a strategy to confront the threat of Combat 18. Bolstered by a rumoured sizeable financial windfall from the US, the party embarked on a twin track strategy of electoral campaigning and going on the offensive against the hardline nazi group.

With a general election possibly less than year away (it was actually held in 1997), the BNP created a "Wake Up Whites" campaign slogan around which it would seek to stand the minimum of 50 candidates needed for a party political broadcast, which the leadership saw as a key requisite for building the party. Each branch was encouraged to find at least one person willing to stand in the election and to begin leafleting the area as soon and as often as possible.

Edmonds was confident of the opportunities the election offered the party. In addition to the TV broadcast, which would allow the BNP to reach millions of people (in a way that was not possible in these pre-internet days), Edmonds also thought that the modern day Conservative Party under John Major had moderated its views so much, particularly on immigration, that the votes of right-wing Tories were up for grabs.

London BNP kicked off its "Wake Up Whites" campaign in mid-July 1995 with what was supposed to be a London-wide leafleting session in Tower Hamlets, but it did not get off to the start the leadership hoped. Arthur had provided us with information of their plans and we circulated them to anti-fascist groups, who in turn mobilised to prevent the nazis from having a free run. The fear of anti-fascist opposition scared many BNP members away, and on the day just 25 turned up, a paltry number for such a significant event. Worse still, with police and anti-fascists scouring the area, the leafleting lasted less than an hour before they retreated for the safety, and comfort, of the pub. Despite all the fighting talk, London BNP members rarely had the courage of their convictions.

A couple of weeks later another canvassing session in Tower Hamlets ended in disaster, when a multiracial group drinking quietly in a pub took offence to the BNP's presence and gave them a good working over with pool cues.

There was further trouble for the BNP when the party held a meeting in the East Midlands for branch organisers and activists to lay out the plans for the General Election campaign and rally the troops for the months ahead. Arthur, and a number of other moles operating inside the BNP, supplied us with details of the redirection point and we duly passed it over to local anti-fascists, who harassed and chased small groups of BNP activists throughout the day.

After much disruption, the meeting went ahead in a village hall in Lockington, near Castle Donnington, in Leicestershire, with 100 people in attendance. Edmonds opened and spoke about the growing potential for the BNP, while Eddy Butler went into his now familiar routine about fighting elections.

The main thrust of leader John Tyndall's speech was to answer criticism of his leadership and the party's failure to move forward, even at the time of Beackon's short-lived council election victory. Facing criticism from moderates and hardliners alike, his main focus of his speech was answering the effective attacks upon him by C18 and the umbrella group it ran, the so-called National Socialist Alliance (NSA).

Tyndall told the audience that he would not have gays and transvestites in the party, and, in response to an accusation that the BNP allowed Jews to join, he pointed out that in the one case where a Jew had been uncovered as a member, they had been expelled at once. "Jews could not join the BNP," he said, "because they have declared war on the party."

He then then turned his attention to C18 and the NSA and their accusation that the BNP and its leaders were not true nazis. "People say I have sold out," he said. "Whilst the packaging may have changed to suit the times, the product stays the same."

Without naming either group specifically, he referred to his C18/NSA opponents as "Hollywood nazis" and said that those who died defending civilisation in 1945 –

C18 literature

by which he meant the Nazi SS and not the Allied forces – must be in terrible distress in Valhalla looking down upon the antics of these Hollywood nazis. He then went on to accuse C18 as being a tools of the state, saying that this was a re-run of what the state did to the National Front in the mid-1970s, conveniently ignoring his own role in the NF's decline.

Tyndall's speech was basically a summary of a five page article he had written for the party's monthly magazine, *Spearhead*, in which he accused C18 of being nothing other than a state operation. He asked his readers why he had been prosecuted under the Public Order Act during the 1980s, yet no-one had yet been held responsible for the highly inflammatory Combat 18 magazine.

"For myself, I can see no logical reason whatever for this failure to prosecute the C18 people other than it suits the establishment to keep C18 in existence."

Tyndall ended by urging his supporters to "shun like the bubonic plague that coterie of big talkers, small doers and fantasy revolutionaries who employ various AKAs but are best known as 'Combat 18'. Whether these people know it or not – and my observation is that most of them are too pea-brained to know it – they are doing the enemies' work."

The BNP leadership was also believed to have been behind the production and circulation of *The Blue Book*, an anonymously-authored publication depicting Charlie and Steve Sargent as either MI5 agents or stupid clowns. Charlie immediately contacted sympathetic BNP branch organisers, urging them not to distribute the booklet. While this was successful in some regions, hundreds were still circulated.

The British far right was buzzing about this open rift. It was now clear to Arthur that the growing divisions between the BNP and C18 had opened up into a huge and quite public conflict. For the past year C18 had been left snipping at the BNP, and winning over its members without much opposition, but now Tyndall was fighting back.

The weekend after the national BNP meeting in the Midlands, Arthur went to a C18 social in Bethnal Green with at least 15 other London BNP members, proving once again that a sizeable contingent of the party's activist base felt quite at ease with a group they were meant to have nothing to do with. While he and others drank, sang and read nazi literature, the leaders of the Croydon BNP branch were huddled over the pool table with Charlie Sargent and Will Browning discussing C18/BNP relations.

***

In the summer of 1995, Arthur travelled over to Hounslow in west London a number of times to campaign for local organiser Warren Glass, who was standing as a BNP candidate in a Hounslow council by-election. While the leafleting attracted BNP activists from across the capital, including the likes of Edmonds, Linda Miller (now Cooper) and Colin Smith, it also brought out people who were also active with C18. Not everyone was impressed by their presence, with Mike Newland being particularly scathing.

The election count brought out those who were not interested in leafleting, including many of the big names within C18, precisely because there was more likely to be a confrontation with their political opponents. Having thwarted an anti-fascist attack on their paper sale the week before, C18 decided to mobilise for the count itself in the hope of a rematch.

The evening got off to a fractious start when a fight broke out within their own mob. One of the main faces out that night was Andy Frain, a notorious Chelsea hooligan, who had just re-emerged after a period on the run in Liverpool, after he had bottled an Irishman in a pub who, it later transpired, was connected to the main crime family in Kilburn in north London.

As the joint C18/BNP mob gathered near the town hall, Frain approached a young skinhead wearing a green flying jacket over a blue football top.

"Is that a Chelsea top?" Frain enquired.

"Of course it is, you muppet," answered the skinhead cheerfully.

The bystanders winced: they knew exactly how Frain would react. Weeks of anxiety were released as the Nightmare punched the young man square in the face, sending him crashing to the floor. Frain pulled out a blade and moved in to finish the job, pulled off just in time by others before he could do more damage.

The nazis knew that the ANL had prepared a picket outside the town hall. Banter between protesters and police was sharply curtailed as news of the imminent arrival of the BNP/C18 mob spread. Officers huddled together, talking into their radios, collecting and relaying instructions, while the demonstrators organised themselves for the usual verbal assault on the nazis. Up the street, the first faces were spotted, but rather than the usual dozen or so, the trickle turned into a stream - about 80 in total.

The eerie moment of silence that followed the sighting of this mob was shattered as the gang broke into a run. The police attempted to restrain them but it was never going to work. A shower of bottles and bricks rained down on the officers and the protesters. The Tactical Support Group, London's specialist riot police, were called into action but took 30 minutes to arrive.

By then the local police had lost control and the damage was done. Many of the ANL supporters, some in tears, fled into the council building to escape the missiles. Less fortunate was the victorious Labour candidate, Les Bawn: he arrived at the height of the violence and, without realising what was occurring, strode towards the entrance. With a shout of "Get him!" the mob made one last surge and Bawn was struck on the back of the head with a brick.

Inside the hall, a couple of national BNP representatives, oblivious to events outside, pondered the absence of their candidate and his local unit. Colin Smith, the party's election officer, turned to Steve O'Connell, the Newham organiser, and asked if he should go and fetch them from the pub. "No, I don't think that would be a good idea," replied O'Connell, who had been in the pub earlier that evening. "I don't think you will like what you see."

Down the road, election candidate Warren Glass was brushing himself down to remove any traces of his involvement in the evening's fracas. Then, to loud applause from his supporters and a raucous rendition of "God Save the Queen", he strolled into the hall to take part in the democratic process. Turning to the press, he blithely disassociated himself from the violence. "The BNP," he asserted, "were not responsible."

***

Meanwhile, John Tyndall had one final card up his sleeve, and it proved to be a good one. William Pierce was unquestionably the most prominent nazi in the world and, as author of *The Turner Diaries* and another neo-nazi novel *Hunter*, probably the most influential and respected. So when Tyndall secured his agreement to speak at the BNP's annual rally, before heading off to Spain for the 20th anniversary bash to mark the death of General Franco (the former fascist leader of Spain), it was quite a coup. It would have been big news regardless, but given C18's own reverence of the American and the story of Robert Matthews, it was even more significant.

Shame then that the BNP could not find a venue fitting for the occasion. Despite their best endeavours, which included trying to book the New Connaught Rooms, a venue adjacent to the Freemason's hall in central London, all they could come up with was the public bar of the New Cotton Inn in Mile End, east London.

As usual, Arthur arrived early to note who was coming in and out. He had a fantastic memory as well as being disciplined enough to make notes on his return home. The audience of 200-300 activists was well down on previous years and reflected the success C18 had had in winning over BNP members and recruits. If that was not embarrassing enough, not all could get into the public bar and at least a third of the audience were resigned to drinking in another room, out of earshot of the rally. Many left in disgust.

David Bruce chaired the meeting and Edmonds spoke first, followed by Mike Newland, but as he rose to speak a young man near the front threw up and staggered out, leaving a trail of vomit behind him. When it came to the regional reports, Warren Bennett, the party's Scottish organiser but also a key C18 supporter, said the IRA was the biggest problem in Scotland, which in turn set off chants of "No Surrender to the IRA!" with lots of foot stamping. This was followed by shouts of "Sieg Heil!" and nazi salutes. Tyndall and Edmonds were both visibly angry.

It was rare that Tyndall would allow himself to play second fiddle at a party event, especially at the annual rally, but in this case he was alert enough to understand William Pierce's currency to party members. Pierce began by comparing the differences between the nazi movements in Britain and the USA, before telling the audience that the FBI assessment that *The Turner Diaries* was a blueprint for terrorism was a compliment. Chants of "Free The Order!" broke out when Pierce mentioned The Order members who were serving very long prison sentences in the USA.

Pierce's wife had a slightly more disturbing experience of the event after she went to use the women's toilets at the pub, only to find it full of drunken BNP louts who could not get into the overcrowded men's room.

Emboldened by Pierce's presence, Tyndall's speech focused heavily on the party's dispute with C18 and the NSA and employed a now well-trodden set of words. "If those who had died on the Eastern Front for the Third Reich could rise up," he proclaimed, "they would spit on the leaders and followers of C18 for the way they had besmirched the movement."

This was greeted by loud jeers from the back of the hall and at least one shout of "Bullshit!" from a key east London member.

While the rally was in many ways a disaster, Pierce's presence was a vital political coup. This, together with the decision to allow a key Tyndall rival, Nick Griffin – who had helped oust him from the NF back in the early 1980s – into the party, encouraged hardliners, including activists from key branches such as Croydon, Leeds and Scotland. Not everyone was pleased though, with both Eddy Butler and Mike Newland leaving the BNP, but all this did was solidify Tyndall's position further. Gradually, some of the party branches that had switched allegiances to the NSA returned.

CHAPTER FOUR: A WEEKEND AWAY

In late August 1995, Arthur joined a minibus of other London BNP activists to travel up to Wales to spend the bank holiday weekend with John Merritt. Merritt had recently relocated with his family with the help of former senior National Front (NF) member, and leader, Nick Griffin. The close friendship between Merritt and Griffin went back to their days in the NF in the 1980s, where both had been part of the faction, which had vocally offered support for Libyan leader Colonel Gaddafi, as well as the Ayatollah in Iran and the American black separatist Louis Farrakhan.

Now Griffin was using Merritt's magazine, *The Rune*, to push his messages and worm his way into the BNP. Merritt's decision to uproot himself from London was actively encouraged by Griffin, who not only helped him find a cheap place to rent in a small village in Powys, close to where he lived, but also found him some work with the Forestry Commission, where he worked as well.

The offer of a weekend in Wales was too good for Arthur to pass by. Not only was it a great the opportunity to find out more about Griffin's political intentions, who was playing an increasingly influential role within the BNP since his re-emergence in frontline politics over the previous couple of years, but he also viewed it as a little mini-holiday with friends. That might seem a strange thing to say, given that Arthur was an anti-fascist spying on his political opponents, but personal bonds were forming between some of them, perhaps unsurprising given that Arthur was seeing the same people two, three or even four times a week.

Croydon BNP member Adrian Woods borrowed the minibus off a friend, who in turn had borrowed it off someone else, and after meeting at East Croydon station the group of 10 set off. Paul Ballard, the Croydon branch organiser, recited a call he had just had from a fuming Combat 18 leader, Charlie Sargent, who demanded that Ballard publicly denounce the anti-C18 *Blue Book*, believed to have been the work of either Tony Lecomber or Mike Newland. While Ballard denounced the publication to Sargent, he had no intention of going to bat for him publicly, though he wasn't quite as forthright in saying that to the C18 boss.

National Front News

This set off a general discussion about C18 more generally, with most of the group openly disparaging about them. Jim Samways, another Croydon member and former paratrooper, said that they were "all mouth and no action". Rob Lowry concurred, adding that an act of recent vandalism by Samways, which had made the front page of the local newspaper, was more action than C18 had ever managed to do. Pat Garratt, from Watford BNP, was more circumspect. While he appeared loyal to the BNP, he was known to have gone to the occasional C18 event and once or twice had even turned up at BNP meetings wearing a C18 t-shirt.

Lowry, meanwhile, recounted yet another beating he had received. By his own admission, he had been drinking in a pub and, without any provocation, began racially abusing a black man having a quiet drink. A white guy came up to Lowry and told him to stop abusing his friend, promptly attacking him.

Swapping such banter back-and-forth, the group finally arrived in Shrewsbury, close to the border with Wales, where they were met by Merritt and his family. While his wife Jenny, who was also heavily involved in the production of *The Rune*, drove the two boys back to Wales, Merritt hopped in the van so he could direct them then across the Welsh border to his new home. Arthur had known Merritt for a year now, but his interactions had been brief and any discussion mainly focused around party activity and politics. Now, up close and personal, Arthur saw a more conspiratorial side. Merritt and his wife discussed at length a recent UFO sighting, with Jenny (incredibly) believing that it was "the Jews" who were coming from outer-space. Merritt remarked that two days after the UFO sighting, the postman had told him that someone was asking where the BNP lived in the area. He clearly connected the two incidents.

The kids were equally alarming. The eldest, who was only five, went on about spies everywhere as though they were bogeymen. He said that he was going to get a machine gun and kill them all.

After settling in at Merritt's new home, which involved putting up tents in a large garden, they all decamped to a nearby pub, which coincidentally was holding a wedding party. For no obviously reason other than being idiots, Samways and Lowry discussed the idea of attacking the wedding party "for a laugh". Arthur winced.

As the drink flowed, so the gossip grew, mainly about other people in the nationalist movement in south London. Several people were slagging off Martin, a local activist in Mitcham, who they all thought was both useless and holding the party back. Several complained that his girlfriend objected to his racist politics and as a result would not let him out often. Adrian Woods noted that he once spent the night there but was so scared of her he kept a knife under his pillow in case she attacked him. Another target of their hatred was Cameron Law, a south London BNP activist who was also very involved with C18. Woods and Merritt were particularly scathing about him, though Ballard was more circumspect. And then there was Tim, from the East London BNP branch, who had just been arrested yet again and considered "a real pyscho" by everyone.

Woods, meanwhile, had actually bought his drum kit with him, presumably with the intention of playing. During the late 1980s he had been part of the National

BNP Croydon Organiser Paul Ballard

Front's drum corps, which would insult the memory of the war dead by leading a fascist march to the Cenotaph on Remembrance Sunday every year. Woods was now keen to get a drum band back together, believing that he would play at nationalist events across Europe, but repeated requests for Arthur to join were met by laughter and ridicule.

Eventually talk turned to Nick Griffin, with Paul Ballard saying that Griffin was intent on building a power base within the BNP, with a view to becoming its leader. While Ballard recognised Griffin was a good speaker and that he would make an excellent leader, he also said: "You can't just join an organisation and expect to take it over."

During a lull in the conversation, Merritt announced that they would be travelling to Leeds the next day, where Griffin would be speaking at a party branch meeting. This caused mixed reaction, with some people excited to meet what was generally considered the second most important BNP branch in the country, after Croydon of course, while others were reluctant to spend another day on the road.

Of course, this was not up for discussion, and the next morning they set off to Yorkshire. Fortunately for Adrian Woods, in light of what was going to happen, he took his drum kit out of the van. He was, however, particularly unpleasant during the journey, telling everyone that they should grab a "race-mixer" off the street and tar-and-feather them. Shockingly, he appeared quite serious. He also told everyone about how he and his mate Squirrel would go "on nigger hunts" together. Arthur did not have much time for Woods before this trip, but now he absolutely hated him.

They were pumped up by the time the minibus entered Leeds. The jovial banter about 'nigger hunts' and attacking their opponents had made everyone much more upbeat about the meeting. The American white power band, People Haters, almost as extreme as C18's No Remorse, was blaring out over the van's music system.

"Jew jew jew jew jewboy – JEWBOY!" screamed the singer's voice as the van arrived at Leeds railway station, with some of the London group providing a backing chorus. "Jew jew jew jew jewboy – AUSCHWITZ!"

They parked up, as arranged, and soon were met by Griffin and some of the lads from Leeds BNP. Griffin told them to wait for further instructions as he and the locals headed off.

A few minutes later, as the London crew sat passing the time, a groups of 30 people walked up the street towards them. Some of the London group initially thought they were fellow BNP and were readying themselves to greet them, but it was Merritt who first saw the Asian lad with them and immediately shouted: "AFA!" – shorthand for "Anti-Fascist Action".

Panic broke out on the minibus. Paul Ballard leapt out of the van to confront the approaching group, as did Rob Lowry and Jim Samways. Ballard then thought better of it and turned on his heals, running in the other direction: he was later caught by some of the anti-fascist group and given quite a pasting.

John Merritt

Tony, another south London activist who was driving the van, attempted to start the engine, but when he saw Ballard jump out he stopped. One of the attackers reached in and promptly grabbed the van's keys. Fortunately he just tossed them across the street, where they were picked up by an onlooker. Some tried to defend themselves from inside the vehicle, throwing punches as best they could, while others simply covered their heads in self-defence, only to be showered by breaking glass.

The attackers were indiscriminate in their violence. Arthur – ironically, an antifascist – was hit on the head by a hammer by what appeared to be the only woman in the other group. The police arrived a few minutes later, but by then the damage was done. They'd all got a hammering, as had the van. The windows were all smashed with the exception of the windscreen – and even that was not for the want of trying.

Shell-shocked, the group stood around licking their wounds and trying to comprehend what had happened. Merritt thought Samways had been kidnapped, while Ballard had been stabbed in the side of the head and had to go off to hospital. Everyone considered the attack on Ballard an attempted murder, as the blade had missed his temple by a couple of centimetres.

Making matters worse, the police (according to the BNP, at least) were more interested in what the group was doing in Leeds rather than taking down details of what had actually happened. Even when an AFA spotter was pointed out circling the area on a motorbike, the police made no attempt to apprehend him. Worse still, a man who introduced himself as a journalist began chatting to the wounded BNP activists. As the police left, he got into the back of one of the cars and simply went off with them. "Special Branch," they all agreed.

By the time the battered BNP group arrived at the Black Lion pub, where the meeting was taking place, they were fuming. While all were concerned about the fate of Ballard, anger was already being directed at Leeds BNP. Not only had they, and seemingly they alone, been sent to a redirection point while local activists had gone straight to the venue, the local branch didn't even provide any security, leaving the London group as proverbial lambs to the slaughter. Worse still, it was widely suspected that the leak, which led the attackers to the train station, must have come from within Leeds BNP.

Arthur's head was aching as the meeting started and as a result, perhaps unsurprisingly, his recollection of the speakers was patchy. Fortunately for us, we had another person in the room passing us information, so we got decent feedback.

While the Londoners were nursing their wounds, the Leeds activists were more focused on events in Halifax a couple of days before. In what had supposed to be a clear-the-air gathering, a massive brawl had erupted between Leeds BNP and Yorkshire/London C18, with several BNP members badly hurt. The evening had been going well until a BNP activist began slagging off C18 and was promptly glassed. The whole pub erupted in violence, with the police being called and arrests made. Charlie Sargent rang some of the Leeds lads the following morning to apologise and to try to smooth things over, but the ill-feeling towards London C18 was palpable.

Back in Leeds, the BNP meeting opened with the local branch organiser apologising to the Londoners for what had happened. He tried to explain that as they had not had any bother from AFA for the previous 18 months, they had probably become too complacent. He also suggested that BNP branches should twin, so they would work together and even attend each other's meetings. He suggested that Leeds twin with Croydon, which initially went down well with the visitors but they quickly changed their minds.

Later, after the formal meeting, the organiser promised to "take out" five anti-fascist targets in retribution.

The main speaker was Nick Griffin, who attempted to appeal to the hardliners and modernisers at the same time. He talked about the "fascist movement" in the context of the nation state and specifically said that he was not opposed to using the word "fascist". At the same time, he argued that the party's aim to stand 50 candidates in the next General Election was correct, as it would bring in huge numbers of new recruits. He did, however, stress that the BNP should not just be about elections, but rather it had to build a power base in a variety of ways, via family as well as vigilante groups – an 'interesting' mix, to be sure.

The mood of the group had lifted as their battered and badly damaged van left Leeds. John Merritt thought the idea of twinning branches was a great idea and they all looked forward to working more closely with Leeds in the future. Arthur totally agreed with this idea, though for very different reasons. The idea of being able to spy on another important BNP branch was too good to pass up.

The van made its way onto the motorway with just the front windscreen intact, and only one working light. Yet luck was still against them, as the increasingly cold activists were temporarily stranded when it ran out of petrol.

Once underway again, it was at a pub stop close to the Welsh border that the conversation returned to the events of that morning. Before long the general attitude towards the Leeds branch had changed dramatically. Some people thought that *Searchlight* had an infiltrator in Leeds BNP, who in turn had passed information to AFA, while others thought the leaking of the redirection point was linked to the fighting between London C18 and Leeds BNP. Others thought that because only Londoners were attacked, a local fascist had deliberately leaked the information in a bid to knock Croydon branch down a peg or two.

Whatever the truth, the general consensus was that someone in Leeds BNP had to have been involved and as a result they wanted nothing more to do with the Yorkshire branch. In fact, they decided that they really couldn't trust anyone going forward and that from then on Croydon branch would increasingly act independently of the London BNP leadership and C18.

Full of drink, they finally left the pub to return to Merritt's new home, where they were going to spend the night before returning home. It was then that van's fan belt came off. In fact, despite a stop in a local garage to repair it, the belt was to come off a further four times. It was 4.30am in the morning when the freezing patriots rolled into Merritt's drive.

CHAPTER FIVE: WE HAVE A MOLE

Our first meeting after Leeds was quite awkward. I really wasn't sure how Arthur was feeling about his undercover role – or even towards me.

He had been struck across the head with a hammer in what had clearly been quite a vicious attack. While it could have easily been worse, it was still not what he had signed up for. I also wasn't sure if he blamed me for the attack. The anti-fascists had obviously been told about the BNP meeting point by someone and while Arthur knew he hadn't been the source, it was clear that the anti-fascists had been tipped off by someone with inside information.

Obviously my main concern was Arthur's well-being, and I was quickly assured that he was physically fine. In fact, even if he did think that I might have been involved in passing over the information that led to the attack, he wasn't saying. He was actually in quite a jovial mood as he retold the story of the weekend, finding the windowless journey back home particularly amusing. We avoided a direct discussion on how Leeds anti-fascists knew the redirection point. I guess that suited us both.

***

The fallout from the Leeds trip was swift and deep. While those present had blamed Leeds BNP, it also made several reconsider their support for, and involvement in, the BNP more generally. Rob Lowry, Adrian Woods and Jim Samways all announced that they were leaving the party and throwing their support behind the National Socialist Alliance (NSA), Combat 18's supposed political wing, believing that only C18's more "physical" supporters could properly protect nationalist events now. Paul Ballard and Pat Garratt voiced a strong desire to stay loyal to the BNP, but several others sat on the fence.

Ripples of discontent were also felt across London after the attack, with furious and frenzied discussions about the mole's possible identity. While none of those caught up in the attack knew of the intended meeting point in advance, that did not stop London BNP activists drawing up lists of possible spies within their ranks. Dissension and suspicion certainly weakened the BNP at the time.

Of course, this also reflected a general paranoia among many of those involved in the British National Party during this time. At *Searchlight* we had reported on internal BNP meetings in some detail. Worse still, there had been a number of physical assaults on BNP activists where the identity of the attackers was unknown.

Press officer Mike Newland was attacked at his home by people he thought were in C18, Michael Davidson lost an eye after being attacked by a gang wielding iron bars while out canvassing in east London, and Alf Waites had his computer (which contained a copy of the party membership) stolen in a robbery on his house. On top of all that, there were now repeated anti-fascist mobilisations to counter BNP activities in east London, with some so specific that they could only have come from information from within.

Arthur stuck with the BNP, keeping a channel open to those who had left, meeting and speaking to as many people as he could. John Merritt, who came down to London the weekend after the Leeds attack, said that he had received a call from C18 leader Charlie Sargent, who told him: "You are either with us or against us, and if you are against us then you are going to get your fucking head kicked in." Paul Ballard, however, had had a far more sympathetic call from the C18 leader to check that he was ok.

Another person sticking with the BNP was south London activist Cameron Law, which was a surprise to many as he was considered close to C18. When Arthur questioned Law's allegiance, he was told that the BNP needed all the people they could get at the moment. Merritt was also surprised, claiming that Charlie Sargent had admitted to him that he had instructed Law to stay close to Ballard and report back on what was happening and disrupt things if required. Whether Sargent actually said that is unclear, but it only added to the unease and suspicion of everyone around.

Merritt rubbished the idea that the attack was an attempt by Leeds BNP to undermine the Croydon branch, claiming if that was truly the case then they would not have organised the whip-round at the meeting to help pay for the damage to the van. However, he also said that he had heard that C18's trip to Halifax that same weekend was an attempt to encourage Leeds BNP to switch allegiance to the NSA, but the offer was rebuffed and that was the real reason for the violence.

He clearly had little time for C18 generally and Sargent specifically, describing him to Arthur as "an illiterate scumbag ... Every other word he says is fuck."

While dismissing some of the wilder theories behind the attack, Merritt did confide to Arthur half an hour later that "we" – by which he was referring to Surrey and Leeds BNP plus Nick Griffin – "are going to take over the party."

Also facing Merritt's wrath was Adrian Woods, who the day before the Leeds attack was slagging off C18 but now was aligning himself to it. "He has bottled it," Merritt fumed. "He is a traitor." He recounted how Woods had told him that the choice facing Surrey BNP was to join the NSA or risk being beaten up on a regular basis. "Maybe we should do him over and then he will come back to us," retorted an increasingly angry Merritt. He went on to add that if anyone from C18 threatened or even attacked anyone from Surrey BNP then without any warning he would "cut them up".

Eventually Ballard chipped in, regretting remaining so close to Sargent after John Tyndall proscribed any association with C18 in December 1993. He admitted this had made it easier for the group to disrupt their branch. He also added that Tyndall had not been too upset with the split within Croydon BNP, as it got rid of the troublemakers while the good people stayed loyal.

It was also clear that Ballard had little time for Woods either, viewing his actions as a betrayal. Ballard attended a hastily arranged activist meeting to discuss the attack, but walked out after Woods had encouraged people to leave the BNP. Croydon BNP had launched an appeal to raise funds for the damage to the van and this had already reached £560, but if Woods asked for the money then Ballard was only going to say it raised £100, with the rest being transferred to *The Rune*.

Ballard had now bought into the view that C18 was a state-controlled operation, a viewpoint which was being widely pushed by the likes of John Tyndall and Tony Lecomber. Ballard relayed Tyndall's view that the link between Charlie Sargent and the nazi-satanist David Myatt highlighted an MI5 link, as "Myatt had been State in the past." Myatt, who was the leader of the secretive group the Order of Nine Angles – which focused on entryism into fascist organisations, in order to pursue a murderous ideology and agenda – had recently become involved in C18 and appeared to be increasingly influential on both Charlie and his brother Steve.

While both Ballard and Merritt thought Tyndall had been ill-advised to write such a public attack on C18 in *Spearhead*, they both felt that he was absolutely right in what he had written. Merritt said that he and Nick Griffin were now going to write a similar piece for the next edition of *The Rune*.

Arthur next caught up with some of those who had decided to join C18's front organisation, the National Socialist Association. They had no animosity towards Ballard or those who were sticking with the BNP, but they simply felt the party had let them down and could not properly defend their events in the future. None of them believed Merritt's claims to have been threatened by Charlie Sargent, who, they claimed, was putting no pressure on anyone to leave the BNP. They should know, they insisted, as they had met up with Sargent and other C18 activists in The Sun pub, in Bethnal Green, soon after their return from Leeds.

Interestingly, they gave Arthur's C18's version of events in Halifax, which was slightly different from that relayed to him in Leeds. Supposedly, only Will Browning – C18's emerging leadership contender – and Kevin Simms accompanied Sargent on the trip, which was more of a social than a planned effort to get Leeds BNP to split away. During the course of the evening, one of the Leeds lads called London C18 "soft southern bastards", whereupon he was glassed in the face by Browning. While a mass fight did break out, it was mainly between Halifax C18 and Leeds BNP, with the London trio – according to Sargent – taking no further part.

They were all insistent that their new allegiance was to the National Socialist Alliance rather than C18 and that the decision was as much to do with frustration at the BNP leadership as it was about the attack in Leeds.

In the space of two weeks Croydon BNP had gone from the largest and most active branch in the country to becoming bitterly divided and split. While some of these divisions were to heal over time, the attack in Leeds and the general concern about moles within the BNP had a profound impact on the ongoing future of this branch.

***

Adrian Woods's new venture was the Surrey Border Front (SBF), an independent group but political aligned to the National Socialist Alliance project of C18. Perhaps paranoid, perhaps cautious, Woods devised a plan to make the SBF immune from the prying eyes of the police. The group would have a coded telephone tree, where instructions were issued through seemingly innocuous messages, so they could arrange meetings without the police getting all the details, and non-members would only be allowed to attend one meeting before they paid their dues or were frozen out. He even had plans for a new magazine, similar to that behind the original idea of *The Rune*, before it got taken over by Nick Griffin and became the vehicle for his return to frontline politics.

Like many of the NSA affiliates, the Surrey Border Front was to have little impact on society. It produced the occasional leaflet opposing the building of mosques in south London and in Chichester, West Sussex, but its followers were largely inactive (apart from several socials). At one point, these followers burnt a cross on public land, but were furious when nothing was reported in local media (the far right has since become adept at using the media to report on their activities, as a means of boosting visibility). At another event, Woods had made some papier-mâché models sculptured to represent black faces, then filled them with red paint and encouraged drunken supporters to stab them.

Arthur tried to straddle all the different factions in order to elicit as much information as possible. He remained in the BNP, but also moved in the NSA and SBF orbit too. On 28 September 1995 he attended an NSA meeting in a pub in Holborn, central London. The audience consisted of C18 leaders, Blood & Honour activists and BNP members. In fact, probably every BNP branch in London was represented there.

In a clear plug to the BNP activists, Charlie Sargent announced that C18 was ready to offer security to all London BNP branches in the run-up to the next election, which most people presumed would be the following year. While this was clearly designed to cause further disruption within London BNP, given that there was no way that the likes of Lecomber, Newland and Butler would accept C18 anywhere near their events, it clearly impressed people in the room, especially Dave King, a BNP member from Newham who had recently taken over organising security in east London.

Adrian Woods

Adrian Woods used the meeting to encourage those still in the BNP to switch over to the NSA, but his advances had little impact. King was obviously chuffed Adrian Woods with his rise within East London

David Copeland and John Tyndall

being so badly hampered by recent anti-fascist mobilisations over the preceding 18 months, it was decided that going ahead was not worth the risk.

In the end, the anniversary rally was pushed back a fortnight to 20 September. Arthur was supposed to be working that day but managed to wangle half a day off so he could attend. After a quick change of clothes, he jumped on the tube and made his way to the redirection point in Bow, where he saw lots of people milling about – BNP members and anti-fascists – but no-one he knew. The one person he did recognise was Julie Waterson, the fearless leader of the Anti-Nazi League (ANL), who was walking around in the company of a minder/photographer.

Rather than approaching people randomly in the hope they were also attending the BNP rally, Arthur decided to ring up a BNP contact to check what was happening. On being told to head to The Swan pub in Stratford, in east London, Arthur caught the overground, arriving in Stratford moments before anti-fascists attacked. There was little actual fighting, more the fight of running and shouting, and the anti-fascists had the nazis on their heels. Standing outside The Swan, bloodied but defiant, was John Tyndall and a small group of supporters, including David Copeland. Arthur immediately presumed Tyndall had been punched or bottled, but it later transpired that as anti-fascists had charged at the BNP, Tyndall had fallen over and hit his head on the curb. Despite being an anti-fascist spy trying to disrupt and even destroy the BNP, Arthur felt a tinge of admiration for the way the BNP leader stood there defiantly as anti-fascists circled the area and police sirens filled the air.

Arthur then looked around, not quite sure what to do. He was mindful that he could be identified as a BNP member and attacked at any moment. He moved tentatively from doorway to doorway, weary of the groups of anti-fascists who appeared to be everywhere. He bumped into the new member, David Copeland, who had been with Tyndall when they got attacked, and the two of them went to a nearby pub for a quick drink and refuge. There, Arthur tried Dave Hill again, but couldn't get through. He then rang Ken Francis, the Newham organiser, who told him to make his way to Bromley-by-Bow, which he did, but by that time everyone had moved on. Arthur and Copeland parted ways, both seemingly going home. Arthur later heard that Copeland had managed to join up with a few others and together had gone into central London with the aim of attacking the Politico bookshop in Westminster because it sold *Searchlight* magazine.

Tyndall was not the only BNP victim that day. Ian Dell, head of BNP security, was badly beaten, as was Mike Barnes, the antisemitic cartoonist from south London. He was part of the Croydon group that had been chased by anti-fascists. While others got away, Barnes was caught and hit.

The fallout from the day was even more severe than what happened on the day itself. Newham BNP basically folded, with Ken Francis getting the blame, and it scuppered their plans to launch the London election campaign. New and seasoned members alike dropped out and a general sense of fear gripped London BNP. This had been the fourth attack on an East London BNP meeting over the past two years, but definitely the worst – not least because pictures of a bloodied party leader appeared in the national media. More significantly, though, the BNP now knew it had a mole within their ranks and Tony Lecomber was on the warpath to discover who it was. But the impact of this was probably not what he expected: the more he hunted for the mole, the more the good and loyal activists came under suspicion and resentment grew.

Despite being a personally scary moment for Arthur, he was buzzing in the weeks following The Swan incident. While he was uneasy at the use of violence by anti-fascists, he could see the consequences it had on BNP members. He had sometimes been frustrated that more of his information was not being used by *Searchlight* or acted upon, but the fact that the BNP anniversary rally had to be abandoned, coupled with the internal fallout, showed that using his information sparingly and strategically was always going to be more effective. While he accepted that we would not be able to use his information publicly for a while, in order to protect him from suspicion, his mind was already turning to disrupting the BNP's Annual Rally later in the year. London BNP was in a mess and this was partly down to Arthur.

CHAPTER SIX: INFIGHTING

London was booming in the 1990s, both economically and culturally. A new skyline was appearing in east London's Docklands, as the business capital expanded out. 'Cool Britannia' reflected this growing confidence and the growing hegemony of liberal middle-class culture. Nick Hornby's book, *Fever Pitch,* personified the changing nature of London's football spectators and 18 years of Tory rule was coming to an end. For the BNP, the heady days of Derek Beackon's council victory in Millwall, back in 1993, was becoming a distant memory, as demographic change was moving the traditional East End to outer London. East London BNP was on the wane, both as a consequence of all this change but also due to the continual anti-fascist disruptions of events and a high turnover of local party organisers. Croydon branch, meanwhile, remained the largest and most active of the party's branches across the capita, but even here there were problems.

Branch organiser Paul Ballard had been arrested for drink-driving but told people that he would claim that he was suffering psychological damage from the disastrous attack in Leeds in August 1995. He wanted to stand down as organiser, but had second thoughts after the widely disliked Croydon activist Steve Wheedon indicated that he was keen to take on the job. After initially planning to set up a chicken farm in Wales, John Merritt – who helped create *The Rune* magazine but had left Croydon in the summer of 1995 to be closer to his good friend Nick Griffin – became disillusioned with Wales and the family had moved back to south London.

Merritt's promised work had not materialised, but the final straw was Griffin racking up huge charges on his phone bill after faxing a large number of documents to the US. In the summer of 1996 Croydon party stalwark and *Rune* cartoonist Mike Barnes dropped out of the party after getting into a fight with Steve Wheedon. Out leafleting one day, Barnes missed out a road they were supposed to cover. Wheedon called him a dithering idiot, causing Barnes to lash out and try to throw a punch. Wheedon was too quick for him and lashed out first, sending Barnes to the ground, kicking him in the head several times. Arthur, Merritt and Pat Garratt had to pull Wheedon off before he caused more damage. As Barnes staggered off, Arthur and others looked on in utter disbelief.

The Surrey Border Front (SBF), launched by Adrian Woods in response to anger at the Leeds attack, was also struggling. The euphoria that accompanied its launch quickly evaporated as numbers dwindled and several key activists drifted back to the BNP. By 1997, it appeared only Woods was left and even he was having a pretty miserable time. In the summer of 1996 he announced that he was no longer

BNP literature

planning to go to any Blood & Honour gigs, after having a third hire van smashed up within a year.

Unlike the Leeds attack, this particular attack was caused by his own side. He had taken his girlfriend to a gig, only to find her ex-boyfriend also there. An argument ensured and the ex, backed up by some of the C18 lads, had smashed up his van. To make matters worse, two of the people who had travelled to the gig in the van fell out with each other and traded blows. The misery was not yet over for Woods. On their way home, he asked everyone to chip in to cover the costs of the damage. No-one gave a penny.

There were two issues which seemed to unite and excite both the BNP and the languishing SBF. The first was a campaign against a planned mosque in Morden, in south London, which the BNP had actively leafleted against while also attempting to launch community meetings against the proposal. While the BNP campaigned publicly, the SBF fly-posted more incendiary anti-mosque posters. What few people knew was that Paul Ballard had produced these posters for Adrian Woods' group.

One BNP activist who caused trouble around this time was Arthur Flinders, or 'Big Arthur' as he was more commonly known. Flinders had a bad temper and would often get involved in scrapes and confrontations. There was one occasion when he lost his rag with a council official at a meeting in Morden Civic Centre over the mosque planning application, telling the man that he was a traitor to his race and that he would end up on the gallows. Then, during one leafleting session, a woman sporting a nose-ring swore at him, to which Big Arthur responded with a stream of obscenities. It was thought best to keep him away from the community meetings to discuss the mosque.

Bob Gertner, a short, balding Croydon activist, was also getting into trouble over the mosque issue. Out stickering against the mosque with another BNP member, Gertner suddenly realised they were being videoed by someone. They set off in pursuit of the man, who appeared to be an Irish Muslim, eventually catching him in a local pub and where they told him he was a race traitor, among other things. They were both arrested and charged with harassment and incitement to racial hatred.

There was also a sense of satisfaction, bordering on glee, over the resignation of Mike Newland, the party's widely disliked press officer, in early 1996. According to the antisemitic cartoonist Mike Barnes, Newland had called it a day in opposition to John Tyndall's desire for a more populist and confrontational approach, as opposed to his own drive for greater respectability. The disagreements came to a head after a meeting of regional organisers in Blackpool, where Tyndall had called for a return to street demonstrations and paper sales. Arthur, however, did point out that Newland had threatened to resign so many times before that we needed to take this news with a large pinch of salt. Sure enough, Newland's resignation threat wasn't as final as it first appeared.

John Merritt, meanwhile, was convinced that there was a mole within South London BNP, given that information he had imprated to only a small number of people had appeared in *Searchlight* magazine. While Arthur was, understandably, alert to any accusations of being an informer, he was not too concerned. He and Merritt got on well and there was never any indication that he was under suspicion. He was also quite blasé about the whole incident, telling us that if confronted, he would simply tell them to "fuck off and prove it".

Paul Ballard was also convinced of a mole within their ranks, though he was less concerned about *Searchlight* than he was about state infiltration. Ballard became increasingly convinced that his old friend Merritt was working for MI5, Britain's domestic security service.

Merritt couldn't do anything right in Ballard's mind and he would regularly moan to others in the BNP about Ballard's behaviour and accusations. While bickering, insecurities and personal rivalries were common on the far right, the growing division between two of the most important figures in the Croydon branch was sending ripples through London BNP. For his part, Ballard saw a sinister motive behind even the most mundane incident. At one branch meeting, Merritt doodled a picture of a Luftwaffe plane attacking a Second World War Allied tank: this was picked up by Ballard, along with numerous other pieces of paper that had been left behind, and chucked in the back of his car. A short while later, the car was searched by police while they were investigating *The Rune* magazine, and they took away away all the material in it. This was proof, Ballard insisted, that Merritt had deliberately left incriminating evidence around, knowing full well that he was about to be raided.

Ballard's paranoia was also being fed by his mum, who would – without any evidence – constantly claim his suspicions were right, and that a BNP activist in east London had – again without any evidence – suggested that Merritt was earning £250 a week from MI5. This led to a confrontation between the two men, with Ballard threatening Merritt was a lump of wood.

In any normal situation we would have been actively encouraging Arthur to spread the gossip around, but in this case the rumours were spreading fast on their own. He was active across the capital, attending BNP branch meetings in east London and south London on a monthly basis, and going to others in north London and west London as time permitted. These meetings generally happened during the week, so allowing for leafleting, social drinks and gigs at weekends.

Arthur's concern for Ballard's mental health grew with every meeting. The Croydon organiser was increasing depressed about the state of the party. Not only had the Leeds attack had a profound impact on him and others in Croydon, but the repeated disruption of BNP events in east London, due in no small part to Arthur's information, saw a steady decline in activity, activists and even a continual churn of organisers.

At a meeting in March 1997, Ballard's paranoia was reaching fever pitch. He claimed that MI5 were playing mind games with him by breaking into his house, moving the position of his toilet brush and then leaving without a trace. In another incident, a BNP member was suspended from his job at a supermarket after being involved in a fight with a black colleague. Ballard deduced that the black colleague was obviously an MI5 plant put in there to cause trouble. On yet another occasion he claimed that "the State" had tried to kidnap him after a Range Rover pulled out sharply in front of his car, but, slightly triumphantly, he told people he got away by taking evasive action. He believed that his persecutors were operating on the direct orders of Prime Minister John Major.

In a bid to shake off his alleged surveillance, Ballard initiated a code system so people could find out locations of meetings and leafleting sessions without having to speak the venue name over the phone. At a meeting in January 1997, Ballard circulated codenames for seven different venues across south London. Morden station was now known as 'V2,' while the Diner Café in Rosehill, a regular meeting point for leafleting, was known as 'M2.' Ballard's paranoia seemed justified after a party branch meeting was cancelled following a threatening telephone call was made to the landlord. While Ballard blamed MI5, which he claimed was tapping people's phones, others pointed the finger at Adrian Woods, the increasingly disgruntled and resentful leader of the Surrey Border Front.

Perhaps Ballard's increasingly suspicious mind was increased through his interactions with Larry O'Hara, a so-called independent researcher who saw spies and conspiracies at every turn. O'Hara had asked *Searchlight* for permission to visit our archive, but on being refused set out on a mission to destroy us by claiming that we were an MI5 front. He even produced a pamphlet claiming that all journalists who had used our information or quoted us in articles were MI5 agents too.

O'Hara was on a mission to expose our sources inside the far right and this led him to collaborate with fascists. In June 1996, in the pub after a leafleting session, Ballard admitted to others that he had supplied O'Hara with information on the far right and possible *Searchlight* moles in return for O'Hara supplying him with information on the anarchist group, Class War. Merritt thought Ballard was making a mistake, while local activist Steve Wheedon suggested inviting O'Hara to a meet so they could beat him up. Ballard defended his decision to collude with O'Hara, claiming that the researcher had already exposed two *Searchlight* moles over the previous few years.

Over the next few months, Arthur was to learn of another south London BNP member who was supplying O'Hara with information on possible *Searchlight* moles and was present when Nick Griffin also encouraged people to send him information on people they suspected. Armed with the information that O'Hara was colluding and even trading information with fascists, we understandably had little time for the conspiracy theorist. Fortunately no-one else did either.

CHAPTER SEVEN: PUTTING THE HOLOCAUST ON TRIAL

From the very first outing with the BNP, Arthur had witnessed, heard and read about the Holocaust being a "lie". Behind its electoral face, the party was riven with deep antisemitism.

A few people in the BNP "admitted" to Arthur that some people might have died in the concentration camps, but they told him that the numbers killed had been grossly exaggerated or that those who died had perished mainly through ill health and disease. The idea of orchestrated mass murder to wipe out an entire race was dismissed by almost everyone he met.

If that wasn't bad enough, Arthur had to sit there and listen to endless jokes about the Holocaust, or "Holohoax" as many in the far right regularly called it, including jokes about Jewish people being turned into soap and lampshades. Holocaust survivors were targeted for abuse and ridicule, while British nazis travelled overseas to photograph themselves visiting concentration camps while striking insulting poses.

Searchlight's boss Gerry Gable came in for particular abuse. On one occasion, Combat 18 figures Steve Sargent and Darren Wells sent Gerry a package from Prague, where they were spending a long weekend away. Inside the box was an old-fashioned suit they had bought from a second-hand shop, along with some chicken bones from a KFC restaurant, a pair of round-rimmed glasses with the lenses smashed, and some dirt and small stones. The accompanying note read: "Just found your grandfather."

Such actions were as nauseating as they were incessant.

Antisemitism and Holocaust denial affected Arthur more than any other racism he heard or experienced. That wasn't to say he was ok with the racist stereotypes and abuse that he witnessed, but he was expecting much of that and had heard it – in a more limited form – from the school playground and the workplace. Holocaust denial, on the other hand, was much more confined to the far-right narrative and given the horrors of six million people being murdered in such an orchestrated and deliberate fashion, it was far harder to deal with.

He probably went through different stages of emotions. Initially it was shock and revulsion. Gradually, over time, he became increasingly immune to it. But then there were times when he doubted his own views and adopted some of the ideas that were all around him during his period undercover. These moments were few and far between, and often punctured by a startling or repulsive comment or action. One of these moments of revulsion occurred when he heard that Nick Griffin had called his two pigs, which he kept on his property in mid-Wales, "Anne" and "Frank". They were named after the wartime Jewish girl who kept a diary of her time hiding from the Germans in a small room in Amsterdam, before she was eventually captured and deported to a concentration camp, where she died. We were equally horrified when he reported that back to us.

***

The Holocaust was the systematic and planned attempt by the Nazis and their collaborators to murder all Jews in Europe. From their accession to power in 1933, Hitler's Nazis used propaganda, persecution and legislation to deny human and civil rights to Jews, before cracking down on their public presence and rounding them up in huge numbers, even before the advent of the Second World War. Over 30,000 German Jews were incarcerated in the Dachau, Buchenwald and Sachsenhausen camps in the 1930s.

After the Nazis invaded Poland in September 1939, Polish Jews were confined to ghettos (small neighbourhoods where people were crammed together in appalling conditions) and the concentration camp system was created and expanded, where hundreds of thousands of Jewish people were killed.

In 1941, as part of the Nazis' "Final Solution", Jewish people in occupied countries were transported to concentration camps across Europe, where they were set to work in awful conditions, often dying through disease, malnutrition or starvation or being immediately killed in the gas chambers. The most infamous concentration camp of all was Auschwitz-Birkenau, where an estimated 1.1 million Jews were murdered. Other significant camps were Bergen-Belsen, Treblinka and Belzec.

In total, an estimated six million Jews died during the Holocaust, the largest and most systematic attempt to whip out an ethnic group in history.

In 1945, as the news of organised mass murder and gas chambers shocked the world, the Holocaust became the primary roadblock to the political resurrection of the post-war far right.

"Many on the far right believed then, and now, that if fascism was ever to rise again from the ashes then the truth of the Holocaust had to be destroyed," writes my HOPE not hate colleague Joe Mulhall. "The original Holocaust deniers were the Nazis themselves who sought to hide all trace of their attempted extermination of the Jews contemporaneously through the use of euphemistic language referring to their 'evacuation' and 'special treatment'."

The vile belief of Holocaust denial - which reared its head even as the fires of the war were ending - relies upon a number of mutually reinforcing "arguments" aimed at turning historical reality on its head. Among them are the ideas that Hitler and the Nazis were not responsible for the outbreak of the Second World War, that there was no Nazi plan for genocide, that evidence of extermination camps was faked, the gas chambers were erected after the war, that the alleged gas used to murder Jews (Zyklon B) was in fact an insecticide used against lice, and the Jews and others who died in concentration camps had perished merely from diseases like typhus.

More significantly though, Holocaust deniers claim that the Holocaust was invented to force Germany to pay for the establishment of the state of Israel (thus attempting to deny legitimacy to Israel) and to silence any opposition to what Israel might be doing to the Palestinians.

The first known Holocaust denier was French journalist Maurice Bardèche, who in 1948 published *Nuremberg ou la Terre promise* (*"Nuremberg or the Promised Land"*), which claimed the "testimonies are not reliable, essentially coming from the mouth of Jews and communists", and those who died did so from disease, while the only gas used in Auschwitz was to kill lice.

More recently there was Arthur Butz, who in 1976, published *The Hoax of the Twentieth Century: The case against the presumed extermination of European Jewry* in 1976; then Robert Faurisson, a French professor of literature at the University of Lyon, who claimed that the gas chambers used by the Nazis to exterminate the Jews did not exist; and a German neo-nazi long resident in Canada, Ernst Zundel; plus the British historian David Irving.

***

One of the most consistently antisemitic and Holocaust denial peddling publications during the mid-1990s was *The Rune,* which started off as the branch journal of Croydon BNP. From its very first edition, antisemitism dripped from its pages.

Issue 1 had a cartoon image on its cover of a large-nosed Jewish man, wearing a top hat featuring a dollar sign and holding a globe – a nod to the antisemitic trope about Jews controlling world finance. The back page of the four-page photocopied newsletter carried a glowing account of Gregor Strasser, who had been a prominent leader of the Hitler-supporting SA brownshirts (until murdered on the Night of the Long Knives). On the front page of issue 5, there was another image of a Jewish man, this time lurking behind a blindfolded blonde-haired woman, with a Union Jack flag wrapped around her waist. The headline read: *"Maastricht: One Final Stroke and Europe Will be Mine"*. The four-page magazine had by now become eight.

What began as a rather amateurish newsletter, produced by Croydon BNP activists John Merritt, Paul Ballard and Mike Barnes, soon developed into a glossy 24-page and increasingly popular magazine among the membership and even the wider far right. This upturn in the magazine's fortunes coincided with the increasing involvement of Nick Griffin, the former leader of the National Front (NF), who was a long-time political ally and friend to Merritt. Griffin had joined the NF as a teenager back in the mid-1970s, before rising through its ranks to become Chairman. He was a hardcore fascist and committed Holocaust denier, though he is perhaps best known for his seemingly bizarre political positions, which included producing an infamous front page of the NF newspaper showing photographs of Iran's former fundamentalist leader the Ayatollah Khomeini, Libya's Colonel Gaddafi, Louis Farrakhan of the hardline black Muslim Nation of Islam, and the NF's own Celtic cross symbol. The newspaper headline said simply: *"The New Axis"*.

Griffin was heavily influenced by an Italian fascist, Roberto Fiore, one of the founders of the Armed Revolutionary Nuclei, an Italian fascist group created in 1977 which was responsible for a string of armed robberies and the bombing of Bolgona railway station in 1980, which killed 85 people. A wanted man, Fiore fled to England where he was hidden from the authorities by Griffin and others. He brought with him a 'Third Position' ideology which rejected both communism and capitalism, and incorporated Julius Evola's aristocratic elitism with the Nazi 'Blood and Soil' philosophy, an idea of a "racially" defined national body (blood) united with a settlement area (soil), championing rural farm life over urban settlements.

In the mid-1980s, the National Front split into two factions, and Griffin was one of the leaders of what became known as the 'Political Soldiers' faction, a term inspired by Fiore's Third Position and defined as someone who devoted their time and energy to the nationalist struggle. It was here that he was to form a close friendship with Merritt. Eventually, in 1989, Griffin's faction left the NF and set up the International Third Position. It was a tiny organisation with little political support, even among other fascists. They did, however, establish a small-holding in France where several of their leading activists moved. It was here that Griffin had an accident with an exploding shotgun cartridge that resulted in him losing one eye. He withdrew from frontline politics for a few years, though continued writing for a number of publications under pseudonyms. *The Rune* magazine quickly became the vehicle through which he plotted his political return.

By issue 10, published in 1995, Griffin was named as *The Rune's* editor, and his influence was immediately evident. It became more extreme and certainly more openly antisemitic and politically uncompromising. The editorial in issue 10 had a sub-heading *"ZOG Watch"*, a nod to the American nazi conspiracy about the so-called Jewish-controlled Zionist Occupation Government. The magazine lambasted the influence of the Board of Deputies, the umbrella body for Britain's Jewish community, and mockingly attacked TV programmes on the Holocaust.

In another piece, Griffin sickeningly labelling the Holocaust the "Holohoax". He went on:

> "I am well aware that orthodox opinion is that 6 million Jews were gassed and cremated or turned into soap and lampshades. Orthodox opinion also once held that the earth is flat ... I have reached the conclusion that the 'extermination' tale is a mixture of Allied wartime propaganda, extremely profitable lie, and latter witch-hysteria."

He also argued that nationalists should produce revisionist material for school children, challenging the orthodoxy that the Holocaust had happened, in order to counter the "indoctrination" they were increasingly being taught in the classroom. *The Rune* advertised its revisionism in a tasteless manner: "It's really very simple and kills ignorant faith in the Holocaust Hoax as effectively as Zyklon-B killed lice and bed-bugs."

In another article in *The Rune*, entitled *"Imagine – or Just Another Crazy Conspiracy"*, Griffin laid out a fictional account of how Jews would plot to retain the "myth" of the Holocaust amid an increasingly sceptical public. Asking the reader to imagine themselves as a Jew, he began:

"You and your colleagues know better than anyone else in the world how important the Holocaust story is to your Cause – and salaries, not to mention keeping enormous subsidies from Germany and the USA flooding into Israel. Not only have you used it for half a century to stifle any criticism of Israel, Jews in general and your own enormous power in your host countries, but it is also very useful in keeping your own people in line. After all, before the Second World War, your Zionist beliefs were rejected out of hand by a majority of Jews. Now all it has takes is a mysterious outbreak of swastika daubing on synagogues and the Stamford Hill diamond dealer and the Crown Heights tailor can be relied on to dig deep for your latest appeal for funds. As your Hollywood friend is fond of remarking (providing he is safely in select company) 'there is no business like Shoah business'.

"But over the last twenty years," he continued, "you have seen this immensely productive scam increasingly threatened by the work of Historical Revisionists."

The article went on to imagine how the Jews might respond, from using Mossad to kill the 20 most prominent Revisionists, to just admitting "the truth" and saying the Holocaust was a con. All these ideas were dismissed in favour of an alternate strategy of giving some ground by admitting some elements of the Holocaust story were wrong, without denying it all. What better person to transmit this message, Griffin argued, than an already "controversial, independent researcher".

"Imagine how the genuine Revisionists would idolise him. And imagine how shattered they would be when he suddenly emerged from some dusty Moscow archive waving a piece of paper which forces him to revise his revisionism – to announce 'I was wrong. Some of the alleged details may have been propaganda, but the Holocaust did happen'. When such an announcement was made, the media would have a field day. Anyone attempting to argue the revisionist corner would be swept away in the tide.

"A brilliant plan, you all agree."

For Griffin, this was not actually an imagined story, it was what had happened, and the compromised Revisionist was David Irving.

***

Arthur was at the BNP's 1997 annual rally when he first saw Nick Griffin's latest publication. On a stall at the back of the hall, alongside back copies of *The Rune*, was a yellow-covered magazine with a massive question mark emblazoned across the cover. *Who are the Mind-benders?* the headline ran, with a sub-heading down the bottom of the page: "*The people who rule Britain through control of the mass media.*"

Modelled on a similar publication produced in the US, *Mind-benders* alleged to expose the sinister group who brainwashed our nation through control of the media. This group was – unsurprisingly (again) – the Jews.

"According to the theory of democracy, 'the people' rule," opened the magazine, before explaining the basic components of liberal democracy.

Griffin's antisemitic publications

"It would be nice it is were all so simple," it continued, before going on to explain that real power lay in the hands of the media, who owned the newspapers and ran TV channels, through which they could dictate the news and steer the public into thinking certain things and being opposed to others. The writer asked:

> "But who is behind it all? Who are the people who determine what is watched on television and printed in the newspapers? This is not so easy a study because a great many of the people concerned operate in the shadows. And even in the case of those whose names are known, what is known about their backgrounds and their connections? Very little."
>
> "For this reason, very few people in Britain are aware of the huge influence over the mass media exercised by a certain ethnic minority, namely the Jews."

What followed was page after page of names and photographs of Jewish people who owned or worked in the media and publishing world. Jewish control of the BBC was (supposedly) demonstrated through the listing of 19 Jewish people who worked for the corporation. Nine Jewish people linked to Channel 4 was seen as proof that it was controlled by the Jews. The "grotesque distortion of popular culture" was blamed on one person - Malcolm McLaren - while David Elstein, then-chief executive of Channel 5, was included to show how that station was manipulated. News Group International, owner of *The Times* and *The Sun*, got a mention too: "Its Chief Executive, Rupert Murdoch, is usually regarded as a Gentile, although he has been described as a 'mamzer Jew.'"

For Griffin, it was trouble enough that the Jews apparently owned and controlled the British media, but just as concerning he felt was how they used this power to manipulate society and forced the public to accept multiculturalism.

> "Students of Jewish influence in the mass media will notice a paradox: while that influence is used, in a hundred or more different ways, to weaken the

national spirit and racial pride of the British people, Jews themselves, in their attitude to their Jewish homeland and to questions of Zionism generally, are to be found amongst the world's most militant nationalists. In other words, what is good for us is definitely not good for them!"

***

At the request of the Liberal Democrat MP Alex Carlisle, the police raided Nick Griffin's Welsh home and Paul Ballard's south London flat in 1997, on suspicion of inciting racial hatred with the publication of issue 12 of *The Rune*. Its cover featured a thick noose, with the headline: *"What has a rope got to do with WHITE UNITY?"*, with an uncompromising editorial calling for hardline nationalism and an attack on Jews.

"An educated and honest position on Racial Realities, including the unmentionable 'Jewish question', and a rejection of Usury. These are the basics of Nationalism. For without the White race, nothing matters; and without ending the banksters' debt swindle, it is impossible to deal effectively with all the other problems."

The magazine glorified Oswald Mosley's pre-war British Union of Fascists, carried Holocaust denial and racist content, and even had an article attacking a project that brought young Germans to the UK.

In another article, entitled *"Unity in Thought"*, *The Rune* quoted several key US white supremacists and nazis, including Robert J. Mathews, leader of the US nazi-terrorist group, The Order, plus prominent US neo-nazi leader William Pierce, author of the *Turner Diaries*, and George Eric Hawthorne, who ran the nazi skinhead label, Resistance Records. The article ended by quoting the "14 Words" – a well-used sign-off for modern nazis first coined by David Lane, who was part of The Order and later sentenced to 190 years in prison for racketeering, conspiracy, and being an accomplice to the murder of Alan Berg, a Jewish radio talk show host killed in 1984.

"To any sane White man today," *The Rune* article concluded, "the only issue is the 14 words: WE MUST SECURE THE EXISTANCE [sic] OF OUR PEOPLE AND A FUTURE FOR WHITE CHILDREN."

While Ballard was meek and quiet during his police interview, the same could not be said for Griffin. He was in a combative mood and unashamedly defended *The Rune*. In fact, he was bullish from the very moment the police knocked on his door, with one officer overhearing Griffin take a phone call during the search and saying: "They're very civilised, more civilised than the Met [Metropolitan police], no Jews or Pakis."

In transcripts of his police interview, later obtained by *The Guardian* under the Freedom of Information Act, Griffin denied that the Holocaust had happened and was convinced that multiculturalism was the result of a plot by international capitalism and Zionism. He went on to claim that the British media was "greatly controlled" by what he called "organised Jewry" and how many of the films made in Hollywood, including Steven Spielberg's, were "anti-white" propaganda.

"We must secure the existence of our race and a future for white children," Griffin told his interviewers, repeating the 14 Words slogan. This, from a man who would later become a Member of the European Parliament.

Griffin then added:

> "Everything I do is related to building a nationalist movement through which peaceful persuasion and through the ballot box can place us in a position whereby those 14 words can be carried out."

Griffin also told his interrogators that he believed that "by the end of the next century the white race will be headed inevitably for extinction". He did not wish to see large numbers of people "from any ethnic group other than British and European stock" residing in the UK, he said. While he had "no antipathy to Jews, as Jews", he reiterated his belief that they had too much control of the British media.

> "It's not a belief, for example, that organised Jewry has a massively disproportionate hold on the mass media; it's a fact. It is my belief that what the mass media is doing in terms of propaganda in this country is overwhelmingly harmful."

The detectives questioned Griffin about a sentence in *The Rune* where he'd written about a "final victory over those who seek to destroy us so that they can rule unchallenged forever over a mass of mongrel slaves". Asked about who he was referring, he replied: "International capitalism and international Zionism."

> "Our grandchildren will be a mass of mongrel slaves, if things are not reversed. If a movement dedicated to preserving the white peoples of the west in their own countries does not come to power then within a very short space of time historically, the white race will cease to exist."

Asked to explain what "winning", used in one of the articles in the magazine, meant to him, Griffin replied:

"Taking political power so as to be able to institute changes, to undo the population shift which has taken place since 1948 with the first Immigration Act, to peacefully and as humanely as possible reverse that and to return Britain to being a homogeneous white nation."

Griffin was then asked his views on the Holocaust:

> "My views are that very large numbers of Jews, certainly, almost certainly hundreds of thousands, were killed during the war for no other reason but that they were Jewish. In the same way that several million Germans were killed for no other reason but that they were German and the people of Hiroshima and Nagasaki were killed for no other reason than that they were Japanese. If you end up with a full-scale war then huge numbers of innocent people are killed."
>
> "But the allegation that there was a systematic and deliberate policy whereby six million Jews were gassed to death is for a variety of forensic and common sense reasons, utter nonsense."

In a glimpse of the combative way Griffin intended to approach the impending court case, he concluded: "I will be delighted if this does come to court to ... discuss the question of ... the lie of the six million, at length."

***

Nick Griffin appeared to relish the prospect of his upcoming trial. This came across in meeting after meeting that Arthur attended during the second half of 1997. Ballard, on the other hand, was far more nervous and worried at the prospect of going to jail.

At a leafleting session during the Uxbridge by-election, held in July 1997, Ballard told Arthur and others that he had already got legal representation while Griffin planned to defend himself. Mark Deavin, who had just completed a PhD at the London School of Economics on the globalist conspiracy behind the formation of the European Community (the forerunner to the European Union), and was politically very close to Griffin, speculated that his friend might try to be represented by American lawyer and far-right activist Doug Christie. When Ballard pointed out that Christie was unlikely to represent Griffin for free, having recently acted for veteran antisemite Lady Jane Birdwood during her trial for antisemitism (and charged her £10,000), Deavin went quiet.

However, it was not long before it was Ballard's turn to go quiet as his very worst fears were confirmed. Deavin announced that Griffin intended to use his pending court case to put the Holocaust on trial.

Griffin confirmed as much during a London BNP meeting a few weeks later. Sporting an eye patch over his left eye, Griffin brandished a copy of the offending *The Rune*, highlighting all the points that had been the object of the police complaint. "It doesn't matter about me and Paul being prosecuted," he told the crowd. Everyone cheered, except Ballard whose anxiety was clearly growing.

At the BNP annual rally held in November 1997, Griffin told the audience that his lawyer had advised him not to speak but he had chosen to ignore them. He said this despite the judge also advising him that speaking publicly about the case might be grounds to deny him bail, so Griffin said that he would not be talking about the case and "was therefore not prepared to talk about green and blue people for fear of upsetting the blue people with yellow spots." Arthur joined in the laughter, though was not entirely clear what he was talking about.

Griffin did say, however, that while he was not looking forward to prison, and would prefer to be on the outside fighting for his political beliefs, he would take heart if activists were exposing what had happened to him.

Later at the rally, Ballard told Arthur that Griffin had planned to call various "Holohoax" experts to appear in his defence, but it was now unclear if he would be able. Rather he might just have to compare *The Rune* to other, more extreme, magazines that were circulating in the far right at the time and where no prosecutions had occurred.

Ballard, meanwhile, was treading a different path and eventually decided to plead guilty in the hope of a lesser sentence. He was clearly scared of going to jail, though used his need to look after his elderly mother as the excuse for this change of plea. He was still convinced that Merritt was working for the police and had set him and Griffin up. He confided in Arthur that he planned to hire a private detective to get to the bottom of his theories about Merritt. Griffin understood his co-defendant's position and was, if anything, quite pleased. The trial could now be all about him.

***

It is hard for someone who has never been in Arthur's position to really understand the impact of racist and antisemitic propaganda hour-upon-hour, week-upon-week and even year-upon-year. In the comfort of your own home, it's easy to think you would be immune. But of course that's not so easy if you are bombarded with these extremist ideas day after day, and even more so when you have to go along with it to protect your cover.

I remember once being told a story from a football copper I knew, who had gone undercover in a hooligan gang for six months. He told me about one of the police officers who went undercover in the Chelsea Headhunters gang in the 1980s, who got so caught up with the life he was leading that he ended up stabbing a rival fan in a hooligan fight. The copper who told me this story did so as he tried to explain the psychological impact of going undercover and how they needed to be tightly monitored and closely supported. He told me about the times when he would return to the station on a Monday morning, after a weekend out with the hooligan firm, and look at himself in his uniform in the mirror with utter disgust.

And so it was only natural that Arthur experienced many wobbles during his time undercover in the far right. There were many times when he would downplay the extremism of what he saw around him, take on some of their views as his own, and even vent some anger at us as though we were on the wrong side.

These incidents of anger or frustration might have been few and far between, but the drip feed of nazi propaganda, racism and Holocaust denial he was exposed to was hard to shake off at times. This, coupled with the stresses of leading a double life, sometimes made things difficult for him. He could even up identifying as part of the group when out with his BNP 'comrades'.

"I did tell some people what I was doing but not very many and their response was not necessarily positive," Arthur would later recall. "I think some of them struggled to understand how a good person could feel comfortable in the company of nazis and extreme racists, irrespective of the fact I was spying on them. So generally speaking, it was best not to tell people.

"Out leafletting or canvassing with the BNP, we'd get abuse and threats, which was fine, that really didn't bother us. There was one guy Ian Dell, who'd shout back at them, 'You're ignorant!' which properly confused them. However, I remember one time we were leafleting in quite a nice estate in I think south London. There was a black girl about my age who I had avoided giving a leaflet but she asked why she didn't get one, so I gave her a leaflet. She had a look and then said to me sadly but defiantly, 'Oh I understand why you didn't give me one.' That hurts even now, knowing that I upset her.

"Away from actually campaigning, I had a lively social life with my nazi friends where we would go out, drink too much, talk about the Zionist conspiracy and the coming race war and possibly do some Sieg-Heiling at various bemused passers-by. I remember one lad who had a wonderful chat up line when he saw an attractive girl: 'So what do you think of the Jews?'

"However, I had a more normal social life too away from National Socialism. Sometimes it was hard to 'unthink' all the nazi stuff, though. Somebody might say something positive about multiculturalism, for example, and there would be a voice in my head saying: 'That's what the Zionist media has fooled you into thinking.'

"My friends in the far right were especially unpleasant about white women with black or Asian partners, though not so much when it was the other way round. So I might be with a group of people and there would maybe be a white girl with a Jamaican boyfriend and all these unpleasant thoughts would be coming into my head and I'd be trying to get rid of them, but they wouldn't go away."

Indeed, in October 1997 Arthur did tell us that he "felt uncomfortable with the idea of race-mixing". While he knew it was a wrong thing to think, this was an example of how he had been affected by being inside the BNP for so long. He even questioned whether he was working for the right side.

He was surprised to be told that this was a perfectly normal response, that everyone who did what he was doing experiences this from time to time and that we would not expect anything else from him. He seemed rather taken aback about by this, but also reassured.

***

In January 1998 *Searchlight* magazine ran a short piece on French Holocaust denier Professor Robert Faurisson, who was speaking at a Croydon BNP meeting shortly before Christmas. Speaking alongside Faurisson was Nick Griffin. As we noted at the time:

> "The handpicked audience included the nazi hate cartoonist Mike Barnes and several BNP/loyalist heavies in London for the anti Gerry Adams protest.
>
> "Many of those present were almost nodding off after an interminable speech by Richard Edmonds, filling in for the guest speakers, who had apparently got themselves lost on the way to the meeting. However, it gave some of those present a chance to browse over the latest batch of hate material, which includes a "Chanucah card" that attempts to make light of the suffering of Holocaust victims and survivors of Auschwitz."

Several members of Croydon BNP went ballistic at this information appearing in *Searchlight* and now knew, for sure, that there was a leak. One person who was particularly angry was key Croydon activist Bob Gertner. Short and balding, Gertner was a party stalwart and diehard antisemite and Holocaust denier. Addressing a party meeting later that month, he promised to break the neck of the mole if he was ever unmasked. His mood soured even more the following month, when *Searchlight*, having been tipped off my Arthur, published an article revealing Gertner's work on the railways. He was hopping mad, and once again promised retribution if he found out who he was. He even told Arthur that whoever it was should be "kneecapped".

Arthur nooded wholeheartedly in agreement.

Things only got worse for Gertner, as two months later he was beaten up outside his home. According to Gertner, three men leapt out of parked van, which appeared to have been parked up for some time, held the BNP man down and stamped on his arm. Adding insult to injury, *Searchlight* published a photo of Gertner, with his broken arm in a cast and sling, along with a caption that he had slipped on a banana. Arthur wondered aloud if we were behind the attack, but after our denials, responded that he would have not been too unhappy on his part if we had, as Gertner was "a slimy piece of work".

***

Griffin's trial was initially scheduled for Wednesday 10 December 1997 and Arthur went along to be seen to give moral support. Joining him outside Harrow Crown Court was party leader John Tyndall, Richard Edmonds and about 15 others. Travelling over from France to give evidence in the court case was the Holocaust denier, Robert Faurisson. Bob Gertner, posing as a journalist, was the only person to get inside, with the others hanging around on the court steps in the cold. With Harrow Crown Court close to a large Kodak factory and business park, there was not even a pub to retire to.

Another person there was Barnaby Ore, a young party member from east London who was short in stature, had short ginger hair and wore round glasses. Ore ran the BNP Education Unit and was responsible for the distribution of Griffin's police interview, in direct contravention to the judge's orders. Ore was clearly trusted by Griffin, as he often stayed at his house in east London before and after party events. Ore told the group that Tony Lecomber had announced at a recent meeting in Loughton, in north-east London, that there was "definitely a grass in the East End" and that he had a suspect but wouldn't say who. Arthur had long thought that Lecomber suspected him, but he didn't seem too bothered by this news.

After a two-hour wait, the court decided to postpone the trial until late April. Fortnuately, that gave time for Tyndall to catch Canadian Holocaust denier Ernst Zundel before he boarded his plane to London, where he was coming to give evidence at the trial.

Faurisson's trip was not a complete waste, as he spoke at a Croydon branch meeting two days later. The meeting was held at a village hall near Wallingford that had been booked by Griffin's solicitor. This was the same solicitor that Edmonds had used for his trial for throwing a glass at an anti-fascist three years before. Almost 50 people were present, which was an indication of the importance of Faurisson within the movement, but also the extent of Holocaust denial views inside London BNP. Edmonds spoke first, enthusiastically telling the audience about Faurisson's own trial for Holocaust denial in Paris, which he had attended a few months before. Edmonds claimed that there were 100 nationalists from across Europe crammed into the court room and Faurisson had "humiliated" the prosecution.

Faurisson, meanwhile, gave an overview of his time researching the Holocaust

Nick Griffin at Harrow Crown Court

and his discovery in disproving the existence of gas chambers at Auschwitz. He claimed that he had spoken to experts in the US who had been involved in the gassing of convicted killers and the process was complex and dangerous for prison staff. Faurisson added that there was no evidence that any German soldiers died of gassing at the camp, which he considered further proof that the death by gassing did not happen. Griffin's trial had shown the limits of freedom of speech in the UK, but it was even worse in France, where there was a specific Holocaust denial law. Griffin, meanwhile, added a few words of thanks to people supporting him, but said that he was unable to say more at this time.

***

Griffin's trial eventually took place at Harrow Crown Court on 27 April 1998 and lasted five days. Griffin ran his own defence – or more accurately ran his political defence. The central pillar was that his political activities, reflected by *The Rune* magazine, were motivated by a desire to ensure the survival of the "white race", which he said was threatened with extinction in less than a century. Citing statistics from mainstream media outlets, he claimed that on current projections the "white race" would soon disappear. Only a BNP government, he argued, would reverse this trend.

He accepted that his magazine was "shrill" and "impolite", but argued that this tone was necessary in order to inspire its readership to take the political action he desired. He also said that *The Rune's* audience included already committed nationalists and not the general public. Therefore it was unlikely to stir up hatred among its readers – especially because the contents were so tame (he said) compared to many other publications around at that time. He specifically called out Combat 18's material, which often carried bomb manuals and hit-lists with encouragement to murder. By comparison, Griffin argued, he was quite the moderate.

He tried to claim that he was motivated by the love of his "race" rather than a hatred over others, and simply wanted to live apart from them rather than rule over them. On the specifics of the issue of *The Rune* edition in question, Griffin claimed that the hangman's noose featured on the magazine's cover reflected the BNP's policy of the restoration of capital punishment for the murder of children and police officers, and terrorist murders. He said it was consistent with other BNP material in circulation at the time, and he produced a BNP leaflet advocating the death penalty for the murder of children as proof.

Next he explained that a reference to "drawing the sword of war" was a metaphor similar to those in William Blake's poem *"Jerusalem"* and was not meant literally. He argued that a reference to "Jamaican immigrant" was nothing compared to what was often in the national papers. To back up his claim, he produced an article in *The Sun* newspaper which described the same man as a "cop-hating Yardie". He described references to "Pakis" as simply a shortened word for Pakistanis and derogatory mentions of Jews was not directed at all Jewish people, but just against a certain type of Zionist politician, he claimed.

But of course all this was a sideshow for the real point of the trial, which was, according to Griffin, a platform to debunk the Holocaust. His first key witness was Faurisson, the leading denier of the Auschwitz gas chambers, who – in the ultimate of ironies – was himself convicted in a Paris court on the first day of Griffin's trial.

Despite Griffin's best attempts, the court refused to allow Faurisson to put the Holocaust on trial for hours on end and instead restricted him to just over half-an-hour's testimony. After setting out his academic credentials, Faurisson explained how he had examined Auschwitz and concluded that the claims of the existence of gas chambers were false. He said that, as a consequence, he had been subjected to severe harassment, violence and legal action which resulted in him being forced to stop teaching for fear of violence.

"Your Honour, I am an arch-criminal," he told the judge, to the sniggering of some in the public gallery. Cross-examining, the prosecuting QC asked Faurisson to confirm that the law under which he had been convicted was a law introduced by the French government against racism, which he did.

The next witnesses were Bexley and Dartford BNP organiser Colin Smith and former party officer Mike Newland, who made out that the BNP was a respectable and moderate organisation and that it was willing to work with black people. Clearly Smith failed to mention the numerous convictions he had, most recently for threatening an off-duty police officer with a hammer while out campaigning for

TONY BLAIR AND JACK STRAW
INVITE YOU TO CELEBRATE
INTERNATIONAL HUMAN RIGHTS DAY
at the
NICK GRIFFIN
FREE SPEECH TRIAL
HARROW CROWN COURT
WEDNESDAY 10th DECEMBER 1997
LIVE BAND: PROF. FAURISSON & THE SCEPTICS
DRESS: MOURNING FOR FREEDOM SUIT
BRING AN OPEN MIND
R.S.V.P. 0410 639214

the BNP in east London. A picture of a teenage Colin Smith, adjusting his swastika armband, was on the cover of *The Other Side of Terror,* the book about the anti-fascist mole Ray Hill, which had first inspired Arthur.

Smith even showed the jury a BNP leaflet aimed at black voters as proof that the party was not a racist organisation. What the jury did not know was that leaflet was mocked up solely for the benefit of the court. To Arthur's knowledge, not a single copy of this leaflet was even handed out. In fact, no-one outside those attending the court case ever saw a copy.

The final witness was Osiris Akkebala, leader of a US black separatist sect based in Orlando, Florida. After being sworn in on the Egyptian Book of the Dead, a notorious occult bible, Akkebala went on to tell the court that Nick Griffin was not a racist but merely wanted a separation of races. Akkebala told the court that he had first met Griffin in the 1980s, when the accused was Chairman of the National Front, and they had worked together for their joint goal of the peaceful separation of the races. He added that he had never experienced any racial hatred in his dealings with Mr Griffin, nor did he find issue 12 of *The Rune* in any way offensive or racist.

Griffin's con trick ended in classic style when he referred to an anonymous Jewish friend who was standing as a BNP candidate in the current elections. This 'friend' was east Londoner Phil Maxwell, had actually been expelled from the party a few years before after admitting he had Jewish ancestry, even though he no longer identified with being Jewish. Ahead of the trial, Maxwell was hastily allowed back in the party to help create a smokescreen for Griffin.

Griffin's plan worked. Even before the jury was sent out, the tone in the court was far more favourable to the BNP man. Summing up, the judge accepted that *The Rune* was not threatening and said the issue at hand was to decide whether there was the accused's intention to stir up racial hatred, and whether the magazine was insulting or abusive or both.

Rather than being "blatant" in its racism, as she had described *The Rune* earlier in the trial, she now said that it was "subtle" and that one had to "read between the lines" to understand its message, and its antisemitism was "disguised" by Holocaust denial. The jury was not fooled though, and saw Nick Griffin for what he was. They returned a unanimous guilty verdict and he was given a nine-month prison sentence, suspended for two years. Ballard, meanwhile, who had pleaded guilty at the outset of the trial, was given a six-month sentence, also suspended for two years.

Arthur had mixed views about the verdict. As an anti-fascist he was obviously pleased that Griffin was prosecuted, but, probably as a sign of how he had become increasingly immune from the racism and antisemitism he would hear on a daily basis, thought *The Rune* was tame (especially compared to other publications that were circulating around at the time). The whole exercise was a waste of time and little more than a show trial to put Griffin away.

CHAPTER EIGHT: MIDSUMMER CELEBRATIONS

Arthur rarely got the chance to venture much out of London, so when he saw an advert for something called Ring-UK – not a mobile phone promotion, but an Odinist midsummer camp held every year in the East Midlands – he jumped at the chance.

The Ring-UK organiser was John Peacock, the British National Party's East Midlands organiser, a veteran activist and Tyndall loyalist. Peacock had a reputation as a hardliner and *Searchlight* magazine would rarely mention him without referring to an incident in which he tried to sell an old German Luger pistol. Arthur was excited to meet him and, when he did, found him a very likeable and friendly guy.

There was, however, probably to Arthur's disappointment, no talk of guns. The event was held in Edale, in the scenic Derbyshire Peak District. The 30 attendees were mostly from the Midlands area and though Arthur thought he had seen a couple of them before at national party events, they were essentially strangers. There was Joe Gould, from Peterborough, a longstanding party activist that Arthur remembered had often given large cash donations at national rallies.

Milton Ellis was also there, a postman who Arthur had read about in the pages of *Searchlight*. The BNP's new press officer, Dr Stuart Russell – who went by the name of Phill Edwards – was in attendance too.

Russell was a rising star in the party, partly because he lacked the obvious nazi baggage of so many of the other senior activists. He was also good at getting the party coverage in local media: he had a knack of sending press releases to local newspapers announcing a new branch or activity supposedly as a result of huge local interest and, without any evidence that this was true, often secured great coverage. On several occasions Russell got front page coverage from gullible newspapers. The resulting media publicity did indeed promote the party locally and generate new enquiries.

Arthur arrived up in Edale in the early afternoon, where he was directed to a campsite on a farm just outside the village, about four miles from the Old Hall hotel. Once they were all there they headed off to a couple of local pubs in Edale for a few drinks and a gossip about movement matters. Many of those present were also involved in the skinhead music scene, so there was a lot of chatter about impending white power concerts and tittle tattle about what was happening in this or that racist band.

A few eyebrows were raised when Arthur said that he was on good terms with Steve Sargent and had attended a couple of National Socialist Movement events.

They all seemed to dislike both Combat 18 factions and did not seem impressed when it appeared Arthur was a supporter of the Sargent faction. Arthur was forced to clarify his comments, and stressed that he just liked Sargent as an individual rather than aligned himself politically.

Paul Burns, who was one of those heavily involved in the Blood & Honour music scene and close friend of Chris Hipkin, who edited *British Oi* and contributed to *Blood & Honour*, two white power skinhead magazines, told the group that he was planning a trip to Germany and then onto the "Polish Butlins" – by which he was referring to Auschwitz, the concentration camp where more than a million Jews were killed during the World War II.

The death camp was depressingly a regular destination for many British nazis, who took great delight in photographing themselves amidst the old chimney stacks and memorial plaques, nicknaming it "Disneyworld". Someone mentioned hearing *Searchlight's* editor Gerry Gable on the radio talking about receiving postcards from Auschwitz, so Burns promised to add another to his collection.

John Peacock, meanwhile, was in a grumpy mood. While he was an unreconstructed nazi, he took umbrage at the swastika flag draped across the tent belonging to two BNP activists that Arthur recognised from the fateful east London meeting the previous year at which Tyndall was attacked. Obviously Peacock's concerns were only to do with the potential hassle it could cause. A couple of years before, the now defunct *News of World* tabloid newspaper ran a piece about another Ring-UK event, claiming it was a paramilitary training camp.

Joe Gould, who had been active in the National Front in the 1970s but then followed John Tyndall when he set up the BNP in 1982, enjoyed telling everyone about a fellow Peterborough BNP activist, who spent his time producing postcards for nationalists to send to Parliament highlighting the allegations of paedophilia against Labour MPs and councillors.

***

Socialising was an integral part of British far right culture. While *Searchlight* would often mock the BNP and C18 supporters for spending more time in the pub than actually doing any political work, drinking, talking and laughing bonded far right activists and created a feeling of community. It provided them with an opportunity to moan about the world around them (often in a racialised manner), plan their activities and dream about the society they wanted to live in. On an individual level, socialising provided friendship to those who for political and/or personal reasons had few other friends.

Most of this socialisaing took place in the pub, but there were also parties at people's homes, gigs around the country and, just occasionally, weekends away like this.

Strangely enough, Arthur enjoyed the social life of being in the far right. Of course there were moments when he found the racist talk disturbing and other times when enjoyment turned to fear of violence, but these incidents aside, he would look forward to catching up with his new found friends.

For the first few years of his infiltration, his social life was primarily with the far right. Of course he had his family and friends outside away from all this, but during a period when he would be out two or three times a week with the BNP, there was little space for anything else. It is not difficult to see how he sometimes viewed his far-right acquaintances – among whom were some of the most hardened national socialists in the country – as friends.

Richard Edmonds, the BNP's National Organiser, exemplified this dichotomy. He was an unapologetic national socialist and Holocaust denier, but also a father figure to so many of the younger BNP members: Arthur included. "I remember his warmth and enthusiasm more than anything else and his immense knowledge of London," Arthur would later recall. It was a view similarly shared by HOPE not hate's Matthew Collins during his years inside the British far right.

***

Well-refreshed, they returned to the campsite where they prepared for a midnight barbecue and listened to a short speech from John Peacock, explaining the purpose of the gathering. "This camp is our way of celebrating the Summer Solstice," he said, before explaining that the Folk-Moot ceremony was designed to "generate a closer bond within our racial nationalist group and is very much about a healthy respect for nature, the seasons and life." Before beginning the ceremony, he told the small crowd that it was fine if they preferred not to participate.

Brandishing a large knife, he began:

"I name this sword the Sword of Truth because in truth we trust. In the name of Odin, Baldur, Frey and Thor.

"Sword of Truth – hallow this Holy Stead and protect from evil."

He then moved around slowly, to face north, east, south and finally west.

"Folk greetings and Sun-Hael!"

At that, Arthur and the others turned and shook hands with one another. Peacock stepped forward, slowly and methodically, and lit a small fire on a makeshift altar.

"We rekindle the Flame of the Northlands, the light of the North – may the light of the Midgard renew the folk-soul of England.

"Fire is the Eye of the Sun.

"By the Fire of Odin may the Folk-Spirit of England awakened.

"May the Sacred Flame of Freedom be lit and never put out.

"The Fire of the Folk is the Fire of the Sun.

"Sun Hael! Hael to the Sun on this longest Day."

Peacock then drank mean from a horn, which he called the Horn of the Mighty, before passing it horn to the person next to him and inviting them to say a few words. Arthur stepped forward, glanced around at those gathered before him, raised the horn and simply said: "For Rudolph Hess."

CHAPTER NINE: 14 DAYS THAT SHOOK LONDON

It began with an explosion. Nails and shards of glass ripped through a crowded open market in Brixton, south London. It was 17 April 1999, the heart of London's black community. Thirteen days later, one bomb had become three in what was to become the most deadly far-right terrorist attack in British history.

The Brixton bomb had been hidden in a 'Head' sports bag. It was comprised of a four-inch pipe filled using flash powder extracted from fireworks and an igniter that acted as the detonator. The crude device was then placed in a cardboard box surrounded by 3kg of different-sized nails and a battery powered timing device made out of an old alarm clock, with the minute hand removed, and a nail hammered in at the 5.30pm mark. That was the time the bomb exploded.

The blast was heard over a mile away, followed shortly after by screams and running feet. Nails had embedded themselves into anything in their path. Shop windows and those of a passing bus were blown out by the force of the explosion. Brixton resident Talent Chioma Mundy-Castle didn't think anyone could have survived the blast as it seemed as if the whole building had collapsed. "There were lots of casualties," she remembers, "everybody was running all over the place trying to find out if their loved ones were safe."

Consultant surgeon Gus McGrouther, who treated many of the Brixton survivors recalls not having experienced a bomb attack like it in London. "The bomb was designed to kill as many people as possible," he would later remember. "It was miraculous nobody lost their life that day."

A former Army officer, Neall Whatley, told *The Guardian* newspaper how he'd tried to comfort a young girl with a nail embedded in her cheek. "It was carnage everywhere. There was one man with severe head, chest and leg injuries."

"I administered first aid to two people," he added. "One was a small child and the other was a security guard from [the supermarket store] Iceland who had severe chest and leg injuries."

The x-ray of the two-year old girl with a three inch nail embedded in her skull, was perhaps the most frighteningly memorable images of the attack.

It could have been a lot worse. The bomber had initially dropped his bag outside the Iceland supermarket, on the busy High Street, half-an-hour before the timer was set to explode, but fortunately a local market trader saw the abandoned bag and looked inside. To his shock, he realised it was a bomb. The bag was moved to a quieter side street, while he and others discussed what to do. The plan was to put it in a large steel bin in an attempt to limit the blast, but another market trader, an ex-

soldier, advised against it on the basis that even more shrapnel could be dispersed.
Their actions didn't stop the bomb, but almost certainly it saved lives.

***

Arthur was drinking with some of his BNP friends when he first heard the news of the Brixton bomb. A buzz of excitement was mixed in with surprise and bewilderment.

He, like some of the others he was with, straight away thought it was a racist or even a nazi attack. "To me it seemed so obvious," he would later recall. Those he was with were throwing around possible ideas as to who might be responsible and whether this was the start of something bigger. There was little anxiety, at that moment, what it might mean for them personally and politically. These concerns would grow later.

While several people did not condone a terrorist attack, there was little sympathy for the injured, possibly because the general consensus (at least among the BNP activists) was that because the attack took place in Brixton, the injured were most likely to be black.

Arthur's mind was spinning. He was horrified at the news, but had to put on a pretence of small enjoyment among his far right friends. He wanted to know if anyone knew or suspected anything, but at the same time he was careful not to ask too many questions. Frustratingly for him, the conversation quickly moved on and was rarely returned to. Perhaps people didn't understand the significance of what had happened an hour before, or maybe they just didn't care.

We were in daily contact with Arthur in the days following the Brixton attack. He was tasked with speaking to as many people as he knew in the BNP, as well as other even more extreme groups, in the hope someone would let some information slip or make an educated guess. By now he was being handled by my friend Dave Rich, from the from the Community Security Trust, a charity which provides safety, security, and advice to the Jewish community in the UK, as I had my hands full running so many sources within C18. I couldn't handle everyone and an agreement was made between *Searchlight* and the CST, with whom we worked with closely, to co-run Arthur and share the information he provided. Dave was roughly the same age as me and we had known each other since the early 1990s. He was fanatical about football and his easy and relatable manner made him a good match to handle Arthur.

Arthur was galvanised by the Brixton bomb. He had been undercover for five years and there were moments when he questioned what he was doing and how long he could carry on doing it for. These doubts had grown in the year leading up to the Brixton bomb and on more than one occasion he said he had wanted to leave. At times this frustration spilled over into resentment and even mild anger, but these tended to be fleeting.

It was always going to be difficult balancing his undercover work ,which in the early years saw him go out two, three or even four times a week, with holding down a job and seeing his own friends. He was, of course, free to stop whenever he wanted, but we had asked him for a bit of time to find a suitable replacement. While we were running as many as 20 sources inside the far right during this time, with at least half in an increasingly divided and fractious Combat 18, having someone in east London was always going to be useful for us. Arthur did not leave, less because of anything we said but because after spending five years with these people, meeting and drinking with them once, twice or even three times a week, leaving this behind was always going to be hard. Totally understandably, and politics aside, he counted many of his fellow BNP members as friends.

Talk of leaving was put aside after the bomb exploded in Brixton. Arthur was energised, focused and determined to help find the culprit - or culprits - before another attack happened. There was no doubt in his mind that this was a racist or even nazi-inspired terrorist attack, though he remembers Dave, initially at least, being more open-minded. "There was talk in the media about a possible link to dissident Irish Republicans or Yardie gangsters but that didn't fit at all," Arthur would tell me years later, echoing the thoughts he had at the time. "There was no reason for Irish Republican terrorists to target somewhere like Brixton and the Yardies were associated guns and knives, not explosives."

He was absolutely convinced that the perpetrator, or perpetrators, came from the far right or had been inspired by far-right propaganda. "This is what nazis in Britain had been talking about doing for years," he said. "Now someone or a group of people had actually gone and done it. They had gone into Brixton and detonated a bomb with the intention of killing and injuring innocent black people and anybody who happened to be there with them. This was ethnic cleansing; it was the race war they had all talked about."

He read the newspapers avidly over the next days, looking for clues for who might be responsible. He made phone calls to the various far-right contacts he knew, in the hope that someone would have news. Everyone was interested, some of them even excited by what had happened, but if they had any suspicions as to who was behind it, they weren't telling him. While the silence of people did little to convince Arthur it was not a far right inspired attack, he certainly came to the view that it was very unlikely to be anyone he knew. Nevertheless, Dave asked Arthur to draw up a list of possible suspects from those he had met over the last five years. It was a long list.

We were asking our other moles inside the far right the same. Obviously our initial focus was on Combat 18, which had long-talked of the need for "race war". But given the number of sources we had inside the group's two factions (by this stage C18 had split) - many at a very senior level - we were confident in making the judgement that this wasn't something approved by the C18 leadership. That said, we could not discount someone acting alone but motivated by the group's propaganda, a model which has become all too familiar as time has gone on.

Publicly, we made an observation of how the Brixton bomb might be heralding a new style of racist attacks. "Previous attacks," we told the media, "even bombings and arsons, have been aimed at rival political groups or individuals but the indiscriminate nature of these attacks would herald a new, and possibly unprecedented, wave of domestic terrorism in Britain".

The implications of this was both serious and frightening.

***

The police had no major leads to go on. While some officers thought that a racial motive was possible, their lack of knowledge of the far right and their failure to monitor them properly in the preceding years contributed to an information black hole and few leads.

Worse still, Special Branch (which was tasked with dealing with far right terrorism) and MI5 had been dismissive of the far-right threat overall, focusing most of their energies to supporting local police forces in assessing public order threats rather than the potential for more extreme violence. In a series of quarterly bulletins on political extremism produced during the late 1990s, London Special Branch was particularly scathing about the far-right threat.

In the absence of any far-right group being obviously behind the bombing, the authorities initially focused on Irish Republicanism. While the IRA had signed up to the Good Friday Agreement the previous year, there were some Republicans unwilling to give up the fight.

A telephone call to the authorities the day after the Brixton bombing claimed responsibility on behalf of Combat 18, but while police received this claim with caution, it did prompt them to launch an investigation into London's extreme far-right groups - if nothing else, to eliminate them from their enquiry. I, among probably lots of others, was approached to see if we had heard anything.

The feeling that the bombing was a far-right attack increased when it emerged that a group calling itself the 'White Wolves' had sent a number of letters to newspapers and magazines serving Britain's minority communities in the days before the Brixton bombing. The Asian newspaper, The Eastern Eye, received a stencilled letter two days before the bomb, saying:

"Notice is hereby given that all non-whites and Jews (defined by blood, not religion) must permanently leave the British Isles before the year is out. Jews and non-whites who remain after 1999 has ended will be exterminated. When the clock strikes midnight on 31/12/99 the White Wolves will begin to howl, the wolves begin to hunt. You have been warned. HAIL BRITANNIA."

Two days after the Brixton bombing, a press agency and *Searchlight* both received calls from a Whitehall telephone box in the name of the White Wolves taking credit for the attack. A day later, *Searchlight* received another letter, again stencilled, with a similar message to the phone call. "C18 did not carry out the Brixton bombing. We, the White Wolves, did."

Our own assessment was that C18 was very unlikely to be behind the attack, at least as an organisation. The leadership of C18 around Will Browning and Darren Wells, who was my most senior mole within the organisation, were as mystified as anyone else about the attacks, and they appeared more concerned that the publicity linking them to the bombing would lead to them being arrested.

Despite these claims of responsibility, and the widely held belief that the attack was racially motivated, the police ended the first week of their investigation no closer to finding the culprit or culprits than they were at the beginning. They were still of the mindset that all motives were possible. Indeed, one theory, which led the police to reach out to their French counterparts, was that there were similarities between this attack and similar nail bombings that had been carried out over there by Islamist extremists.

***

On Saturday 23 April, a week after the first attack, a second bomb exploded just off Brick Lane, in the heart of London's East End and the city's Bangladeshi community.

The bomb was built in the same way as the Brixton device. This time though, it was primed to explode at 6pm when (we later learned) the bomber thought most people would be milling around the area.

Two things happened that, mercifully, limited the damage. First, the bomber had not realised that the busy Brick Lane market was held on a Sunday and not a Saturday, so the area was fairly deserted when he got there. Frustrated, he decided to drop the bag containing the bomb in a side street and head home.

The only other option would have been to disarm the bomb and take it home, which he had no intention of doing. Like Brixton, the bag was spotted by a member of the public and thinking the owner had dropped it by mistake, they decided to take it to the police station around the corner. However, much to his annoyance, the police station was closed so he took the bag back to his car where he peaked inside. On seeing the nails all packed into a box, the man presumed the bag belonged to a workman, so he decided to take it to another police station but

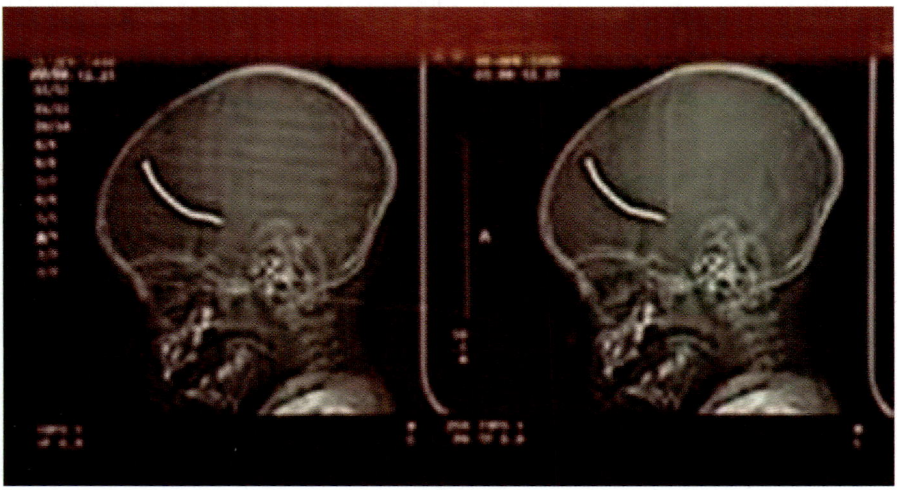

X-rays show a nail from the Brixton bomb embedded in an infant's brain

that too was also closed.

It was only then that the man remembered the nail bomb that had exploded in Brixton the week before and realised what he was dealing with. Stepping away from his car, he rang 999 to report the package. Moments later the bomb exploded in the car boot, throwing the vehicle several feet in the air. Fortunately it had exploded in a deserted side street and beyond shop windows being blown out, there were no serious injuries.

***

It was abundantly clear to everyone that the two bombs were connected and the motive was racial. The leader of Tower Hamlets Council, Julie Mainwaring, also denounced the bombing. "Brick Lane is the heart of the East End's Asian community," she declared. "It appears that someone out there has chosen to attack our people again. It's almost certainly linked to the Brixton bombing."

Oona King, the area's local MP, reminded us that racial hatred and violence were not unusual in Britain today: "I think people failed to realise it, but the black community is living every day in fear of racist violence". Even the police were saying publicly that a racist bomber, or bombers, were on the loose.

As police forensic specialists sifted through rubble and debris seeking clues about the manufacture of the bomb and anything that would identify the bomber, one theory emerged that the attacks were sparked by the recent February publication of the findings of the inquiry by Sir William Macpherson into the murder of black teenager Stephen Lawrence. Oona King shared these sentiments, telling journalists she blamed "a white backlash against the Stephen Lawrence report for the Brick Lane blast".

Fears were growing that more attacks might follow. By 25 April the media had changed their tune. From describing the bombings as random violence, they now began using phrases such as "race terrorism", "years of racial conflict", "Race bombers strike again", "Neo-nazi thugs who stir up the East End" and "New bomb raises fear of racist campaign".

Shaken by the apparent racist campaign, ethnic minorities across the capital were living in increasing trepidation of further attacks. The communities targeted were understandably left shaken. "Nobody feels safe around here anymore," one eyewitness told journalists.

***

Any lingering doubts about the bomber's motives were quickly dispelled by the Brick Lane bomb.

"Everyone knew now that it was racially motivated and this individual or group was going to carry out more bombings unless they were caught first," Arthur recalled. He felt powerless and frustrated at his, and *Searchlight's*, perceived inability to stop the attacks. Dave reassured him that there was a lot they could do, and were doing, but Arthur remained doubtful. Dave told Arthur it was just a case of plugging away, listening out for any chatter, catching up with people on the phone.

Given the absolute silence we were hearing, both from Arthur's contacts in the BNP and our other sources in groups like C18, Dave told Arthur that the bomber could well be based outside the capital. And so it proved to be. The last thing Arthur expected was the bomber to be someone he knew.

Arthur continued to make calls to his nazi friends, again trying not to make his agenda too obvious, but still no-one seemed to know anything.

***

A couple of days after the Brick Lane bomb, *Searchlight* uncovered a 15-page document that had been written a few years before in the name of the White Wolves. We had never heard of this group before and nothing had come out from them since, so perhaps it was all a coincidence, but the language of the document, coupled with the anonymous letters and calls in the name of the White Wolves, suggested a link was possible.

The document was far more serious than the infantile abuse of most of the Combat 18 propaganda. There was also a coherent rationale behind it, so lacking in most of the other material in circulation at the time.

"Every nation has the absolute right to defend itself, its land, its identity. A nation is a living thing, not just a collection of individuals, and just as a nation can thrive so it can die. So who we are to target? Not necessarily the politicians or media who have waged the undeclared war. They are paid well for their treachery and are, in the main, replaceable. Besides, the public wouldn't understand such actions as relevant to them, so wouldn't take sides.

"Our main line of attack must be on the immigrant communities themselves, the black and Asian ghettos. If this is done regularly, effectively and brutally, the aliens will respond by attacking Whites at random, forcing them off the fence and into self-defence. This will begin a spiral of violence which will force the Establishment's hand on the race issue.

"The British people will fight, but not if we offer them only the soft voting option. WE must point them in the right direction by taking the necessary action to start the spiral of violence which will ultimately include even the reluctant, forcing them to fight. The victory will come from them once they have no other option, but the initiative must come from us. There are a dozen Belfasts and a hundred Londonderrys in Britain today, they're just waiting for a spark.

"It is true that the immigrants are innocent of any recognised crime individually, but collectively they make up an invading army which threatens the birthright of children and the unborn generations of our folk. Their presence spells the death of our people, so if they must be forced out with extreme violence, then so be it."

The White Wolves document went on to detail possible attacks and counter-surveillance tactics. It encouraged supporters to form small cells of two to five people, but also to continue life as normal. "If you are already a member of an

The Admiral Duncan pub moments after the bomb blast

established Nationalist party, stay with it. A sudden exodus of members to [White Wolves] activities would be a dead giveaway."

The White Wolves document was classic leaderless resistance, an idea of small cells operating independently in order to evade police infiltration and clampdown. If one cell was caught, nothing would lead the authorities to other cells. "We do not believe that we alone can win the race war, but we can start it," it concluded.

The authorship of the document was unknown to us when it was written back in 1995 and it remained a mystery to us as we hastily researched for anyone using the name "White Wolves". The C18 group in the north of England had called themselves the same name, but we discounted them as suspects as we knew their leader, Del O'Connor, had moved to the US after falling out with C18 leader Will Browning in 1998. This did not stop the media going into overdrive about O'Connor and splashing photos of him with firearms extensively across their front pages. Unfortunately for O'Connor, the attention led to the US authorities realising that he had overstayed his holiday visa and he was promptly deported back to the UK, where he was arrested on his arrival.

We had no proof that the individual or group using the name White Wolves was behind the bombing. It seemed quote possible that a person or group of people were using the name to create fear or perhaps to launch their own terrorist action. It also seemed an amazing coincidence that the first White Wolves stencilled letters appeared just a couple of days before the Brixton bomb.

Adding to the growing anxiety, a letter was using the name White Wolves was sent to *The Chad*, the local newspaper in Mansfield, Nottinghamshire, a few days after the Brick Lane bomb. It warned of an imminent attack on the Chesterfield May Day event, one of the largest May Day gatherings in the country, usually held on the first Monday in May. On the same day that the letter arrived, the Mansfield Unemployed Workers Centre was attacked in broad daylight. The night before the Chesterfield May Day demonstration, a car was stolen in a nearby town. After a car chase, the police recovered the vehicle and found a large amount of explosives and other components for making a time-delayed bomb. The two male occupants fled. It may have been a coincidence, but nevertheless, it was very worrying. X-rays show a nail from the Brixton bomb embedded in an infant's brain

***

The fear among London's minority communities was palpable after the Brick Lane bomb. The concern was made worse by the hoax calls that were made across the capital. In Hackney alone, there were 40 scares after the bombing. In east London police carried out a controlled explosion on a suspect car, only adding to unease in the local community.

The bomb in Brick Lane reinforced the threat to London's diverse communities, yet out of the apprehension came a determination to resist. In Southall, in the west of London, supporters of The Monitoring Group, an anti-racist group initially formed in west London in the early 1980s, acted as stewards to patrol the local shopping streets. In north and north-east London, volunteers from the Community Security Trust provided a similar service in areas with a high Jewish population. For both groups, their presence was to reassure local residents as much as it was to search the area for possible devices.

***

The big breakthrough for the police was a consequence of the bomb originally being discovered prior to exploding in Brixton. As the market traders were discussing what to do with the possible bomb, a man thought he would help himself to the nice new 'Head' sports bag and made away with it. He had survived the explosion uninjured, but worried that he might be accused of involvement in the attack, he had jettisoned the bag on the pavement outside Boots, on the High Street.

With the bag intact, police had a vital lead. Scouring the CCTV cameras, they eventually found the bag, and a young man carrying it who was wearing a white baseball cap. The image was sent to specialists in to NASA, in the USA, for enhancement. Eventually, they had a picture of their man.

On 30 April 1999, the media released an image of a suspect and asked for the public's help in identifying him. The head of the anti-terrorist branch, Deputy Assistant Commissioner Alan Fry, told the media: "We have someone who is clearly recognisable; someone knows him ... [and] he must be caught."

Arthur was in a local supermarket when he first caught sight of the *Evening Standard* newspaper. Emblazoned across the front page was the CCTV image of the presumed Brixton nail bomber. Above the photo ran the headline: "Nail Bombs – Do You Know This Man?"

Right away Arthur thought it could well be a BNP man he had met a number of times, but didn't know well: David Copeland. But he wasn't definitely sure. The picture was blurred and Arthur hadn't seen Copeland for 18 months. He was also conscious that he might be seeing what he wanted to see out of a desire to catch the bomber. Compounding his uncertainty was the thought that although he knew Copeland hated black and Asian people, he didn't really ever seem like a potential nazi terrorist. Indeed, Arthur knew Copeland from the BNP and while many in there were nazis, most of the openly violent nazis were in more extreme groups.

Arthur raced home to watch the news and there were the same CCTV images from Brixton on the BBC News. He switched over to ITV and there he was again – the suspect who looked like David Copeland. The more he looked at him the more convinced Arthur became. Slightly shaking with both fear and excitement, he pulled out his phone to ring Dave, but before he could find the number, his own handset rang. "Hi," said Dave.

Even before Dave could finish asking if he had seen the CCTV image of the bomber, Arthur blurted out the name David Copeland. Of course he was not 100% certain, but there was a striking resemblance. There was no time for chit chat: Dave had a call to make.

After conferring with the rest of us, a call was made to the police with Copeland's name and the address we had for him in Barking, east London. Unbeknown to us, the police had already received a called from Copeland's workmate, Paul Mifsud, who had also recognised him from the CCTV, but our information was the first to confirm a far-right connection.

Sadly, the police were unable to act on the information before David Copeland set out with what became his third bomb. He had been intending to go on the Saturday after the Brick Lane device, in keeping with his two previous bombs, but with the police releasing the CCTV image he knew time was limited. At 6.37pm on Friday 30 April, in the crowded Admiral Duncan pub in Soho, heart of London's gay community, another bomb exploded. This time three people were killed – including a pregnant woman, Andrea Dykes, and another 73 injured, 13 of them seriously, including Dykes' husband Julian.

Consultant surgeon Gus McGrouther was on duty again that day and will never forget what he witnessed. "As these patients came in, one at a time, we began to realise just how serious this was. They had quite horrific injuries," he would later recall. "It was like a war zone.

The injuries in this attack were far more serious than the earlier bombings. Partly this was because of their close proximity to the bomb blast and being in a confined

CCTV image of Copeland

space, but also because Copeland had allowed his pet rat to urinate and defecate over the nails, leading to several of the victims to endure nasty infections.

David Copeland was arrested at his home in Cove, Farnborough, just hours after the Soho blast. A police search of his room revealed bomb-making equipment and nazi paraphernalia. Arthur heard the news that an arrest had been made on the radio on the Saturday morning. The news report gave a name, but it was not Copeland's. "Oh well," shrugged Arthur, guessing he was wrong about the identification.

A short time later, Dave rang Arthur to tell him that it was indeed Copeland who had been arrested. "But I heard them give another name," replied Arthur, somewhat puzzled. "The press had the name of the person who lived in the bedsit before Copeland,"

Dave explained. "It is definitely him." That evening, Arthur attended a party at the home of one of the nazis he knew.

"Most of the people there were hardcore National Socialists," he would later recall. "As well as the BNP there were people who were who had been involved in Blood & Honour, the National Front, the Ulster Defence Association support group, and even the Ku Klux Klan. I think there was also a strange man who thought it was a good idea to attack Anglican Churches on the grounds that 'Judaeo Christians' had built their churches on the hallowed ground of Woden. So, people were pretty well connected, but if they knew anything about the bombing they weren't saying."

There was excitement in the air at this meeting. Some people openly expressed support for the bombings and hoped that whoever had been arrested was only one member of a wider terrorist cell and that his comrades would attack another target that night. They then discussed who would, or even should, be next. One person said "the blacks", another said "the Asians". Others still suggested "the Jews" or "the Reds".

There was little sympathy for the victims of the Admiral Duncan pub, and several shared jokes about "legless gays".

As the party came to a close, one woman remarked sadly: "Well, I'm sorry there were no more bombs tonight."

Arthur made his way home, disgusted. The bombing campaign had re-energised him and reminded him of the importance of his work for us. He felt dirty listening to these comments, but he also knew that he needed to be there to hear them, and if that meant laughing along to some of the disgusting comments, then that's what he had to do.

Just hours after Copeland's arrest, the police were confidently asserting that Copeland was acting alone and had no connections with any nazi organisations. "It is understood he was acting alone for his own motives," David Veness, Assistant Commissioner of the Metropolitan Police, told journalists. Arthur, and we, knew different.

David Copeland at a BNP event in 1997

CHAPTER TEN: THE MAKING OF A NAZI BOMBER

Arthur knew David Copeland probably as well as anyone else on the far right. That wasn't a boast, more a simple statement of fact. Even though the two only saw each other seven or eight times during a six month period in 1997, they often talked and on a couple of occasions shared a pint together. Copeland was a loner and didn't mix much with most of the others. He was almost always the youngest at a BNP meeting or leafleting session and the age gap, plus his own social awkwardness, kept him apart.

Copeland had joined the BNP shortly after the 1997 General Election and Arthur first met him while out campaigning in the Uxbridge parliamentary by-election that summer. Copeland was just 20, living over in east London and was super enthusiastic. There was no indication that he had been involved in any far-right group before, though he spoke positively of Combat 18, particularly in relation to the Dublin riot in 1995, when England fans forced a friendly international to be abandoned after they began ripping up chairs and hoardings and throwing them onto the pitch, which C18 leader Charlie Sargent had boasted his group had caused,.

His political views appeared more moderate than most of the others in the BNP at the time. "Basically he hated black people," Arthur was to tell me in September 1999. "His racism was overt, but at the same time he probably wasn't that different from a lot of other white working class lads at the time. He would regularly use the words 'nigger', 'paki' and stuff like that."

He obviously fitted in with most of those around him, though Arthur cannot remember Copeland saying anything at that time about Zionism or the Jews. "I remember once or twice people bringing up Zionism and Jewish conspiracies but he didn't indicate that he agreed or disagreed. I think it was something new to him."

Copeland's political immaturity, at least in far-right terms, was borne out by two incidents Arthur reported on at the time. The first was how Copeland was left quite distraught by the death of Diana, the Princess of Wales. While virtually everyone else active in the BNP at this time was quite disdainful of the monarchy and Diana in particular, Copeland appeared devastated by her death. "Even though she was shagging an ugly Arab," as he told Arthur.

In late October 1997, Copeland attended a Newham BNP branch meeting held at The Albert pub, in Greengate Street. The keynote speaker was Alexander Baron, a supposedly independent researcher who spent most of his time attacking *Searchlight* and railing against the power of British Jewry, both topics close to the heart of virtually every BNP member. Despite this, and Baron's close relationship with Nick Griffin, he was not widely liked by the party membership, with many thinking that he looked Jewish himself. Copeland also took a great dislike to Baron, on the basis that he "looked like an Arab". Clearly his national socialist beliefs, and related Jewish conspiracies, were yet to be formed.

Copeland was an eager member of the BNP, though, and often complained to Arthur that the party was not active enough. He wanted to be out more often and would take people's telephone numbers and chase them up for activities to join.

There was nothing particularly unusual about Copeland. He loved music, Oasis in particular, and talked enthusiastically about his job working on the Jubilee tube line extension. During one conversation, he even offered to fix Arthur up with a job there too. He lived alone in east London, didn't talk about his family and came across as someone who had a lot of friends. He was not aggressive in his manner, and aside from his regular and casual racism, he never gave any indication that he was thinking about terrorism or extreme violence.

***

Copeland: I knew people would get hurt. Maimed. Killed. I didn't fantasise about killing people. I never have done, I don't get off on that. I fantasise about the chaos and disruption that's caused.

Police: Right. So you knew that when you put that bomb out that people would get killed?

Copeland: I was just like a robot. I knew it.

Police: You knew they'd be killed.

Copeland: I thought they would be.

Police: You knew that people would be seriously injured?

Copeland: Yeah.

Police: Right. Why did you put nails in them. What did that mean to you by putting nails in the bombs?

Copeland: It means they'd smash windows, stick into people and maim people and kill people.

***

David Copeland was just 22 when he unleashed the bombs that killed three and injured more than 200 other people. Motivated by a virulent hatred towards ethnic minorities, which was compounded by a vehement homophobia, the allure of nazi ideology was all too compelling for Copeland. Since childhood he had been consumed by inferiority complexes and crises of sexuality and masculinity. The ideas of the far right were to play on his anxieties and sense of powerlessness in a way that culminated in death, destruction and tragedy.

Copeland was not alone in having an unhappy childhood or psychiatric problems. But few perpetrate the amount of violence that he did. The ideas he possessed and the hatred he felt towards others did not come only from within. The fuse that ignited and directed the anger within Copeland was his involvement in the far right.

Copeland was the second of three boys. He was born on the outskirts of west London, but when he was four his family moved to a semi-detached suburban house in Yately, Hampshire. From his birth there had been concerns about his development, initially over the size of his testicles and later over his lack of height. These factors, coupled with an inferiority complex in relation to his two brothers, played heavily on his mind as he grew up.

An underachiever at school, he sought to make an impression. But suffering from low self-esteem, he was always the loner. He could never quite fit in.

His insecurities were exactly those that the far right seeks to exploit through its caricatured version of masculinity. A web of violence, explicit heterosexuality and strong masculinity underlie most far-right groups. The last two were lacking in Copeland's own life, and this was the image he desperately wanted. He yearned to belong.

In spring 1997 Copeland moved to London. His father had arranged a job for him with engineering contractors on the Jubliee Line extension. With racism already embedded in his mind, he found east London very different from the life he left behind. It was during the General Election campaign that summer that Copeland made his first contact with the British National Party.

For six months he was an active member, attending meetings and participating in leafleting campaigns across the capital. Though a member of the Newham branch, he joined a BNP election team in Uxbridge and heard Nick Griffin, now party leader, speak in Redbridge.

After an aborted anniversary rally in Stratford, scene of the now infamous photograph of himself and the BNP leader John Tyndall, Copeland joined three other members in attacking Politico's bookshop in Victoria – the target of their hatred being *Searchlight* magazine, which was stocked in the shop.

Since his childhood, Copeland had harboured a strong revulsion towards gay people. Because of his size, he had been paranoid throughout his youth that his family thought he was gay. The court heard of his fear of using public toilets and that he carried a knife in case gay men approached him.

***

Copeland: I went down Old Compton Street, I wanted to make sure it was the right pub I was after. I wanted a queer one. A gay one, whatever you want to call it.

Police: Have you got a problem with gays then?

Copeland: Yeah, I have

Police: Why?

Copeland: I'm just very homophobic. I just hate them.

Police: Why?

Copeland: I don't know. Just do you know.

Police: There must be a reason?

Copeland: I've got a thing about homosexuals. I just don't like talking about it, if you know what I mean. I choose the gays because I hate them. Yep, that was personal.

Police: The tape doesn't show it, but when we speak to you about the gays you have to close your eyes and you seem quite intense there David.

Copeland: Yeah, I just don't like them. I just don't like them, yeah. I'm completely straight, yeah. Don't worry about that.

Police: No, no, no. It's not a problem, but it seems to upset you. I don't know why it upsets you. It upsets you enough to plant a bomb.

***

The virulently homophobic BNP clearly fanned the flames of his hatred towards gays. Within the group, any roles that did not conform to a rigid version of masculinity, or to what was considered a normal and healthy sexuality, were strongly maligned. This could culminate not only in overt abuse but also physical violence.

But while the BNP offered an introduction to the far right, Copeland wanted more. Frustrated at the lack of activity in the BNP, he drifted away. A year earlier he had watched the television scenes of the Centennial Park bombing at the Atlanta Olympics with unconcealed excitement. He imagined carrying out a similar strategy at the Notting Hill Carnival. His time in the BNP brought that dream a little closer to reality.

Copeland joined the BNP against a backdrop of growing far-right militancy in this country. Even though the BNP had split from C18 by the time Copeland joined the party, the idea of 'race war' was firmly embedded in the minds of most people active during this period. Hardline racist and antisemitic material was regularly on sale at BNP meetings for much of the 1990s, even after C18 was proscribed. Members would sit in BNP meetings, including at the all-important Annual Rally, wearing C18 and Blood & Honour t-shirts, and activists shared allegiances between the BNP and BNP football card the C18-controlled umbrella group, the National Socialist Alliance.

A football card used as a BNP fundraiser. Copeland picked Southampton

Holocaust denial was also almost universally accepted within the party, and if anyone actually believed the Holocaust happened, then they kept quite about it. The BNP magazine *Spearhead* advertised books promoting the theory of race war and the story of the US nazi-terror group, The Order. A leading

BNP organiser, Mark Payne, changed his name by deed poll to Mark Mathews, after Robert Mathews, the US nazi who led The Order and died surrounded by a raging fire and FBI bullets during a shoot out in 1984.

***

It was soon after leaving the BNP that Copeland attempted his first bombing campaign. First learning of the internet while in the BNP, he spent long hours in an internet café in Victoria, searching the web for useful sites. He had downloaded *The Terrorists' Handbook*, an online document which contained instructions to make bombs, and set about trying to build an ammonium nitrate (fertiliser) bomb, similar to the high explosive device used in the Atlanta Olympic Park bombing of 1996. It failed; frustrated, he gave up.

However the lure of the far right was never far away and within a couple of months he was back in contact with the BNP, first with Tony Lecomber, himself a convicted bomber, and then with Barnaby Ore, a young east London activist who Copeland had befriended during his time as a member. But by now the BNP was too tame for his views and, having read in the newspapers about high-profile National Front marches in Dover, he decided to make contact with the NF. Ore was less than keen to hand him over to a rival organisation and suggested that if he wanted something more hardline he should contact the National Alliance, the infamous and powerful US neo-nazi group led by William Pierce.

Writing under the pseudonym Andrew MacDonald, the former Physics professor had written *The Turner Diaries*, a fictional account of one man's fight against the American system. It was among Copeland's few books he possessed at the time of his arrest. Set in the late 1990s, *The Turner Diaries* depicted a right-wing underground army taking up the battle with the American government, which it claimed was under Jewish control. A race war developed after the government outlawed the right to bear arms and attempted to enforce racial integration. Leading the revolt was a white underground movement called The Organization, with a secret leadership known as 'The Order'. Members conducted a terrorist campaign, from the blowing up of FBI buildings to a rocket attack on Congress. Supply lines were cut as the economic infrastructure of America was slowly destroyed. Finally the white population won its battle, but only after Israel was destroyed by nuclear weapons.

Described by some as a modern-day *Mein Kampf*, *The Turner Diaries* became a core text for thousands of neo-nazis throughout the world. It inspired William McVeigh, the white supremacist who planted a bomb at a federal building in Oklahoma city in 1995, which killed 169 people. Copies of the book were also found in the possession of the National Socialist Underground killers, a three-person terrorist cell in Germany which murdered 10 people and carried out a string of armed robberies. The book also inspired Pavlo Lapshyn, a Ukrainian PhD student who murdered an 82-year-old Muslim man in Birmingham and planted several bombs at mosques across the Black Country in 2013.

The Turner Diaries introduced the term ZOG – the Zionist Occupation Government

– to describe its conspiracy theory of a Jewish-run society, a myth adopted by nazi movements in several countries. While the Jewish conspiracy has long been a central plank of far-right thinking, *The Turner Diaries* provided it with a demonic catchphrase, and the acronym ZOG became ubiquitous in extreme far-right circles.

"Everyone read it," Arthur told me back in 1999. "I think it's been said that John Tyndall's autobiography [*The Eleventh Hour*] is the bible of the BNP. That's quite clearly baloney. Equally, I don't think *Mein Kampf* is either. *The Turner Diaries* is the closest in that people may not follow the strategy, but it's the book people are most enthusiastic about.

"From a far-right perspective, reading the *The Turner Diaries* you get a certain amount of satisfaction, of reading details of blacks, Jews, race-traitors and so on being killed. And when you are frustrated about the way society is going then it's a good tonic."

The fact that Tyndall felt he needed William Pierce to speak at the BNP's annual rally in 1995 speaks volumes for the importance of the man amongst British nazis and the almost widespread appeal of *The Turner Diaries* and the theory of race war it espoused.

***

Copeland: I want them [ethnic minorities] out of this country. I'm a National Socialist. Nazi, whatever you want to call me. I believe in the master race.

Police: But you're saying to us that you're a loner. You are not part of any organisation?

Copeland: No, I wouldn't trust any of those idiots. They're just a bunch of yobs, that's all they are.

Police: How would you obtain this state as an individual then?

Copeland: Well, I'd just be the spark, that's all I would plan to be – the spark that would set fire to this country. Cos every nutter out there now, if he wants to get on the news, he's gonna have to blow something up. They're all thinking about it. If you've read *The Turner Diaries*, you'd know [in] the year 2000 there'll be an uprising and all that racial violence on the street.

Police: So, your aim was that just to plant bombs and hurt people?

Copeland: That's right. My aim was political. It was to cause a racial war in this country. There'd be a backlash from the ethnic minorities, then all the white people would go out and vote BNP. Do you know what I mean? It'll be obvious.

Police: That's how you understand it.

Copeland: If I were a white person with kids in London and they had all these blacks and Asians coming after you with knives and what have you, what are you gonna do? Put up with it? No, you don't. You'll vote them out.

***

Copeland was by now branching out politically. Browsing the internet, he came across a tenet called Christian Identity, a far-right theology that turned traditional Christian teaching on its head and claimed that the Anglo-Saxon and Nordic "race" of northern Europe and the US was the lost tribe of Israel, while the Jews were the spawn of Satan and black people were sub-humans or mud people – terms Copeland would himself use later.

When he came across a sticker for something called "the National Socialist Movement" (NSM) in central London he thought he had at last found his political home. Launched a year before as a splinter group from Combat 18, the NSM was one of the few openly nazi groups in Britain at the time.

The NSM had been launched in the summer of 1998 by David Myatt, an extremely eccentric man who was also the founder of a bizarre nazi-satanic cult, The Order of Nine Angles. Myatt first became active in far-right politics back in the early 1970s while at university, and after a public absence re-emerged in the mid-1990s to become a guiding influence behind Charlie Sargent and his brother Steve, the C18 leader. After C18 split, with Browning wanting to follow a terrorist strategy and Sargent wishing to pursue a more political strategy, Sargent had then been arrested for the murder of a rival faction member. In the ensuing chaos, Myatt and Steve Sargent set about forming the NSM.

"The flag of the NSM is the swastika, and the NSM proudly and unashamedly upholds the political creed of National-Socialism," declared its *Aims, Strategies and Tactics* document. These aims were:

"To make known the truth about National-Socialism – its noble idealism, and its principles of honour, loyalty and duty; To encourage Aryans to live in an Aryan way by them striving to uphold the National-Socialist values of honour, loyalty and duty; To encourage the creation of an Aryan homeland as a practical alternative to the decadent anti-Aryan society of our times, so enabling Aryans to live freely and healthily in accord with their natural and healthy customs; To build the foundations for a National Socialist revolution and thus create a National-Socialist State."

Myatt did not believe that National Socialism could be achieved through the ballot box and throughout this period wrote numerous papers and articles advocating terrorism and a strategy of tension. Years later, Myatt and his secretive Order of Nine Angles group were influential in a new wave of nazi terrorism through groups like UK-based National Action and Sonnenkrieg Division, and the US-based Atomwaffen Division. At the time of writing this book, eight people with links to O9A have been convicted under terrorism offences in the UK and at least five in the US. There are three more O9A supporters awaiting terrorism trials in the UK, while in America a US Marine is awaiting trial after being charged with plotting to murder members of his own military unit.

In his writings *System Breakdown: A Guide to Disrupting the System*, widely considered a terrorist manifesto, Myatt called for a terrorist campaign: not a few "wasteful and pointless" attacks on isolated targets but instead a prolonged attack on society, tantamount to a strategy of tension. He wrote:

"It means persistent and calculating pressure applied to the whole structure of everyday life – and it means that a power base has been built which can supply the

David Myatt confronted by BBC journalist Graeme McLagan

dedicated people needed to mount and sustain such pressure over a period of many years. Tension within certain communities can be raised by 'direct action'.

"Members of covert action groups should infiltrate themselves into organisations, groups, businesses and other concerns to either (a) sabotage it from within, or (b) obtain useful hardware. All covert direct action organisations must be prepared – at some time in the future – for armed conflict with the forces which aid and support the system."

In 1998 Myatt also wrote another pro-terrorist essay called *A Practical Guide to Aryan Revolution*. Chapter titles included 'Assassinations', 'Terror bombings' and 'Racial War'. A copy of this essay was found in David Copeland's flat at the time of his arrest.

***

The emergence of this new group pricked our interest at *Searchlight* and at the first opportunity we encouraged Arthur to get involved. In late November 1997 he went to an NSM meeting in Chelmsford. There were 25-30 people present, few of whom Arthur knew. Steve Sargent, the brother of C18 leader Charlie, chaired the meeting and opened by thanking everyone for coming. He had expected a few more to come, especially from Yorkshire, but, in his words "they clearly hadn't bothered to turn up".

Sargent spoke about the split within C18, between his brother and his erstwhile lieutenant Will Browning, dismissing claims that Charlie was a police informer. The truth, he told the audience, was that Browning was the actual informant. He also claimed, with no proof at all, that Browning was the author of an anti-C18 booklet published back in 1995 and not Tony Lecomber (as everyone had presumed). Arthur tried to maintain a straight face. He knew that the Sargents and Browning hated each other, but to claim that Browning had produced an anti-C18 booklet at the height of the group's power was stretching it somewhat.

The speakers were Steve Rowland, the National Front's south London organiser, who announced: "I'm a British Nationalist, but I have no problem with people who choose to call themselves National Socialists," to applause from the audience. Tony Williams, a former National Front activist and close confident of Steve Sargent, was next up. In his mid-to-late thirties, Williams wore a ponytail and was well spoken, or "posh" as Arthur was to report. He was also, in Arthur's view, "a bit nutty". He immediately launched into a tirade against people "calling us [the NSM] Hollywood Nazis" – by which he meant John Tyndall and others in the BNP. He said that he was "proud to call myself a National Socialist and a member of the NSM". He went on to say that the main thing holding the far right back in Britain was a lack of belief that they could form a government.

"But I do believe the NSM can form a government," he concluded.

Williams then turned to a subject closer to the hearts of most in the audience – Jews. He said racism was natural and good, but then in the next sentence claimed that the real racists were the Jews. To illustrate the point he read out a letter from *The Jewish Chronicle*, the main weekly newspaper serving Britain's Jewish community, from a man complaining about racism among British Jews. "How dare you call me a racist, Mr Jew!" he screamed. The audience clapped in delight.

The final speaker was NSM leader David Myatt. It was the shortest speech of the afternoon, lasting less than five minutes. He said that it didn't matter that there were so few people at the meeting, because those that were there were all such wonderful people – "the cream of Great Britain." In the pub afterwards, Myatt admitted that the size of this meeting was twice that of the previous one.

Arthur made his way back to London in a buoyant mood at his successful infiltration of the NSM. He had been worried that he wouldn't know anyone there, but there were a couple of people he recognised and he had found it quite easy to chat to those present. That said, he was hoping that Charlie Sargent and close friend Martin Cross would be sent down for the murder of Will Browning's friend Chris Castle, who had been stabbed to death in Sargent's mobile home in Harlow at the beginning of 1997. The trial, which took place at Chelmsford Crown Court in early 1998, had formalised the split within C18.

***

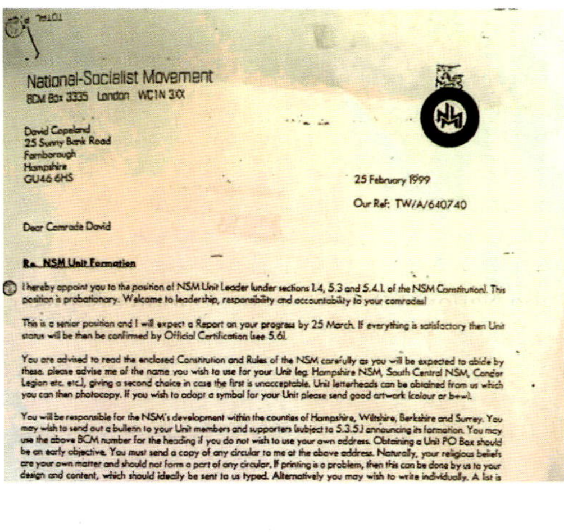

National-Socialist Movement
BCM Box 3335 London WC1N 3XX

David Copeland
25 Sunny Bank Road
Farnborough
Hampshire
GU46 6HS

25 February 1999

Our Ref: TW/A/640740

Dear Comrade David

Re. NSM Unit Formation

I hereby appoint you to the position of NSM Unit Leader (under sections 1.4, 5.3 and 5.4.1. of the NSM Constitution). This position is probationary. Welcome to leadership, responsibility and accountability to your comrades!

This is a senior position and I will expect a Report on your progress by 25 March. If everything is satisfactory then Unit status will be then be confirmed by Official Certification (see 5.6).

You are advised to read the enclosed Constitution and Rules of the NSM carefully as you will be expected to abide by these. please advise me of the name you wish to use for your Unit (eg. Hampshire NSM, South Central NSM, Condor Legion etc. etc.), giving a second choice in case the first is unacceptable. Unit letterheads can be obtained from us which you can then photocopy. If you wish to adopt a symbol for your Unit please send good artwork (colour or b+w).

You will be responsible for the NSM's development within the counties of Hampshire, Wiltshire, Berkshire and Surrey. You may wish to send out a bulletin to your Unit members and supporters (subject to 5.3.5.) announcing its formation. You may use the above BCM number for the heading if you do not wish to use your own address. Obtaining a Unit PO Box should be an early objective. You must send a copy of any circular to me at the above address. Naturally, your religious beliefs are your own matter and should not form a part of any circular. If printing is a problem, then this can be done by us to your design and content, which should ideally be sent to us typed. Alternatively you may wish to write individually. A list is

By late 1998 David Copeland was a committed nazi. In a confession written after his arrest, he said: "I bombed the blacks, Paki's, Degenerates. I would of bombed the Jews as well if I got a chance." In Broadmoor, a high-security psychiatric hospital, he ranted against the "Zionist Occupation Government" that was conspiring against him.

Having moved back to Hampshire in 1998, after suffering panic attacks while working in London, Copeland had been put in touch with the local NSM organiser, Kirk Barker. Barker had an unenviable record for violence, having served a three-year sentence for his part in an unprovoked racist attack on Asian waiters in Buntingford, Hertfordshire in 1992.

Copeland was unimpressed with Barker and, although he soon replaced Barker as the local NSM organiser, he soon dismissed any thoughts he had of recruiting Barker to his terrorist campaign. For his part, Barker was equally dismissive, claiming Copeland was a religious nut.

Within weeks of joining the NSM Copeland had become its Southern Regional Organiser, responsible for recruiting members and organising local activities. Of course the title was quite grand for an organisation that only had 20 members and a further 80 supporters. Within days of becoming organiser, Copeland began his preparations for his bombing campaign.

With little hope of attracting others to his plans, Copeland entered 1999 determined to go it alone. Having re-read his internet bomb manuals, he decided on a more moderate, but deadly, device to the one that he had tried to build the previous year. Buying components at local shops and experimenting in a nearby wood, he put the finishing touches to his campaign.

Three months later, he calmly set off on his bicycle to Fleet station, in Hampshire, from where he caught a train to Clapham Junction in London. From there it was a short taxi ride to Brixton. Strapped across his back was a dark sports bag containing a primed bomb set to explode at 5.30pm.

***

Copeland: Personally, I wanted to get caught, be famous of some sort.

Police: What does fame mean for you?

Copeland: If no-one remembers who you were, the you never existed.

Police: It would be remiss of us to ask why you did it?

Copeland: To spread fear, resentment and hatred. I am a Nazi, I admit that.

***

The court at his trial later heard how Copeland had hoped to start a race war with his actions. "I believe in a real master race," Copeland declared. His race and country came first and he wanted Aryan domination of the world. While Copeland would like to be remembered as the nazi who tried to ignite a race war, one cannot separate his politics from his personal problems.

His inferiority complex over his size and failure to have a girlfriend was exploited by the likes of the BNP, who gave him a target and a scapegoat for his anger. It also provided a remedy for his crisis of masculinity through its continual outbursts against gays.

Self-frustration was transformed into anger at others. Once he had political justification for his feelings, he had the impetus to kill. It is therefore little surprise that Copeland was attracted to the far right. He was typical of a disaffected young male alienated from society. He lacked an identity that assigned him any status of power. He was a loner who found refuge and status through racism and white supremacy. Through adherence to the politics espoused by fascist groups, a new identity emerged. It was an identity that empowered him by positively identifying with the status of the white male. Within the BNP and far-right groups generally, race is absolute.

Copeland's "whiteness", elevated to a higher status by the far right, gave him the feeling of superiority that he felt he lacked within mainstream society. Nothing else mattered. Because nazis prioritise race over any other factor, by virtue of his skin colour Copeland was able to feel special.

In Broadmoor, a psychiatric assessment of Copeland concluded:

"He has developed delusional beliefs which are connected to his low self-esteem and concern about his sexuality and he took an interest in extreme rightwing and fundamentalist Christian ideology. His attitude to others and more recent offending behaviour shows evidence of arrogance and lack of empathy and there are significant sadist elements to his thoughts and behaviour."

***

Copeland has claimed that it was his destiny to kill. He wanted to ignite a race war in order to facilitate a BNP-led government. He may have had the background and mental state that allowed him to commit such heinous crimes, but the ideas came from elsewhere.

The BNP and other far-right groups provided the lethal ingredient to a dangerous recipe. The mixture of personality disorder, sexual insecurities and crises of masculinity with virulent racism and white supremacy proved deadly in a man who was very much a loner. He wanted to be special, and was desperate to be remembered. When informed by police during his interrogation that a third person had died as a result of his bomb in Soho, he could only reply: "Does that make me a serial killer then?"

***

Britain's nazi groups all publicly condemned the three April 1999 London bombings and moved fast to distance themselves from the perpetrator.

The BNP described the events as "a wicked nail bomb campaign", while Combat 18 leaders told the press of their disgust at the indiscriminate nature of the blasts.

However, not everyone was just content to condemn the attack. The National Front claimed that the bombings were the natural result of Britain's multicultural society, telling the media:

"We are not completely surprised that such a scenario has come to pass. For many years now, the long suffering white communities across London and our other major cities have been ignored, oppressed and victimised by successive British governments and the controlled media ... branded as idiots at best, reviled as violent thugs at worst. Is it any wonder then that some individuals feel the need to resort to acts of violence to get their message across."

Most groups saw the dark hand of "the State" involved. The skinhead leaders of the Blood & Honour movement thought this was a state plot to close down their music operation, while the BNP saw it as an attempt to undermine the the party's European election campaign. The BNP noted on its website at the time:

"Who gains from this affair? Some neo-nazi individual or group who dislikes us for our legitimate [sic] democratic approach to the dismantling of British society ... The left who wish to use the bombings against us in a reverse of the manner Hitler used the burning down of the German parliament building, by a crazed former communist individual, to justify a crack-down on left-wing groups. Thirdly, the Government, which can present itself as opposed to terrorism, a repository of law, order, and civilisation, and, like the left, use public outrage to suppress politically incorrect views."

In its monthly magazine *Spearhead*, the BNP even suggested that the bombs might have been the work of the Security Services, in a bid to justify the banning of the party. Citing the revelation that Charlie Sargent, C18's original leader, had been working as an informant for the police, *Spearhead* concluded: "Even with Sargent in prison, it is quite feasible that the State is still guiding or using the organisation it helped create."

The BNP went into almost total amnesia over Copeland's links, publicly denying any association to the media. Arthur rang Ken Francis, the party's Newham organiser, shortly after Copeland's arrest, asking if this was the same guy who had been in East London BNP. Francis looked through database but claimed that no-one with that name had been in the branch. A few days later, Francis rang back to clarify his earlier statement. He had spoken to Tony Lecomber, who reminded him that there had indeed been a member with that name, but that this 'David Copeland' had left the country some time ago so it was clearly a different person.

Others were equally forgetful. And few, if any, said anything about the victims, which had included hundreds of innocent people. True, David Copeland kept himself to himself and rarely mixed with others, but for everyone to have "forgotten" him was a bit much. But it was a good lesson for a re-energised Arthur, and a timely reminder as to why he had went undercover in the first place.

CHAPTER ELEVEN: OLD WINE, NEW BOTTLES

"Back in 1968, when the repatriation policy since associated with British Nationalism [compulsory repatriation] was first popularised, it was possible to think in terms of the repatriation of all non-whites within one parliamentary term. In the light of the huge numbers which have flowed in every year since, however, that is clearly no longer practical.

"I used to think otherwise, then to hope otherwise, then to kid myself otherwise, but this is the truth.

"If we continue to ask for something which the British people at their present dumbed-down level of racial awareness will not give, then it will not happen, and even what little we have left will be lost forever. It's not a matter of anyone selling out, it's a matter of realpolitik."

- Nick Griffin, *Spearhead*

Writing in the BNP magazine *Spearhead* in late 1998, Nick Griffin proposed that the party abandon its policy of compulsory repatriation, signalling the most dramatic and fundamental shift in policy in the party's history. Focusing on expelling illegal immigrants and "voluntary repatriation", Griffin believed the BNP would finally have a "saleable" policy on race that could attract the support of large swathes of the British population, many of who would reject the party's (then) current position of forced repatriation of ethnic minorities born in the UK.

Citing a conversation with farmers in north Wales, Griffin wrote: "Even these desperate men still don't think it would be right to force people who have lived here all their lives to go home to a place they have never seen".

Not only that, but the perception of what compulsory repatriation meant also alienated potential supporters: "Repatriation at bayonet point which, under the circumstances, is the logical result of that word compulsory," is how Griffin explained the likely outcome of forcible repatriation. Placing the emphasis on voluntary repatriation would remove the "very upsetting images of whole families being dragged, kicking and screaming, from their homes" he claimed. Of course, Griffin hadn't changed his true belief in a white Britain, but was merely trying to publicly make it more moderate and acceptable to the British public.

***

From the moment Arthur first heard of Nick Griffin it was clear that the former National Front leader had leadership ambitions. In fact, it was one of the most poorly kept secrets around. Griffin's route into the BNP was through its Croydon branch, initially writing anonymously in *The Rune*, but before long he was adding his byline and speaking at meetings.

Arthur had a lot of time for Griffin, and found him an impressive speaker, despite his hardline and incessant antisemitism and Holocaust denial. "He wasn't mad," Arthur was to later recall, which was in fact a compliment when compared to some of the other people he met during this time. "He came across as intelligent and confident, and he had a good grasp of detail, which wasn't true of John Tyndall."

Ironically, though Griffin came into the BNP through the Croydon branch, it was with the more moderate activists in east and north London that he was to build his political base within the party. Nick Griffin was a regular topic of conversation within London BNP branches, with many more seasoned activists nervous of his involvement because of his hardline and factionalist past (helping to split the National Front).

For others it was just a matter of time when he made his move on the leadership position. In 1997 he formally joined the party. He would have probably made his move earlier if his leadership ambitions had not been exposed in the national media.

***

Nick Griffin's 1998 *Spearhead* article was written in response to internal criticism of Mike Newland's appearance on a Talk Radio show hosted by James Whale. It was listened to by an audience of over two million people, and offered a seemingly more moderate alternative to official BNP policy.

"It's all a question of numbers," Newland told Whale, explaining that party's first priority was to expel "illegal immigrants" and then offer grants for other people to return to their country of origin. He went on to say that if the numbers remaining did not "threaten our identity" then perhaps they could stay.

Griffin's six-page defence of Newland's position in the *Spearhead* was part of a coordinated attempt by some within the BNP to change party policy. It came only a month after the *British Nationalist*, the party's monthly newspaper, published a statement asserting that the BNP was not a white supremacist party or even racist, the latest in a series of articles in BNP publications calling for a more moderate and respectable image.

Accepting that the nazi and extremist image had badly affected their party, those pushing this line hoped a more conciliatory tone would eventually deliver the kind of electoral success that far-right groups on the European continent had already achieved, but which was so lacking here. Making no apology for this change in strategy, Griffin provided the reader with an alternative plan for reducing the "non-white" population in Britain, which he estimated would take between 10 and 15 years to complete – three consecutive terms in government.

According to Griffin, the first term of a BNP government would see an immediate halt to immigration, then the expulsion of all illegal immigrants and the overseas aid budget channelled into funding voluntary repatriation. The second term would see the repatriation programme expanded and linked to beneficial "trade agreements" with countries that were likely to receive the exodus from Britain, which Griffin thought would be welcomed by many Afro-Caribbean and Asian people living here. It was only after this process that compulsory repatriation would be considered, he claimed, and then only with the consent of the British people in a referendum.

Even then, Griffin accepted that the image of people being dragged out of their houses would remain so repugnant for many people that it would be best all round for the BNP only to discuss the removal of illegal immigrants and voluntary repatriation. "Isn't that easier to sell than compulsory repatriation for all?" he suggested.

Of course, even this supposed "moderation" was very far removed from reality and did little to hide the nasty and virulent racism underlying the core of the BNP's beliefs. Still, traditionalists in the party were uneasy with this proposed change in policy. While Arthur thought this might improve the party's chances of getting members elected, many of the London activists he knew expressed deep disquiet and even saw it as a political sell out.

"It was not that long before," recalled Arthur, "that we'd be driving round in Richard Edmonds' battered old van, laughing at his strong belief that one day they would be in a vehicle supplied by the state [presumably after the BNP took power], with 'Bring out your niggers' blaring out over the loudspeaker."

While that might have been wishful thinking for Edmonds and the others, many London BNP activists did change the party slogan –'Stop Immigration, Start Repatriation' – into much more forceful chant of 'Stop Immigration, Start Extermination'. Arthur would remember the looks of horror from passers-by as they shouted that from the van.

John Tyndall, unsurprisingly, voiced some concern about any change in policy, though he accepted Griffin's insistence that this was a change in presentation rather than actual policy. He grudgingly acquiesced: "Providing that the bottom line of a restoration of the white Britain that our grandfathers knew is not compromised."

***

Griffin's new pragmatic approach to the party's immigration policy was in sharp contrast to the image he'd been keen to promote over the previous few years. Writing in *The Rune* during 1995 and 1996, he'd insisted that there could be no compromise on the BNP's beliefs or tactics.

In a long article in issue 11, he'd set out his stall against the modernisers who wanted to dilute the nationalist message and those who sought compromise in the hope of nationalist unity.

"The would-be builders of a 'mass party' must understand that it is inevitable that their apparent addiction to the ballot box quite rightly arouses the contempt of everybody who sees that the democratic process is a hollow sham and that electoral success is the result, not the cause, of power. At this stage of the game, elections are there to provide limited opportunities to build our power-winning machine. The actual percentages gained is of little concern.

"And they must grasp the fact that our struggle is revolutionary. While we need electoral success to provide a constitutional rubber stamp to make the change-over acceptable to the police and army, there is much more to a revolution than plonking a couple of hundred Nationalist bottoms on the plush benches of the den of thieves and traitors in Westminster."

Unity was important to him, but only around a firm set of beliefs and policies. To back up his case, he quoted Hitler's *Mein Kampf* in rejecting the idea of a 'patriotic coalition'. To drive home his point, the cover of *The Rune* depicted an attractive blonde-haired woman, with an obvious-looking Jewish man brandishing a large knife lurking in the shadows. "Your daughter, Your wife, Your future: the nightmare will go on until we unite," ran the cover headline.

Later in the same article he warned against right-wing populism. "Yes, seek to be popular," he wrote, "but recognise that populism – which starts with thoughts of trimming policies, avoiding holding election rallies in areas which might cause Asian riots, sneering at skinheads and acquiescing in the Holocaust lie – is the kiss of death."

"The electors of Millwall," he concluded, "did not back a Post-Modernist Rightest Party, but what they perceived to be a strong, disciplined organisation with the ability to back up its slogan 'Defend Rights for Whites' with well-directed boots and fists. When the crunch comes, power is the product of force and will, not of rational debate."

***

In the November 1996 Nick Griffin was approached by a former SAS soldier asking him to a meeting with a French colleague. Griffin told them:

"Before we first met, I thought, well, this could well be *Searchlight* anti-fascist magazine, it could be British television, it could be Mossad, or it could be British intelligence. It could be all sorts of different people... No-one from the other side could sit in a room for three hours and talk as we talked and not say something which would make me think... No-one from the other side understands how we think. To be one of us, not at our level, it's impossible, but the street level with no hair, it's no problem. When you realise that, when you take on board how genuine you are, it gives you a certain encouragement and inspiration."

A couple of weeks later, and over several bottles of expensive wine and a leisurely £200 meal in a Telford hotel, Griffin was asked for his vision for the future of nationalism in Britain. With a degree of smugness, he added:

"The extent to which I'm involved with the BNP is known only by a very few

> folk, very few people indeed."

He was enjoying the attention: he was, after all, being fêted by representatives of Jean-Marie Le Pen's Front National, the main far-right party in France. With the offer of substantial funding being dangled in front of him, here at last was his chance to make something of the far right's electoral potential and, by extension, himself. He told his guests:

> "I've been expecting an approach from the Front National in two years' time. I was slightly thrown by the fact that it was two years early, but to me that symbolises the uniqueness of the Front National."

Griffin explained that the likely election of a Labour government in the near future would be followed by a dramatic rise in the fortunes of the extreme right, in much the same way that the National Front flourished under a Labour government in the 1970s. With the correct organisational structure in place, Griffin told his French host that within five years the BNP could be winning council seats across the country and regularly retaining its deposits in parliamentary seats.

This is what his hosts had hoped, and expected, to hear they told Griffin, explaining that their extensive research had concluded that he was the man to improve the fortunes of British nationalism. Griffin's ego suitably stroked, they concluded the lunch by asking him to write a paper on how we would bring nationalist success to the UK. So excited was Griffin, he even offered to write it there and then.

Ironically, Griffin's initial suspicions turned out to be true. He was being set up ITV's investigative show, The Cook Report together with *Searchlight*. Over the next five months Griffin met what he thought were representatives of the Front National on 34 occasions, even inviting one of them into his home several times. While Griffin was to eventually rumble the plot, it was not before he offered a blueprint for his path to power.

Within a week of the first meeting, and with the offer of £100,000 funding on the table, Griffin had produced his document and a second lunch was arranged. *"The Current Position of the Nationalist Movement in Britain – With Proposals and Costings For Its Rapid Improvement"* was a seven-page document, which was followed shortly afterwards by another six-page report answering a number of questions that we had raised.

Scoffing at the BNP's current strategy, Griffin took little interest in its election campaign, refusing to stand as candidate and doing no campaigning. "Our most important task over the next two years is to build our internal political and economic infrastructure," he argued. A process of political education for selected recruits – "agitprop" – and a network of small businesses to employ these people was his solution.

But the crucial problem, Griffin foresaw, was what had always plagued the fascist movement in Britain: the lack of any intellectual base.

> "Britain does not have the tradition of intellectual fascism, which is such an important factor in many other countries. While I do have a number of proposals to help rectify this deficiency, the truth is that this is a handicap which we can never overcome completely."

To recruit a more middle-class base, Griffin suggested the formation of a New Right project, including a new publishing house, targeting public schools and the Oxbridge universities, offering training seminars and the production of white power CDs, which would bring in money and supporters. This would not only attract the necessary recruits but provide the BNP with "a 'fifth column' within the establishment".

Of course, at the centre of his plan was Griffin becoming leader of the BNP.

> "I didn't, to be honest, expect the reaction I've had, which has been within a year, people from John Tyndall downwards, to say well, you're the next leader of the BNP. I hope it doesn't sound big headed."

Griffin proposed an uncompromising hardline strategy for the party and was scathing about those in the organisation who wished to make the BNP more respectable.

> "The popularism in British nationalist circles means the idea that if we change our image the Jews will not say bad things about us, therefore you perhaps don't talk about repatriation, you just talk about stopping immigration, then the television will not say bad things about us. It's a slippery slope, you start on this and you end up back in the Conservative Party.
>
> "The BNP should not try and appeal to middle-class notions of respectability, which take issue with the fact that a minority of nationalists wear large boots and short haircuts, or that the BNP activities often 'provoke violence'. It is more important to control the streets of a city than its council chamber."

Tony Blair's impending electoral victory was, Griffin believed, part of the Jewish conspiracy.

> "Blair's administration, Tony Blair's whole campaign is financed by Jews. Oh yes, it's unbelievable."

While attacking Jews in general, Griffin had specific hatred for the former Liberal Democrat MP, Alex Carlisle, who had reported *The Rune* to the police. He was:

> "This bloody Jew, our local MP, who organised the raid [on Griffin's house] whose only claim to fame is that two of his grandparents died in the Holocaust."

Griffin set out two areas of potential growth for the BNP, as he saw it. The first was the establishment of "Radio White Europe", which he considered the "single most important item on the agenda between us at this stage". The second was a move into the (highly profitable) white power music scene.

> "The collapse of C18 [Combat 18] – human shit – leaves a big gap in the music scene over here. Whoever fills it will have access to large sums of money and a significant amount of influence over the future political direction of the next generation of nationalist activists."

Perhaps Griffin's most audacious idea was to merge the BNP with the National Front, possibly calling the new group the British National Front. He of course would be leader, with Wayne Ashcroft, then chairman of the Young National Front and the NF's West Midlands organiser, becoming his deputy. The NF, he told the undercover reporters was: "...a pitifully small organisation with such low grade people", but it still had a household name.

It was no surprise that Griffin eventually twigged he was being played. The only shock was that he failed to do so sooner, given that it took five months into the undercover operation to do so.

He had been invited to France but on checking the ticket with the travel agents, he learnt it had been booked by Calton TV, the makers of The Cook Report. He had been approached by a company whose name he knew to be false, using an obvious mailing address and advertising a fax number that did not work. There was no way of checking our credentials: he was simply told that our mission was so secret that the FN would publicly deny knowledge of it. Besides, we also convinced him that it was in everyone's interest that he mention our approach to no-one. Clearly happy to keep the £100,000 on offer to himself, he had agreed to talk and put down his thoughts in writing.

Once uncovered, Griffin tried to make the most of revealing the sting, but few were fooled.

"Griffin fell for it, hook, line and sinker," said Wayne Ashcroft, confiding his views (to yet another undercover reporter!). "He's not clever," he added. "He's Cambridge University and all this nonsense, but that doesn't make him a natural political leader."

Paul Ballard agreed, telling Arthur that the sting had set back Griffin's leadership ambitions.

***

The BNP's modernisation plan collided with its national socialist membership at the party's Annual Rally held in late November 1998. Three hundred and fifty people gathered at the Stourport Manor hotel, in the countryside just outside Worcester.

By BNP standards it was a well-run event. It was only two hours late and just a few activists were left stranded at the motorway service station due to the inefficiency of West Midlands organiser Keith Axon, who was co-ordinating the re-direction point. With most of the audience dressed in jackets and ties, this was certainly no repeat of the party's 1994 rally, when several supporters had turned up wearing Combat 18 t-shirts. Nor were there the drunken members that had so rudely interrupted the American nazi William Pierce's speech in 1995, less still the Sieg-Heiling lunatics that greeted John Tyndall as he rose to speak at the party's rally in Bethnal Green in east London in 1991.

All that said, there was still plenty of nazism on show. As Arthur was browsing the stalls, Tyndall marched up and began complaining about the space given to the nazi CDs on sale. It was clear from his body language that he wished they had not been there at all. Arthur soon understood why. One BNP fundraising CD pictured a nazi figure saluting skinheads and with song titles such as "Vote with a Bullet". To try to placate the BNP leader, one of the stall holders offered him a free CD as a peace offering, but Tyndall angrily waved it away and stormed off.

Compèring the rally was the monotone John Morse, a longstanding member and loyal Tyndall supporter. In a change from previous years, there were no international speakers at the event, instead the focus was on regional organisers outlining the reports from their areas. The report for the South West region was given by George Jeffrey, who focused heavily on the work in farming communities, and then it was over to veteran Keith Axon, to give a report for the West Midlands.

Speaking for the East Midlands was Stephen Belshaw, who Arthur remembered as a former C18 activist and friend of the racist bully Simon Chadwick. Belshaw's description of Peterborough's MP as "goofy" was quite ironic, given that was how many people depicted him, especially decked out in his ill-fitting suit.

"There is only one thing for these paedophiles", he told the crowd. "A long length of rope." The applause had only just died down before he continued: "It's time to send the immigrants back where they belong." As the dinosaur wing of the BNP howled with delight, Nick Griffin, Tyndall's heir apparent, sat on his hands. 'New' BNP still had a long way to go. Clearly relishing his newfound popularity with the audience, Belshaw gave a cheeky wave as he was encouraged to end his speech.

Belshaw was not alone in making inappropriate remarks. Phill Edwards, speaking about the party's Media Monitoring Unit, could not help remarking about a Jewish woman working for the Commission for Racial Equality: "Cohen – now that's an interesting name isn't it?"

He continued in much the same vein: "The only place for Indian and Bangladeshi families to develop is in India and Bangladesh." Chris Jackson, representing the North West region, also got in on the act. While supporting Griffin's new line on voluntary repatriation, he could not resist telling a sick joke about Holocaust survivors.

The most practical speeches came from Barnaby Ore, Richard Edmonds and Griffin himself. Ore spoke about the BNP's video operation, saying how it intended to produce a new recruitment video called "Introduction to the BNP". He also hoped the unit would soon be in a position to produce a quarterly video magazine. Meanwhile, Edmonds spoke about the forthcoming European elections, though he was still unsure how many candidates they needed to qualify for a party political broadcast. He did talk excitedly about BNP literature being distributed free by the Royal Mail to 20 million homes.

Griffin, meanwhile, announced a new party campaign, "Equal Rights For London's Whites", which, to Arthur, sounded like a rehash of the "Rights for Whites" campaign of the early 1990s. Griffin also announced an intention to target small businesses, with party literature being sent to 18,000 such enterprises in the next few months. A more adventurous project was the mailing of a free CD to young people on their 18th birthday. Sharron Edwards, from just outside Kidderminster, who was a rising star in the party along with her husband, spoke about the importance of women in nationalism. Meanwhile south London's Bob Gertner, who was in charge of the party's Instant Response Unit, a team of activists drawn from across London who would go to set events inside and outside the capital, spoke on the success of their recent intervention on the huge Countryside March, organised by the Countryside Alliance to oppose the Labour government's plans to ban foxhunting and undermine rural life. They'd also had success at country fairs, he said. Surprisingly, he failed to mention how they were thrown out of the most recent fair they had attended, in Warwickshire, a couple of weeks beforehand.

It was David Bruce, an old timer from Hertfordshire, who provided the audience with some light relief, as he decided to wander off the stage while compèring the fundraising appeal. Unfortunately for the man who many BNP members suspected was Jewish, a not uncommon charge within the party and reflective of their obessive mindset, he only succeeded in pulling the microphone out of its socket. When he tried to clamber back onto the stage he tripped and almost fell flat on his face.

The afternoon allegedly raised £12,000 – though almost all in the form of IOUs. Sidney Smith from Enfield, who conveniently was not there, supposedly pledged £2,000, while Griffin (or his mother who accompanied him) dipped into the family coffers to give £2,800. Bob Gertner, the London rail worker and Croydon activist, pledged £1,000. Tyndall, rather embarrassingly, put up only £50.

The real talk of the meeting was of the leadership challenge that everyone anticipated was coming. Tyndall's speech was therefore greeted with great anticipation. Arthur, like others, was not to be disappointed. By default or design, Tyndall gave the only truly political speech of the afternoon. Blatantly copying Oswald Mosley's oratorical mannerisms, he launched into an attack on the Board of Deputies of British Jews, claiming that they were behind the cancellation of several BNP venues both that year and the previous.

"As far as the BNP is concerned any ordinary person of the Jewish faith who keeps to himself has nothing whatever to fear from us," he told the audience. "But", he added with some venom, "we will not tolerate any minority in this country, Jewish or otherwise, dictating to British people where they may or may not hold their meetings in their country."

To huge cheers he continued: "We have reached the point now where we are not going to take this lying down any longer. If these people want to fight with us then a fight they shall have." Tyndall added that the Jewish community was "the most powerful pressure group in the world."

Tyndall was working up quite a sweat, and the audience was loving every minute of it. Yes, the Media Monitoring Unit was all well and good but derogatory comments about blacks, Asians and Jews was what they wanted to hear. And Tyndall wasn't letting them down.

"It is amazing to me that the politicians are always talking about Europe and the great European ideal, and yet these are the very people who have been busy over the past 40 years bringing the Third World flooding into Europe to occupy our homelands," he spouted, his hands gesticulating wildly.

Criticising the plethora of anti-European groups that would be competing for the nationalist vote in June's European elections, Tyndall dismissed them for not being racist:

"What on earth is the point of fighting for this country's freedom and sovereignty if at the end of it all the British nation is lost anyway through immigration, multiracialism and interbreeding? In the European elections we have to fight not only the treason of the mainstream parties but also the bogus patriots who come waving their little Union Jacks but are quite happy to see huge tracts of our land becoming the outposts of the West Indies and Asia."

If there was any doubt about the real views of the BNP towards immigration, then these were dispelled. Tyndall had worked the crowd into a frenzy, feeding them a diet of antisemitism and raw racism. They enjoyed his speech so much that he was the only speaker to be given a standing ovation. Griffin glumly rose to add his half-hearted applause but it was noticeable that he was the first person in the hall to sit down.

***

Arthur had friends in a number of different far-right groups, many of whom had been in the BNP with him at one time or another. Others he was in touch with through correspondence or attending their events.

In January 1998, he learnt that the National Socialist Movement (NSM), a Combat 18 splinter group led by Steve Sargent, brother to former C18 leader Charlie (who had just been found guilty for the murder of a rival faction member), and the nazi-occultist David Myatt, were organising a counter-protest to the annual Bloody Sunday march, an annual pro-Irish Republican demonstration in London.

Arthur had been to the occasional Loyalist event and counter-demo over previous years, but he was never that interested in the Loyalist scene. This event pricked his interest and he discussed with Dave Rich about going. Arthur initially suggested that he ring Steve Sargent to get the details, but Dave asked him to hold off. We didn't want to risk Arthur getting arrested, or indeed beaten up, if there was a clash with the ascendant C18 faction led by the violent Will Browning. It was decided he would go to the National Front counter-demonstration instead.

The NF event was a pretty pathetic affair, with only about 20 NF supporters and 10 Portsmouth hooligans initially turning up at the rendezvous point outside London Bridge station The NF group was led by Terry Blackham, a man with an unenviable reputation for violence and himself a convicted Loyalist gunrunner. After a quick drink, they made their way up to Holloway Road in north London and began to loiter along the main road in preparation for the Republican march, by which time their numbers had swelled to 80. Ironically, among those now were Steve Sargent, David Myatt and the small NSM contingent that we had been keen for Arthur to avoid.

While most of those there were not known to Arthur, there were a few familiar faces, including Tower Hamlets BNP organiser Dave Hill, Watford activist Pat Garratt and east Londoners Linda and Alex Cooper. Also there was south London NF organiser Steve Rowland. As the Republican marchers filed past, shouts and screams roared out from the far-right group. A line of police prevented any disorder, though no-one really seemed intent on a fight.

Retiring to the pub near London Bridge where they had started the day, Arthur sat with Linda and Alex and reminisced over their old BNP days. Over came Alan Winder, a former member of the Royal Artillery Intelligence and more recently 'Grand Dragon for the Realm of England, leader of the Knights of the Invisible Empire' – or in layman's terms, the Ku Klux Klan (KKK). Both Alex and Linda had been part of the group, but turning to Winder said: "There wasn't much to leave, was there Alan?"

Winder accepted that the KKK in Britain, a chapter of the US KKK, had run its course, which had not been helped by a recent media exposé He donated the remaining money to the NF and other activities he saw as worthwhile. The only example he gave of KKK activity was "cross-burning to wind up the blacks".

Arthur remained in regular contact with Linda and Alex, attending parties at their flat and even going on a National Front Remembrance Sunday demonstration in November 1998.

***

Nick Griffin announced his decision to challenge John Tyndall for the BNP leadership early in 1999, though there had been some shadow boxing between the two for several months. Tyndall proposed a change to the constitution to strengthen the position of the leader and place a five year minimum membership for anyone wanting to stand as leader, which of course would have had the effect of ruling out a leadership bid by Griffin. The row exploded into the open at a two-day BNP leadership meeting held in early February at a hotel in the West Midlands, with furious exchanges between the two men.

Purple-faced with rage, Tyndall demanded an immediate vote of confidence from the meeting, but even some of his closest allies, such as Richard Edmonds and John Morse, felt this was premature. Griffin distributed an open letter accusing Tyndall of being an obstacle to the BNP's further progress and openly announcing his challenge for the leadership.

Responding to Tyndall's proposed constitutional changes, Griffin letter pulled no punches.

> "This summer you will be 65, the age when it is usual to begin to take a slightly back seat role. You will recall that, late in 1996, we discussed our relationship and the timescale of your relinquishing the party leadership. You said then that, if things were to go very well for the party in the year after the general election of 1997, so that we could see 'real and rapid progress on the path to becoming a mass movement,' you visualised continuing as leader for perhaps up to five years. Conversely, you said that, if things did not go that well, political reality would dictate that you should have over the reins to someone else 'in about two years' time."

While Griffin saw many advances, such as the creation of their Instant Response Group and their countryside campaigns, "none of these constitutes rapid progress... Accordingly, therefore, to your own criteria, it is time for a change."

The contest was on.

News of Griffin's leadership bid swept through the party, helped of course by *Searchlight*, which gave a running commentary of the growing split. We were helped by Arthur, who fed us a constant stream of information from both factions. This included a series of letters written by Griffin to others, which had been supplied by Ballard. Richard Edmonds responded to Griffin's initial letter by imploring him to withdraw his nomination.

Griffin wrote back three days later, stating that he would be prepared to withdraw his nomination if Tyndall agreed to several demands, among which were a call for a full member meeting in the summer to discuss and agree to constitutional changes, the creation of an Advisory Council, the appointment of a party auditor, and that Tyndall stand down in July 2000 and accept the post of President. The new interim leader would be, of course, be Griffin himself, and new elections would be held in the summer of 2001.

> "I hope that you will agree, and will do what you can to persuade him to accept the proposals outlines above would be better than fighting the kind of bitter campaign heralded by his self-destructive letter of 9th February, a campaign which would seriously damage his standing in the eyes of the membership, and which he would undoubtedly lose."

Of course, Tyndall rejected Griffin's proposals and the scene was set for a summer showdown, though there was a brief lull in the campaign due to fighting the European elections, which were to be held in June.

Croydon organiser Paul Ballard felt torn. On a personal level he was friends with Griffin, though politically he was closer to Tyndall. On 2 June, on behalf of the Croydon branch, Ballard wrote to Griffin warning of the dangers of a serious split in the party and asking if it were better if he was the "de facto number two in the present BNP rather than leader of half of it." Griffin wrote back expressing his sympathy and understanding of Ballard's position, but given Tyndall had rejected his proposed phased handover, he had little option but to challenge him.

The election campaign proper began in late June, but it was clear to everyone that Griffin was likely to win. That obviously did not stop either side from campaigning and this became increasingly fractious and negative. Branch meetings held in the final weeks of the election campaign took on an extra dimension as supporters of both camps jockeyed for position and influence. Arthur was tasked up with going to as many meetings as he could across the capital, and during August and early September 1999 he attended meetings in Croydon, Newham, Dagenham, Waltham Forest, Barking & Dagenham and Enfield.

The Enfield meeting, held on 8 September, was particularly interesting. It was billed as a debate between Tyndall and Edmonds on one side and Lecomber and Griffin on the other. Arthur and 30-40 others met up at Cheshunt railway station and waited for the venue details to be released. There were people from both the Tyndall and Griffin factions there, but everyone seemed on friendly terms – at least on a superficial level. This was probably helped by the fact that Tyndall skipped the re-direction point and went straight to the venue, while key lieutenants Edmonds and Ian Dell went to the public toilets and seemed to stay there until everyone moved off.

Inside the meeting itself, the atmosphere was quite different. It was tense and clearly divided. To the Chair's surprise, Griffin pulled out at the last moment, leaving it to Lecomber to fight his corner. When Tyndall and Edmonds entered the room, Tyndall and Lecomber completely blanked each other. After their speeches,

Lecomber applauded the BNP leader, but Tyndall and Edmonds did not reciprocate.

Before the meeting officially started, Lecomber and a couple of his close friends handed out a sheet entitled: *'Awkward Questions'*, listing six questions Lecomber wanted people in the audience to ask Tyndall. They included 'Why is friendship conditional on unquestioning loyalty?', 'Why did it take two years for Tyndall to proscribe C18?', 'Why has no-one seen the books?' and 'Why are legacies required to be left to Tyndall personally?'

Edmonds was the first up, and bizarrely began by reminiscing about when he was a boy and that there were "no brown faces around and everyone was happy." He then went on to say that the BNP had been through many ups and downs over the years, but Tyndall had steered them through it all. He even held up a copy of the famous *Daily Mirror* front page, placed by *Searchlight*, which carried the photo of a bloodied BNP leader and David Copeland at the 1997 aborted rally in Stratford.

"We still don't know how the Reds found out the arrangements for that day," he said, "as only a few people in the party knew about it."

He said that the photo, connecting the nail bomber to the BNP, was probably the most challenging incident that they had had to deal with and had been released by *Searchlight* two years after it had been taken for maximum effect. He then told the audience that as soon as the story broke, Tyndall liaised with Edmonds, Newland and Griffin and between them drew up a press statement with three main points.

The first was that this had been a public meeting and so anyone was invited. The second was that the BNP was the only party to advocate capital punishment for killers. The third point was that the BNP hoped justice would be done and if Copeland was the bomber [this meeting happened before the trial took place] then he should be punished. Edmonds claimed that this three point statement neutralised the potential damage the bombing could have done to the BNP and was testament to Tyndall's leadership. For that reason alone, he argued, people should vote for Tyndall.

Lecomber was next up and began with a jibe at Edmonds. He reminisced about his own childhood in Hounslow, where there were lots of brown faces. But, he added: "I'm not as old as Richard." He then launched into an attack on Tyndall's record, demolishing any claim the BNP leader might have to the party's biggest success – the 1993 Millwall by-election victory. This success, he told the audience, was down to Eddy Butler and not Tyndall.

"If you ask Tyndall what 'Rights for Whites' means, he'd say 'a bunch of blokes standing on street corners shouting Rights for Whites.'" Of course, he said, it was a sophisticated electoral campaign.

When Lecomber apologised to new members for the division the leadership election had caused, Ian Dell interrupted and shouted: "The trouble is coming from your side!"

"Nick Griffin is the flair and vision candidate," Lecomber continued. "People are leaving his meetings enthused about the possibilities for the party throughout the country. In contrast, Tyndall's meetings are negative, based on attacks on Griffin!"

By now, Lecomber had become very emotional, shouting out his words and looking as though he was about to cry. He said that there was going to be a purge in the party, and that he, Griffin, Newland and others would be kicked out if Tyndall won.

"Griffin," he concluded, "is the unity candidate, the only man who can hold the party together! If he wins, he wants Tyndall and his supporters to stay in the party."

Tyndall had been scribbling furiously during Lecomber's speech. When it was his turn to speak, he didn't hold back. The previous speaker, Tyndall began, had claimed it was the Tyndall camp that had been bad-mouthing people.

"What rubbish!" he bellowed. "Nick Griffin has been bad-mouthing me for a long time." Apparently, so the BNP leader claimed, Lecomber had used a Enfield branch meeting at the beginning of the year to say that Tyndall was "an alcoholic".

"When Griffin came into the party I believed that there was a lot to this man," Tyndall thundered. "But I also had my misgivings and so Griffin was effectively put on probation. I then heard that he was going all around the country promoting himself, but it all came to a head with The Cook Report. Everything became clear. And yet still, Griffin had the gall to deny in *Spearhead* that he wanted to be leader!"

Lambasting Griffin for being a manipulator, Tyndall then said: "Griffin used [Wayne] Ashcroft. I don't think he had any intention to make Ashcroft his deputy, but he was cynical enough to tell him that he could have that position." Tyndall said that the leadership election was badly timed. He said he had been "working his balls off" for the European elections, realising that any slip up could ruin their best-laid plans. "Yet all the time, Griffin was going up and down the country speaking and promoting himself."

Tyndall then turned to his own motivation for remaining as party leader.

"I'm not continuing with the leadership of the party for personal satisfaction," he claimed. "Elements of the job are rewarding but that doesn't make up for the hard work." He added that he would very much like to hand the leadership over to a suitable replacement and concentrate on writing, both for *Spearhead* and on an idea for a political novel. He dismissed age as a factor, claiming that he ran three miles each day, and five when it was cold.

Lowering his voice, and pausing for effect, Tyndall then brandished the same copy of *The Daily Express*, which carried a front page story about the police cracking down on the far right, that Edmonds had also used as a prop, to claim that that MI5 was behind Griffin's leadership bid.

"No-one in Griffin's camp are actually working for MI5, but people are pulling strings and there is a whispering campaign going to divide the party."

That said, and to counter Lecomber's claims, he also promised not to purge Griffin and his team if he won.

Tyndall ended his speech with one final attack on his opponent. "Griffin will destroy the BNP!" he roared. "As NF leader he was a complete failure and there was split after split. He will do the same to the BNP!"

The question and answer session following his speech descended into acrimony. Arthur Flinders said that "all this New Nationalism stuff is rubbish" and that they were never thugs beating up black people. Arthur thought this intervention was quite

American historian Deborah Lipstadt. Photo: International Committee of the Red Cross (ICRC)

Ironically, Irving seemed better-viewed than Griffin among some party members. "I think that even amongst people who thought that Griffin was the best person to lead the BNP, there was a realisation that he was very much a player, taking a good salary and expenses out of the party," said Arthur. "Whereas David Irving was very much a man of integrity, who was doing this for the common good as well as trying to clear his name."

London BNP supporters were regular attendees to Court 73, where the case was being held. The most regular attendee was railway worker Bob Gertner, who appeared to have taken time off work so he could be there as often as possible. Arthur knew Gertner well, but had little time for him. He was a hardcore antisemite and a thoroughly unpleasant man.

Others who would also go regularly were London BNP stalwarts Arthur Flinders and Ron Smith. Flinders was particularly confrontational and took great delight in upsetting anyone he could. On one day he sat with an American Holocaust revisionist paper displayed on his lap next to an Auschwitz survivor. To a young black man in the audience he loudly proclaimed: "One day the truth will come out. It's the biggest fraud in history." The BNP members were heard laughing loudly about gas vans as they left court. Their admiration for Irving was voiced loud and clear.

Arthur went to just one day of the trial, out of personal interest but also in his role as mole, to show support and be seen. The public gallery was fairly sparse on the day he went, with only Bob Gertner and a few individuals who had come along to what they thought was an interesting trial. While these people appeared to be politically unattached, they all wanted, and expected, Irving to lose. As part of his cover, Arthur made his support for Irving clear, much to the discomfort of some of these seated around him.

The start of proceedings was delayed that day because Irving had forgotten some papers and had to go back to his home in Mayfair to collect them. Once he was back, Rampton wanted to prove that Irving was in attendance at a particular far-right event in the USA; Irving felt that this was a waste of time, because he never denied being there anyway.

Much of the day was spent discussing the burning of bodies in the ovens at Auschwitz and, specifically, how many could be burnt within a certain time frame and how natural body fat could aid this process. It was a pretty grim discussion and Arthur felt very uneasy about it, not helped he thought by the very partisan nature of the debate.

Looking across the court at Deborah Lipstadt, Arthur thought she had a lot of

David Irving. Photo Allan Warren

people with her, but nevertheless she looked weary and stressed. Arthur felt empathy for her, despite the fact he couldn't let his feelings show. She was a brave woman and shouldn't have had to be in that situation.

David Irving, by contrast, was very much alone. He had no legal team and to Arthur's knowledge only himself and Gertner in the court as supporters. Arthur privately found that amusing. Of Irving's two supporters, one was a spy. "Irving had put forward views that had caused incredible hurt to survivors, their families and the wider Jewish community," Arthur remembered. "However, I am not going to lie, I could see the bravery in him."

Arthur was also interested in the barrister acting on behalf of Lipstadt and Penguin Books, Richard Rampton QC, though this was more because of his role in representing the McDonald's food chain against two of his personal heroes, the environmental activists Helen Steel and Dave Morris, who had been sued by the restaurant chain in the so-called "McLibel" trial (over leaflets about the chain). As a result, Arthur had very mixed feelings. Rampton, as Arthur saw it, was with the good guys this time, but he was still going to be very well paid for his work.

***

It might seem ridiculous to someone who has never been in the company of antisemites and Holocaust deniers, but the continual drip-drip of propaganda can turn heads.

"Looking back, surrounded by people who were convinced Holocaust deniers, who had well-practised arguments, who seemed to have a good grasp of detail and who above all pushed forward the idea that people who did believe that the Holocaust happened were naive, I continually questioned whether the Holocaust did happen," Arthur admitted to me many years later.

"However, I always quickly came to the same conclusion that indeed it did: that is to say, many millions of Jewish people and other minorities died through mass murder and neglect and that the order came from Adolf Hitler.

"I can remember a BNP leafletting session where activist Big Arthur Flinders was laughing about a documentary where a witness told how a Jewish man arrived late at the station and how he had actually ran after the train that was his intended transport to a concentration camp. In Flinders' mind this exposed the absurdity of Jewish people being forced to go to the camps and ultimately the gas chambers. I admit I considered what Arthur Flinders had to say, but quickly came to the conclusion that the Jewish man believed that he would be in more trouble if he missed the train, if he was complicit with the Nazis, then if he would survive the war.

"If there was any danger of me being convinced by people like Big Arthur, then my *Searchlight* contact Dave was a great help. Rather than simply saying the Holocaust deniers were liars, he would take on their arguments. He would say for example that [infamous denier] Fred Leuchter did indeed carry out tests on rubble from Auschwitz and find no traces of cyanide, however that's because he was testing rubble from the wrong buildings."

***

On 11 April 2000, after 36 days of hearings and in front of 150 journalists, Mr Justice Gray found in favour of Deborah Lipstadt and Penguin Books, and against David Irving after the publication of Deborah Lipstadt's *Denying the Holocaust.* In a stinging judgment, he said:

> "Irving is one of the most dangerous spokespersons for Holocaust denial. Familiar with historical evidence, he bends it until it conforms with his ideological leanings and political agenda. A man who is convinced that Britain's great decline was accelerated by its decision to go to war with Germany, he is most facile at taking accurate information and shaping it to confirm his conclusions. A review of his recent book, *Churchill's War,* which appeared in *New York Review of Books,* accurately analysed his practice of applying a double standard to evidence. He demands "absolute documentary proof" when it comes to proving the Germans guilt, but he relies on highly circumstantial evidence to condemn the Allies. (114) This is an accurate description not only of Irving's tactics, but of those of deniers in general."
>
> "Irving has for his own ideological reasons persistently and deliberately misrepresented and manipulated historical evidence; that for the same reasons he has portrayed Hitler in an unwarrantedly favourable light, principally in relation to his attitude towards and responsibility for the treatment of the Jews; that he is an active Holocaust denier; that he is anti-semitic and racist and that he associates with right wing extremists who promote neo-Nazism."

Writing in *Searchlight,* my old colleague Kate Taylor proclaimed that Justice Gray had ruled "in favour of history, truth and reason" and wrote that the judgment showed that Irving, as well as other deniers, were "manipulators and distorters who refute the truth in order to serve an ideological agenda" that was "very often neo-nazi in content".

While she conceded that the judge's verdict would not stop Irving or other deniers from publishing their offensive views, "the verdict will deny Irving and his followers mainstream legitimacy and credibility".

From the moment the judgment was announced, it was clear Irving was a broken man. When he rose to speak following the verdict, he was visibly shaken. For once the arrogant tone was gone; the booming voice was muffled. His voice shook as he asked the judge for leave to appeal. "I need time to gather my thoughts and regain my strength from this," he told the judge.

Arthur was not surprised by the verdict, though.

"It was very much what people expected, but of course people were disappointed. Some people hoped that Irving could seize the opportunity to prove that the Holocaust did not occur or was vastly exaggerated or at least the order was not given by Adolf Hitler. More realistically, perhaps, some hoped the judge may have found that Irving had not intentionally lied and we could then spin this as David

Irving defeating Deborah Lipstadt and hence proving that the Holocaust did not take place."

The BNP itself was silent. From a position of lambasting Irving for his moderation only a few years before, with one eye on the ballot box the newly-crowned leader of the BNP was now desperately trying to present himself in a more respectable light. Whatever he privately thought, admitting his support for Holocaust denial in public wasn't in keeping with his new BNP image.

But the court case could not be ignored so completely. While bending over backwards to ensure that they couldn't be considered Holocaust deniers any longer, Griffin could not ignore the issue altogether. During the trial the BNP called for an open debate on what had happened during the Second World War.

> "The victims of Hitler's regime, and their kin, are constantly infuriated that their fervently held beliefs are challenged, and often – sometimes without reason – feel that the war dead are being insulted ... May we suggest a five year programme among historians to resolve this matter, with free debate and discussion?"

The same could not be said of former leader (and Griffin rival) John Tyndall, who wrote an article in his magazine, *Spearhead*, condemning the result. Under the title *"Justice Perverted"*, Tyndall criticised the historian for even taking the matter to court in the first place.

> "Long ago, I made myself a golden rule in the struggle against the dominant 'liberal' establishment: keep away from the courts."

Within that context, he really couldn't understand why Irving would have brought the case in the first place, as he was clearly going to lose from the outset – given the forces he was up against.

> "Reading Mr. Justice Gray's summation, one might have imagined one was reading a transcript of one of the Stalinist show trials in the darkest days of Soviet tyranny instead of the proceedings of the High Court in London. Irving quite clearly was an ideological 'enemy of the people' and had to be sent to his own Siberia."

However, he concluded the article with a degree of sympathy with Irving, something most in the BNP would share.

> "We find ourselves disagreeing with David Irving, but his type of bravery is a rare treasure in the country Britain has become. We must hope that others derive inspiration from it, and we wish him all good fortune in his future endeavours to promote the truth as he sees it."

***

Some years later, on a Saturday afternoon, Arthur was walking down The Strand in central London and saw what appeared to be a gathering of anti-fascist protestors, mingling outside the High Court, surrounded by journalists and the police. He quickly realised that they must be filming something, as the High Court would be not in session that day.

It was only later that he realised that they were filming the movie "Denial", a Hollywood film based on the Irving libel trial, featuring actors Rachel Weisz as Deborah Lipstadt and Timothy Spall playing Irving. He approached the well-known British actor Tom Wilkinson, who was playing Richard Rampton QC, but he proved less than talkative. Despite being shunned, Arthur very much had sense that he was looking back into his past.

CHAPTER THIRTEEN: PANTOMIME SEASON COMES EARLY

Arthur knew it was going to be more than just *a meeting*. And it was one that he did not want to miss. The BNP leadership was split and the October 2000 gathering in Tipton, in the Black Country, was going to be a key showdown.

On one side was Tony Lecomber and others loyal to party leader Nick Griffin. On the other were Steve and Sharron Edwards, the Black Country duo who were the respectable and moderate face of the BNP. The pair had previously been in the National Democrats, a split from the National Front, before switching over to the BNP, where they soon became a poster family for party literature and earning a reputation for strong community politics. Alongside them were most of the West Midlands branches and Mike Newland, the former press officer who had become the party's National Treasurer under Griffin. Even the 135 mile distance from London was not going to keep Arthur away, as the BNP faced a potential split.

***

Griffin's leadership victory had been built on a promise to modernise the party, to make it more respectable and (therefore) more electable. However, from almost the start he set about strengthening his own position and undermining his rivals. He marginalised BNP founder John Tyndall and moved his key lieutenant Richard Edmonds and promoted his own team into key positions. Lecomber also began purging pro-Tyndall supporters at a regional and local level. Rather than expanding democracy within the party, Griffin actually began consolidating power with rule changes and executive action.

Allegations of financial mismanagement and impropriety began to stalk the new leader. While Mike Newland, who had been appointed treasurer after Griffin's victory, had access to the accounts he had no oversight into the party's fundraising project account, the Trafalgar Club, which was controlled by Griffin and his mother Jean. Newland alleged that the Trafalgar Club was little more than Griffin's private slush fund.

In addition to the vagueness over party accounts, Griffin was also accused of using party finances for his own personal gain. The BNP paid for an extension at his home, big enough to host the party's ruling executive meetings, plus a £1,500 payment to Tony Lecomber, which was later passed off as a loan but just happened to be the exact amount Lecomber had personally donated to Griffin's leadership campaign, and also the cost of the purchase and repairs to a number of vehicles which were then sold through a private enterprise run by Griffin himself.

Against the backdrop of financial impropriety, Griffin also moved against the party's Deputy Chairman, Sharron Edwards, and her husband Steve. They were among the most popular and hardworking activists in the organisation and under their stewardship the Black Country BNP had made huge electoral advances in the region.

When Sharron Edwards took up Mike Newland's concerns over the lack of financial transparency, Griffin moved to suspend her and also her husband over a series of seemingly trumped-up charges. Their suspension also rather conveniently meant that neither could stand in the forthcoming West Bromwich West parliamentary by-election, caused by the retirement of the-then Speaker of the House, Betty Boothroyd.

Incensed by what had happened, the BNP branches in the West Midlands unanimously decided to take action and called a "Unity meeting" in the hope that a huge turnout would force the leadership into reversing its decision.

***

The meeting was held at the Tipton Leisure Centre and although portrayed as a "Unity" rally, it was anything but for party leaders, who must have felt as though they were attending a show trial.

Fearing the event, and the growing groundswell of unrest, attempts were made to persuade members to stay away. Writing in the BNP's October *Organisers' Bulletin,* under the title "One to Miss", Griffin claimed there was "no need for a meeting" as he was willing to allow both of the Edwardses to re-join after a six-month "cooling off period". While this proved unacceptable to the membership, Griffin thought it was more than adequate. "Go if you must," Griffin wrote in his bulletin, "but don't expect anything worthwhile."

Griffin went on to urge London organisers to "strongly discourage their members from attending the depressing and pointless meeting on Saturday. With so much constructive work to do we've got to avoid unnecessary trouble."

Unfortunately for Griffin over 100 BNP members defied his call to stay away. While most of the audience was from the West Midlands, and most of these were strongly supportive of Steve and Sharron Edwards, many others came from further afield. Arthur travelled up with a sizeable contingent from London, led by Richard Edmonds, and there was a smattering from elsewhere. Few present were neutral on the matter, but many, like Arthur (albeit for different reasons than most), went because they expected fireworks to fly. Ian Dell, for example, the party's Chief Steward during the first couple of years of Arthur's infiltration, had not been very active for quite some time, but he told Arthur that he wasn't going "to miss it for the world".

There was a hum of anticipation as the meeting was opened by the Chair, south Wales activist Dave Jones. After a quick introduction, he handed over to Mike

Newland, who immediately launched a tirade against Griffin. Apologising for backing him for leader, Newland described the BNP boss as the biggest crook he had ever come across. He went on to describe Griffin as an "asset stripper", someone who repeatedly ripped off "nationalist" (read: extreme far-right) organisations for personal gain.

He told the audience that rather than breaking from the past, Griffin was simply continuing the regime of incompetence, financial mismanagement and nepotism that he had inherited from John Tyndall. Newland explained how Griffin was being paid £125 a week by the party, a relatively small amount even back in the summer of 2000, but this was supplemented by a variety of side projects he was involved with via the party. Lecomber, meanwhile, was being paid £110 a week, boosted by government benefits for the low paid, but after complaining to Griffin an additional £100 a week was found. Newland then claimed there was no accountability over the party finances and no accounts had been published or even fully disclosed to him as party Treasurer.

The final straw for Newland was an advert for "Affordable Cars" in the party newspaper *Freedom*, which gave the impression that this was a party enterprise and that the party would receive any money made. However, Newland explained it was a private enterprise run by (and for) Griffin. The PO Box behind "Affordable Cars" (which sold second-hand cars) was personally run by Nick Griffin and its bank account was actually in Griffin's father's name. Newland took this complaint to Sharron Edwards, the party's Deputy Chairman, and she in turn raised it with Griffin. The party leader responded by suspending Newland for three months.

Newland concluded by announcing that there may be a bid to replace Griffin as leader in the near future. An obviously embarrassed Sharron Edwards, widely tipped among the audience as the only obvious candidate, grimaced with annoyance.

Lecomber responded for the party leadership. He was the only member of the BNP Advisory Council – which had voted unanimously to expel the Edwardses and Newland – to appear at this stage of the meeting. His speech led to howls of derision.

There was little solace for Lecomber in what was otherwise a torrid afternoon. To cries of "bullshit", "stand down", "rubbish" and "he's lying just like Tony Blair", Lecomber defended the decision to expel the trio. Instantly judging the mood of the audience, an increasingly angry Lecomber claimed there was no need for this meeting as Griffin had already agreed to the Edwardses' return. But it was clear from his repetition of the charges of disloyalty and theft against Sharron Edwards that this change of mind had been forced upon the leadership against its will. He then went on to give various convoluted reasons as to why either one or both of the couple shouldn't be the party's candidate in the forthcoming West Bromwich West by-election. Few were buying it.

The speech was difficult for many in the audience to hear, not to say even embarrassing. At one point, the party's former election guru Eddy Butler turned to the barrister Adrian Davies, who represented several far-right figures during this time, and within earshot of Arthur said: "Let's just let him bury himself in the hole he's digging."

Sharron Edwards, Steve Edwards and Mike Newland

Lecomber finally lost his temper and began screaming at the increasingly hostile audience and swearing randomly at hecklers. When Charlie Bough, a veteran activist from Cannock, objected to the swearing, Lecomber responded with "you do fuck all". One woman pointed out that Bough had health problems, to which Lecomber replied: "I don't give one."

Griffin had yet to appear, leading to increased annoyance among the audience. "His name means nothing in the West Midlands," complained one local activist. West Country organiser Bruce Cowd summed up the view of many in the room when he said that the meeting was pointless without Griffin being present. "So I am prepared," Cowd told Lecomber, "to wait until 11 or 12 at night - you get on the phone, get Griffin down here and get Steve and Sharron back in the party".

Around the room murmurs could be heard that Griffin could not be much of a leader if he didn't have the bottle to show up.

After Lecomber sat down, it was the turn of Sharron and Steve Edwards to speak. Sharron poured out details of personal and financial loss as a result of their involvement in the party. She claimed that both had lost their jobs, adding that journalists had been camped out in the reception of her work for weeks trying to get a story on her. Finally, after some German clients protested, her boss bowed to pressure and sacked her. She denied the allegations made against them and even called up someone in the audience who had been at the supposed reconciliation meeting: they told that crowd that Lecomber's recollection of events were nonsense. While she accepted that Griffin was now willing to readmit them to the party, the conditions attached made them unacceptable.

Sharron Edwards' speech was littered with references to the need for unity within the BNP, and ended by her recounting a story about a young girl who had been gang-

CHAPTER FOURTEEN: A NEW DAWN

Nick Griffin survived the Tipton meeting by promising to allow Steve and Sharron Edwards back into the BNP. No sooner was the meeting over he set about tightening his grip on the party and reneging on his words. Wounded by the open rebellion against him, especially by those who had supported his leadership only a year before, Griffin's best course of action perhaps should have been more conciliatory – but that was not in his nature. His decision to impose himself as the BNP candidate for the West Bromwich West by-election, and his resulting poor vote, only further alienated him from party activists. In fact, the 794 votes he secured, 4.2% of the votes cast, was only 13 more than his bitter rival Steve Edwards had polled in a single ward six months before.

Quite understandably, the Edwardses were not bought off by Griffin's promises at the Tipton showdown and continued their call for fundamental change to his increasingly dictatorial and vindictive leadership. In a letter to branch organisers a few weeks after the meeting, Sharron Edwards set out her views.

"It is now clear that Party Chairman Nick Griffin has gone back on his signed agreement to 'unconditionally re-instate' us at the Unity Rally and will not accept Steve Edwards as West Midlands Regional Organiser," she wrote.

"The Party leadership are using the constitution as a pretext for asset stripping hard earned local funds, provided by local people for campaigning in their communities, but now being seized to pay head office salaries.

"It must be realised that, over the next few weeks, tens of thousands of members' money could be paid into central funds (via Mike Newland's old PO Box, which is now under the control of Tony Lecomber, and not Chris Green, the assistant treasurer dealing with receipts) by unsuspecting members, thus providing a substantial fund at the mercy of an unscrupulous leadership involved on Tony Lecomber's own public admission in tax and benefit fraud, clearly spelt out by barrister Adrian Davies in his report on the Trafalgar Club finances."

She ended the letter in an openly defiant manner. "The survival of our Party depends upon a leadership that works within the law, and enjoys the members' respect and support, counselled by an advisory council that takes responsibility for the proper running of the party, not one that gutlessly allows impropriety (not to say flagrant illegality) to discredit our Party and perhaps destroy it altogether."

At a subsequent West Midlands organisers meeting, also attended by organisers from South Wales, it was unanimously agreed that Griffin had to go. However, Steve and Sharron Edwards appeared reluctant to challenge Griffin themselves, so all the

The Oldham riots were triggered by BNP and C18 supporters attacking Asians in their homes

talk was of supporting John Tyndall if he decided to contest the leadership again. The former leader had his own base of support in the party and was becoming increasingly vocal in his own opposition to Griffin's leadership style.

"The irony was that under John Tyndall and Richard Edmonds, the BNP was much more overtly nazi, but they were also much more easy going," recalls Arthur. "Nick Griffin and Tony Lecomber realised that you needed to keep the nazism and fascism out of the way, at least publicly, but they had a much tighter grip on the party. They valued loyalty before ability."

Longstanding and quite able activists and senior organisers were regularly overlooked for key party roles, with Griffin increasingly promoting younger, more inexperienced members instead. Two people who were given plum roles within the party was Mark Collett, a Leeds-based activist who became Young BNP leader, and Kent-based member Paul Golding, who became the new head of communications.

"Many BNP activists would joke that Nick Griffin was sexually attracted to Paul Golding, which was why Golding rose to prominence so quickly," remembers Arthur. "However, I am quite sure that Griffin liked Paul because he was a 'Yes Man,' whereas much more experienced and able people like Steve and Sharron Edwards were pushed out of the way for speaking their mind."

Nick Griffin fleeing the 2003 election court in Oldham

This, Arthur claims, was quite different from how the party was run under Tyndall. "After Griffin took over, John Morse told me that Tyndall had tolerated people he actually disliked because they were a benefit to the party. Whereas Griffin and Lecomber wanted any dissenters sidelined or expelled. Disgruntled BNP activists would say that Griffin was no better than Tony Blair, though to be fair, Griffin could see the stupidity of invading Iraq.

"There was definitely less violence happening and generally speaking when it did occur, it seemed to be small groups of anti-fascists going to the homes of BNP members. Still a lot of people around who were involved in football hooliganism though."

***

Events in Oldham, Greater Manchester, in April 2001, transformed Griffin's fortunes and the direction of the BNP. After months of growing tensions and minor clashes between white and Asian gangs, violence exploded on the streets of the old mill town on the evening of Saturday 26 April. About 60-80 far-right activists, mainly Combat 18, BNP and football hooligans, had met up earlier in the day with the intention of provoking trouble with rival Asian gangs. The police were mobilised and kept the groups apart, but at 5.30pm, as the far-right group began to thin out, the police stood down. An hour later, an argument in a street between some school-aged kids, led to three taxis full of C18 and BNP members racing up to the area and randomly attacking Asians in their houses. This was the "trigger", as a judge later described it, for three days of rioting.

The BNP was jubilant. To them it proved the inherent dangers and incompatibility of multiracial Britain and it brought race to the fore of the political agenda. Arthur remembers Oldham as a turning point. "Then BNP felt that its time had come," he would later recall. "People were excited."

By coincidence, or then again perhaps not, Nick Griffin was standing in Oldham East and Saddleworth in the 2001 General Election, which was only weeks away. The party used the riots to press home its racism, demanding that Asians – and Asians alone – pay for the costs of the riots and that a 'peace wall' should be built to divide the communities. While Griffin talked peace and moderation to the national media, locally the BNP was stressing the incompatibility of large immigrant communities and the violence they threatened. Amid extensive local and national media coverage, Griffin secured 16.7% of the vote in the election, a record for the party.

The Oldham riots were quickly followed by disturbances in Burnley and Bradford. The BNP was key to winding up tensions in all three areas prior to the riots, with Griffin even holding a meeting in Bradford attended by 150 people the night before the riot there. The party benefitted massively. The riots shook the complacency of the London media and political elites that multiculturalism might be working well and only highlighted the deep divisions, suspicions and rivalry between communities – especially white and Muslim – in many northern towns and cities.

A couple of months after the Bradford riot, 19 hijackers flew three planes into the World Trade Centre in New York and the Pentagon. The War on Terror had begun and the BNP switched focus from racial nationalism to Islam.

***

Arthur cannot remember any specific mention of Muslims or Islam prior to 2001. Up until then, the talk was just of Asians and Blacks. Indeed, the party's whole Rights for Whites campaign in east London through the 1990s simply mentioned just Asians and immigrants. "An immigrant was an immigrant," remembers Arthur, "and most BNP members thought they were all controlled or manipulated by the Jews". All that changed in 2001, as party literature and Griffin's own speeches began warning of the dangers of Muslims and the incompatibility of Islam in Western countries.

Within a few weeks of the Twin Towers attack, Arthur was out distributing two anti-Muslim leaflets, which was part of the party's new 'Campaign against Islam' initiative. One of these was called 'An Islamic Britain: a cross to bear?' which was to be placed in churches alongside Christian Aid and other such leaflets. "People were generally enthusiastic about these leaflets," Arthur told us at the time, though it was not without more light-hearted – and offensive – moments. On one leafleting session, in Morden, a confused woman said to one BNP leafleter: "Thank Christ you're here, God must have sent you. You are the gas man, aren't you?" To which the leafleter replied: "No, but we will be when we get in power."

Support for the anti-Islam turn did not eradicate Jewish conspiracies, with many BNP members still believing that the Jews were really behind the Twin Towers attack. However, most people were shocked to hear that US nazi William Pierce, the leader author of *The Turner Diaries* and a speaker at the 1995 BNP annual rally, actually thought the attacks were a good thing, seeing it as a strike against the (supposedly) Jewish-controlled US government. Richard Edmonds shared this outrage, but soon began making excuses for Pierce.

At a London-wide BNP meeting held a few months later, Griffin's change of tactk was obvious, with the main focus of his speech now about the dangers of Islam. He told the audience that when black people moved into an area muggings and crime might go up, but they did not fundamentally change the local community. The same could not be said of Muslims.

The threat from Muslims, Griffin would say, was inherent in their religion. "Al-Qaeda are Islamic extremists, they're good Muslims who have read the Quran properly," he said. "Those Muslims who really do want to get on with British people are bad Muslims." Griffin backed this up by quoting from the Qu'ran, which he said divided the world into two – a Muslim world and a warzone, where Muslims needed to fight to make it Muslim.

Griffin would repeat these warnings at subsequent meetings, including one as troops were preparing to invade Iraq. "If this stupid war goes ahead," Griffin told Arthur and other London BNP members, "there'll be gangs of Muslims out taking revenge on English people."

The 9/11 attack and the subsequent invasion of Iraq changed everything for the BNP, and for society at large. "On the evening of September 11th," remembers Arthur, "someone told me 'things will never be the same again' and I knew she was right, though I probably didn't realise just how big a game changer this would be for the far right and those opposing them.

"People inside the BNP still feared and hated Asian people for being Asian, however now increasingly they also hated people for being Muslim.

"In the build-up to the invasion of Iraq and then the war itself, there were a few BNP members who couldn't resist the excitement of Royal Marines and British Army soldiers invading an Arab country and RAF Tornadoes and Royal Navy warships bombarding Arab targets. However, the overwhelming view of BNP members was that Tony Blair had made a massive mistake in supporting George W. Bush's invasion. Whether Saddam Hussein still held weapons of mass destruction or not, most felt that Iraqis would not willingly accept people from predominantly Christian nations as occupiers.

"I did have one amusing moment, watching BBC television with the wife of a BNP member: we witnessed the US soldiers pull Saddam from his underground hideaway and she remarked, 'He looks just like Catweazle!'

"But much like the Left in Britain, most BNP members I knew could see that Bush

newspapers/leaflets we produced in the early 2000s

and Blair were heading for disaster, creating a vacuum in Iraq and whether they cared or not about the much larger Iraqi death toll, they could see that Blair was sending many servicemen and women to their deaths. Unlike the Left, they believed that there was some sort of Jewish/Zionist strategy behind all this."

The BNP reaped the political rewards of the 2001 upheavals when it won three council seats in Burnley in the 2002 local elections, though the party was helped by all-out elections, which meant voters were choosing three councillors per ward. There were other good results for the BNP around the country, though fortunately no further council gains. The party polled 35% and 30% in St James and Chadderton South respectively in Oldham, 28% in Townend Farm in Sunderland, and 26% in Castle & Priory in Dudley.

The BNP only stood 21 candidates across the whole of London and a third of those were in Bexley. In a sign of the party's changing fortunes in the capital, its highest vote was 16% in the Canning Town North ward in Newham. In Millwall ward in Tower Hamlets, where the BNP won a council seat in 1993, it polled just 9%. With council victories and rising votes happening in the north and Midlands, the political importance of London BNP, for so long at the heart of the party, was on the wane.

***

Griffin put a lot of political capital into new pro-countryside campaigning, partly because he could use it to show that the party was concerned about issues other than race, but also because the countryside, and rural living was an issue that had long been at the heart of his political philosophy. The BNP produced a couple of editions of the *Countryman*, an eight-page magazine that was distributed free. It was regularly put out by the party's Instant Response Group (ISG), a team of activists led by Croydon-based Bob Gertner, at country fairs and stalls in market towns.

In March 2002 the ISG was out in force on the huge Countryside Alliance march in London. Under the slogan 'Liberty and Livelihood' two separate demonstrations converged on Whitehall to hear a series of speeches denouncing the policies of the Labour government, which they believed was undermining rural life. While the Countryside Alliance had intended the event to get across a myriad of issues, the powerful foxhunting lobby managed to push its cause to the fore, so that the main purpose of the demonstration seemed to be to defend hunting against a parliamentary ban.

Arthur was part of the BNP team that was out on the demo and he found it quite a different experience. They were able to operate openly without much fear of abuse or anti-fascist violence, their audience was conservative – politically and culturally – and almost exclusively white.

The BNP members must have been filled with excitement at the prospect of giving out copies of their free newspaper, *The Countrysider*. Prepared specially for the day, the frontpage banner over-optimistically declared *"one million countryside centurions on the march"*. BNP supporters carried bundles of the newspaper, which they handed out at several points on the march.

The party claims to have distributed 46,000 copies, though the true figure was considerably lowers. *The Countrysider* contained a mish-mash of anti-Labour and racist material. For some reason the eight-page newspaper required four editors, Nick Griffin, Darren James, Clive Wakely and Martin Wingfield.

"The old parties," they proclaimed, "with their addiction to using our taxes to help foreigners and foreign causes have failed Britain. So the only thing to do now is to get ordinary, decent Britons like us joining together and building the new party that is committed to restoring our freedoms and to putting their own people first."

A major issue for *The Countrysider* was (so-called) "white flight" – white people moving out of the cities into the countryside. The newspaper said: "They are mostly white, middle class, city folk – ordinary people who, in the main, are sick to death of living in our increasingly alien, cosmopolitan, overcrowded, congested, polluted, crime-infested urban centres ...

"More fool the 'white flighters' seeking a new start in the country: little do they realise that Blair's Babylon is coming to a town near them, it's only a question of time!"

It was on this demo that Arthur first met Mark Collett, the leader of the Young BNP and a member of the party's ruling Advisory Council. Collett was a rising star in the party, confident, brash and extremely loyal to Nick Griffin. In May 2002, while in his third and final year studying at Leeds University, he also coordinated the BNP election campaign in Bradford before joining the party staff on a full-time basis. Arthur and Collett exchanged a few words, but Arthur was later to admit that he couldn't remember anything from the conversation.

The meteoric rise of Collett appeared to have come to a crashing end after he featured on a TV programme admitting he was a nazi sympathiser and was inspired by images of German nazis "Sieg Heiling" in the streets. *Young, Nazi and Proud* was an hour-long documentary that examined the new, respectable face of the BNP. For eight months, programme maker David Modell chronicled Collett's political and personal life. What emerged was an intriguing insight into the mind of a man who hopes one day to lead the party.

Collett boasted of his support for Hitler's Germany, said he would prefer to live in 1930s Germany than in many cities in northern England, and declared that he could not understand why people should find images of German soldiers giving nazi salutes upsetting. Collett was also shown squaring up to Anti-Nazi League protesters at Leeds town hall, confidently canvassing voters in Bradford and giving articulate interviews to television stations. Yet he was also revealed as insecure, vain and a social misfit.

"Collett was a case study in artless, idiotic arrogance. Pumping iron semi-naked in his basement and getting a little too animated about watching 'a brain-dead white slag' snogging a black man suggested there was something a little repressed about the boy," noted Gareth McLean in *The Guardian* review of the show.

In one of the most revealing insights into his character, Collett discussed with much bitterness the break-up of a relationship. After attacking his former girlfriend, he told filmmaker Modell: "I like to break people. When you've broken them and sucked that last bit of life out of them. That's it.

"When people say that I am evil, yeah I am. But it all depends. I'm either the sweetest angel or the most evil being you've ever encountered. It just depends which side you push me. Never kill people. Push them to the point of despair where they do it themselves because that's when you've really won."

In another scene, the arrogant Collett told the reporter: "Hitler will live on forever and maybe I will too."

Among his more illuminating quotes had been one suggesting Nazi Germany was a better place to live than modern Britain. "I honestly can't understand how a man who's seen the inner city hell of Britain today can't look back on that era [Hitler's Germany] with a certain nostalgia and think yeah, those people marching through the streets and all those happy people out in the streets, you know, saluting and everything, was a bad thing.

"Honestly now, would you prefer your kid growing up in Oldham and Burnley or 1930s Germany? It would be better for your child to grow up there."

Arthur and others in London BNP were incredulous and left incandescent at the programme. It was bad enough that Collett was voicing his national socialist views in public, which was contrary to the image the party was trying to portray, but it was his arrogance that really disgusted them.

"Everyone was livid," Arthur reported back to us immediately after the programme was aired. "People were particularly angry where he talked about 'breaking people'." Others were annoyed that the programme deflected attention away from the BNP's remarkable second place in the Mayoral election in Stoke-on-Trent, which occurred in the same week. Some of the more senior figures in London BNP pressed Tony Lecomber about who had given the authorisation for Collett to appear in the documentary, but Lecomber pleaded ignorance. Others demanded that he be sacked from the party.

A week later, London activists had a chance to air their frustrations to the party leadership at a London activist meeting, addressed by Lecomber and Nick Griffin. After the main speeches, and during the Q&A session that followed, several people vented their fury, both at Collett but also at Griffin for the failure to discipline his protégé. Some even suggested that Collett was a plant, sent into the party in order to discredit them, while others thought he should be expelled for just being a complete idiot. Arthur stood up and said he thought it all reflected badly on Griffin himself. There was a murmur of agreement from around the room. Pat Garratt, a long-time party member from Watford, went on to say that it was the most damaging programme there had ever been about the BNP, as Collett came across as so loathsome.

Despite publicly stripping Collett of his Young BNP leader role, the leadership ignored the views of the overwhelming majority of party members and decided to stick by him, and on Sunday 10 November, less than a week after the programme was aired, Collett shared a platform with Nick Griffin at a party meeting in Bradford.

Four months later, Richard Edmonds was billed to speak at a party meeting in Basildon, when he was 'uninvited' literally a few minutes before the meeting was due to begin, in preference for Collett, who just happened to be in the area. What made Edmonds' mood even worse was that Collett gave a dreadful speech, which included several references to going out drinking and getting pissed with his mates. Edmonds thought this, and comparing immigrants to 'cockroaches', juvenile.

North West London organiser Ian Edward, an ex-National Front activist who was now an increasingly senior figure in London BNP, phoned the recently installed London organiser, Chris Roberts, to relay the unhappiness many felt toward Collett and specifically the quality of his Basildon speech. Roberts dismissed his concerns, saying the speech was "terrific" and "fantastic". When Edward then asked him what Collett was doing down south anyway, he was told that he was around for a disciplinary hearing resulting from the Channel Four documentary. However, Roberts admitted that the hearing didn't actually happen as Griffin hadn't turned up. Rather than proceed anyway, the rest of the disciplinary panel, which consisted of Tony Lecomber, Chris Roberts and his brother Barry Roberts, decided not to proceed.

When Edward relayed this conversation to Richard Edmonds and others in London BNP, there was little surprise. "I met Chris [Roberts] for the first time when he was 17," recalled Edmonds. "He had 20 years off and comes back as London organiser!"

***

Just as many of the BNP activists from the Tyndall era began to slowly disappear, through political frustration at the Griffin leadership or merely moving on with their lives, so new people came in. One of the most important new recruits was Chris Roberts, who, from virtually nowhere, was appointed London and Essex organiser, a full-time position made possible after a career in the City. In 2002 he announced that he had arranged a two-year contract with the BNP, which would see him lead the party into the 2004 Greater London Assembly elections. Very quickly, however, he was wondering what he had let himself in for. He told Arthur during one campaign activity that the only decent branches in London were Waltham Forest, Redbridge, Croydon and North West London. The east London branches of Hillingdon and Newham had collapsed, other branches in west London, north London and south-east London were barely functioning.

His pessimistic view of the job was compounded by two poor council by-elections in his first few weeks of being in position. The BNP polled just 49 votes (2.1%) in the Heathrow Village ward, Hillingdon, and 87 votes (4%) in the Blackwall and Cubbitt ward in Tower Hamlets. Despite these poor results, Roberts saw great potential, both in the quality of many of the new enquiries approaching the party but also in untapped areas of support like Lewisham.

Roberts had a brother who was also in the BNP, and two daughters, who had been told in no uncertain terms that no African blood could enter the Roberts bloodline. He told Arthur, in some irritation, that the previous week one of his daughters had announced that she was not going to marry a black man, but instead was going to marry a Jew.

Another new member was Melinda Coalhurst-James, a woman in her 30s with long blond hair. While she appeared new to the party, she was not new to far right politics and was deeply antisemitic and a strong supporter of John Tyndall. She described herself to Arthur as a "National Socialist" and expressed her delight when she saw old photos of Tyndall in his paramilitary uniform and swastika armband.

Coalhurst-James was scathing about most people she met. Bob Gertner was, in her eyes, “a half-red Polack with a Jewish surname” and is “definitely an infiltrator”, whereas Nick Griffin was only “probably an infiltrator”. She was even more derogatory about the South American partner of another BNP member, who she referred to as a “mongrel”. At one BNP meeting, Coalhurst-James almost traded blows with Linda Miller, which resulted in her getting thrown out of the party.

***

On Sunday 9 March 2003, Arthur attended a London-wide BNP meeting which was ostensibly to launch the party’s 2004 Greater London Assembly campaign, but in fact it turned out to be a rally point for all those who felt disaffected and excluded by the ‘new’ BNP. The meeting was held in an upstairs room at The Roding pub, in Newham, with the redirection points being both East Ham and Upney tube stations.

There were 106 people present: Arthur remembered the names of 56 of them when debriefed by Dave. Most of those present were old timers, people who had been in the party as long as Arthur and often longer. In fact, for Arthur, it was as if he had been transported back to his first BNP rally nine years ago. With John Tyndall were his old allies Richard Edmonds, John Morse, Ian Dell and Peterborough-based Joe Gould. From Croydon branch there was Paul Ballard, Steve Wheedon, Frank Walsh and Bob Gertner, while from Lewisham there was Barry Roberts, brother of Chris Roberts, who was also there, and Tess Culnane. From east London BNP branches there were Dave Hill, Ken Francis, Barry Osbourne and Linda and Alex Cooper.

Annoyingly for everyone present, there was a police van parked outside and police were photographing everyone entering and leaving the pub. Dave Hill's fury was evident. He said that the police had rung him a few days before the meeting and asked him where and when the meeting was. When he asked them how they knew about the event, they said that Tony Lecomber had told them.

The meeting was held in a large upstairs room, which had been decked out in flags and posters for the occasion. John Morse was selling the latest copy of *Spearhead*, which had been largely banned from party meetings, and a well-known West Ham football hooligan manned the literature stall, which consisted of back issues of *Spearhead*.

Chris Roberts was the first speaker and largely stuck to script. He spoke about the "enormous opportunity" the BNP had in London, particularly in light of the anger of many Labour voters to the unpopular Iraq war and the continuing disillusionment of many Tory voters. The BNP could provide an alternative outlet for these voters if, and only if, the party could get its act together both with funds and activism. "It is up to you people," he said, looking around the room, "to get everything covered."

Edmonds was up next, and began with a quote from Dickens. "It was the best of times, it was the worst of times," he said, reflecting on the history of Britain and what it had become. Of course, Edmonds being Edmonds, 95% of his speech focused on the worst of times – and in this case the state of the country, mass immigration and tales of black nurses with AIDS working in the NHS. The best times, he concluded, was when people began to fight back and he namechecked the recent successes in Burnley, where the party had three councillors, and Stoke-on-Trent, where the party had come second in the city's mayoral election.

After a short break, which gave the audience a chance to refill their glasses and empty their pockets for the collection, John Morse introduced the main speaker and "founder of the party", John Tyndall. From literally his first sentence, the gloves came off. Arthur reported back to us that Tyndall "gave a very robust and bitter speech attacking the current BNP leadership." However, he didn't mention Griffin's name once, but instead merely made references to "our leadership".

Tyndall was frequently interrupted by applause from the audience, especially after he directly criticised the party leadership. As Arthur recalled at the time: "Very few people did not join in the applause, and throughout there was a real sense that the audience was on his side."

The former party leader began his speech by reminding the audience that he was born in Bromley, so London was very close to my heart. "But like a lot of people," he went on, "I've joined the white flight to Brighton & Hove," which he described as "pooftaville".

"I am determined," he added, "that a homosexual will never stand as a candidate for the BNP."

Then it was on to the real meat of the speech. "For three-and-a-half years I have held my counsel on what is happening in our party, but I can do that no longer." Holding up a copy of the party newspaper, *Freedom*, opened to an article about a BNP candidate with a black son-in-law and mixed race grandchildren, he continued: "I want to make it clear that I have great sympathy for anyone who finds themselves in the position of this unfortunate man. But, according to *Freedom*, we shouldn't feel sympathy for him, we should feel pride that someone with these conditions should be standing for our party. Our Chairman [Griffin] has held himself as a champion of democracy, particularly during the leadership election, but where was the consultation here?

"On the next page we have Mr Singh attacking the idea of religious hate laws. So in other words, he supports the existing race laws and therefore would support the fact that myself, John Morse and other members have been imprisoned for expressing their views.

"I've never been a person who believes we should be completely uncompromising and should go around with badges saying 'I'm a racist' or knocking on doors saying 'hello, I'm your racist candidate'. However, there is a certain point that you can't pass and we've long reached that point. Like other people, I've been imprisoned and beaten up – but I should mention my beating was a mere tickle compared to other peoples – and I have not put up with these things to see Mr Singh writing articles in our party newspaper."

Tyndall concluded his speech with a clear message to the party leadership: "I won't stand for anything less than a totally white London and a totally white Britain." He sat down to an standing ovation from the entire audience. Arthur couldn't ever remember Tyndall, or anyone else in the party for that matter, receiving such an enthusiastic ovation after a speech.

The speech whipped up the audience and many of the questions that followed were related to the party's increasing moderation. "Where is this all going to end?" asked Barry Roberts, Chris's brother. "Will we have black members in the party?" Chris mumbled a response, whilst Tyndall was more forthright. "I really don't think it's in the interests of a party such as this to have black members. It's only going to cause strife."

London activist Paul McHale wanted to know where all this was in the manifesto. Again, Chris Roberts refused to answer and reminded people that this was a meeting to launch the GLA campaign. By now, the audience was in total rebellion and had little time for Chris Roberts' defence of the party. Ray, an elderly activist, started shouting obscenities at the party leadership, with south Londoner Lee, responding by shouting back: "It's the wrong time to be doing this." Just as John Morse appeared to be restoring order, Peter Shaw put up his hand and immediately opened up a new angle of attack. "I've worked in Bournemouth getting things going but the party leadership seem hell-bent on destroying everything." Lee then shouted at Shaw, and a slagging match ensued between Lee, Peter, Ray and an increasingly irate Dave Hill. Amusingly for Arthur, none of them were actually defending Lecomber, who had been a target for much of the abuse, but they simply disliked each other.

Hill then jumped on the stage and said people were reluctant to name names and they seemed to think they shouldn't make it personal, "but I'll name one name, and that's Tony Lecomber.

"Tony Lecomber accused me of being an MI5 agent," he continued, to a stunned audience. "I've been through a lot this year. I've got an iron gate in front of my door, and Tony Lecomber's a convicted bomber!" He then proceeded to demand a show of hands against Lecomber and people began raising their hands, before Roberts stepped in and stopped it in its tracks. "This is not a meeting against Tony Lecomber or Nick Griffin," he pleaded, "This is about the GLA." Luckily for him, Tyndall backed him up and the room returned to order once more.

Matters only got worse for Roberts after he took home the evening's collection, which Dave Hill and others objected to, fearing that the money would not find its way into the GLA campaign fund. Hill went round to collect it, much to Lecomber's objection and he instructed Roberts not to hand over the money because "Hill is a thief". Undeterred, Hill went round, this time accompanied by his mate, big burly Bob James, and literally just took or stole the funds (depending on which version you wanted to believe). Lecomber was furious, and demanded that Roberts make a statement to the police. However, it seemed as though Hill had got there first and made his own complaint about Roberts. Fearing arrest, Hill quickly passed the £200 onto someone else in the BNP, who paid it in to their account, thus heading off any police investigation.

The BNP got their revenge though and expelled both Hill and James from the party. As a final dig, they revealed James's real name as Robert Jeffries.

***

Under Griffin, the BNP dispensed of the longstanding Annual Rally for a three-day event called the Red, White and Blue festival, based on a similar event held by Jean-Marie Le Pen's Front National in France. The first took place near Oswestry, in Shropshire, in August 2000 and was attended by only a couple of hundred people. The second was held on farmland near Llanerfyl, on adjacent land to Griffin's own property in Wales. Arthur was one of about 300 people who made the trip, though arriving at the venue was not easy as police had set up two roadblocks on the approaching roads to collect everyone's details, checking them against a list of ticket holders that Nick Griffin had supplied to police beforehand. Some even had their vehicles searched. Souring the mood of attendees even more was the incessant rain, which seemed to fall over the entire weekend and meant that many of the planned activities were cancelled.

The speeches were as to be expected, with most predicting great things for the party in the very near future. Mick Treacy, the party's Oldham organiser, spoke about how in 2000 the BNP only had two members in the town and now they were counting votes in their thousands. The person giving the Scottish report was actually English and the London report was made by someone Arthur had never seen before.

The evening's entertainment kicked off with a children's play about a wild boar that terrorized the people of Durham, until the animal was slain. The only problem was that the kids appeared scared of the narrator, a role carried out by a Darlington BNP member, and so when he put the microphone to their faces they appeared reluctant to talk. The (English) Scottish organiser recited an Old Welsh poem, which he claimed was the oldest British poem. Kitted out in a kilt and Celtic attire, he held a spear which he kept thumping on stage for dramatic effect. However, this was rather spoilt when he hit Griffin with the spear by mistake. Few people ventured outside for the fireworks display, and those who did quickly returned.

The highlight of the evening was Stigger, a guitarist who had been a key performer on the Blood & Honour circuit for many years. After performing several ballards, some of which he dedicated to the BNP, he was urged to perform some Skrewdriver covers, the most infamous white power band he performed in with legendary frontman Ian Stuart Donaldson. Many in the audience roared with delight as Stigger sang *'Hail Victory'*, and shot out their right arms in nazi salutes. Others, including Griffin, gave V for victory salutes, though as their right hands were stretched out in front of them, it looked like a sea of Sieg Heiling.

The evening got worse as the music gave way to comedy. Chris Telford, an activist from the north east, was introduced by Griffin himself: "He's not red or white, he's blue." With that, Telford began a stream of racist and sexist gags. However, the loudest laughter was when someone in the audience shouted "taxi for one please!" after one particularly unfunny joke. The show descended into chaos as the microphone was passed around the crowd and people took turns in telling jokes. At first they were all racist jokes about blacks and Asians, but as soon as people got more confident they moved onto antisemitic jokes, including some about the Holocaust. West London activist, Warren Glass, made one particularly unpleasant joke when he said: "A man with a crocodile walks into a pub and asks 'do you serve niggers?' The landlord says yes, so the man says 'well, I'll have a pint, and a nigger for the crocodile." Griffin was present throughout and laughed as much as anyone.

The event the following year was substantially bigger and much more successful. This was held in Swaley, Lancashire, not too far from Burnley. Arthur estimated that there were over a thousand people in attendance, making it easily the party biggest event he had been at. The setup was also much more professional than the previous year, with a large marquee erected for the main speeches and a large campsite nearby. Two burger vans replaced the one from the previous year, and there was also another van serving a hog roast. The Saturday entertainment was also certainly less interesting, but it was also of a far lower quality.

Nick Griffin's speech was billed as the highlight of the weekend, and he arrived to classical music and the audience chanting 'Nick Griffin's Nationalist Army.'

Quite modestly, he said that it wasn't his nationalist army but that of the party members. He claimed that the BNP was now the party of old Labour, while also encompassing the patriotism of the Conservatives. He attacked the Iraq war, even offering sympathy to those civilians being killed in the Allied attacks and promised a future BNP government would buy conventional crops from Afghan famers so they wouldn't have to grow opium. The speech ended with a rendition of Jerusalem and the release of 1,000 balloons.

Of course, the event wouldn't have been complete without its internal tensions and infighting. London Regional Organiser Chris Roberts didn't come because he had fallen out with Griffin, while North West London organiser Ian Edward said that if he had turned up he would have only got drunk and punched the BNP leader. John Merritt told Arthur that he had largely dropped out of the BNP after Ballard accused him of being an infiltrator.

***

Within unrest in the air and the whiff of rebellion getting every stronger, Griffin and Lecomber decided to finally move against Tyndall in a mid to pre-empt a leadership challenge. For added measure they also planned to expel Richard Edmonds and John Morse, the three men who ran the party until 1999.

The decision was taken at an extended BNP Advisory Council meeting in July 2003 and within three days an organisers bulletin was sent out detailing the charges. Six charges were levied against Tyndall, including being a disruptive and undermining influence in the party and of conspiring to produce and distribute *Spearhead,* a publication that had been proscribed earlier in the year.

Far from emerging out of a position of power, Griffin's actions appeared to be the work of a panicked man. While Tyndall had long been an irritant to Griffin, he had always been careful to direct his criticism towards the leadership while preaching loyalty to the party. Griffin had obviously hoped that Tyndall would walk of his own volition at the party's increasingly moderate tone, but he did not and in the end, against the backdrop of growing disquiet at his leadership, Griffin felt forced to push him out.

Griffin and Lecomber had become increasingly concerned in recent months at the growing disillusionment among many party members towards the leadership. While they would have expected nothing less from the decreasing number of Tyndallites left in the party, this unease had spread to formerly loyal activists.

In Scotland, the Edinburgh organiser, David Edgar, and Glasgow stalwart, Steve Cartwright, had both resigned in disgust over the party's adoption of candidates with black relatives. The London region had become a virtual no-go area for Griffin and the thoroughly-despised Lecomber. All bar two of the London organisers signed a petition drawn up by Chris Roberts calling on Griffin to remove Lecomber from any position of influence over London and Essex BNP.

Making matters worse was the feeling among many London activists that the following year's Mayoral and London Assembly elections would be largely

Eddie Izzard adds his support to the HOPE not hate campaign

ignored by a leadership obsessed with prioritising the European elections. It was no coincidence, some said, that Griffin was keen to make the European elections a priority because he was due to top the party's list in the North West.

Even in the South West, a strong pro-Griffin region, there were murmurings of discontent towards Lecomber. His rude and abrasive manner was thoroughly disliked among local organisers. But it was in the all-important North West region where opposition was reaching fever pitch. Burnley, Clitheroe, Pendle, Bolton, Rochdale and Stockport BNP branches were all led by organisers hostile to Griffin. In Blackburn, it was only Lecomber's intervention on two separate occasions that prevented local activists deposing Robin Evans, a Griffin loyalist and local councillor, from his position as branch organiser. The first move to oust Evans, supported by branch organisers from across Lancashire, contributed to the resignation of Chris Jackson as regional organiser.

Even more alarming for the party leadership was the rapturous reception given to Tyndall when he spoke at a Halifax BNP meeting in June. Sharing the platform with Tyndall was Richard Mulhall, one of the party's two councillors in the town.

Ill-feeling towards the party leadership was made even worse by the increasingly antagonistic behaviour of Tony Lecomber. Never known for his social skills,

Lecomber became even more divisive and confrontational, dismissing people's concerns, being rude and unhelpful to new members and organisers and increasingly vindictive. Ken Francis, who had become another critic of Griffin, was expelled from the party for having a South American partner, though she had been around for years and even been to party meetings.

Less than a month after the charges were issued, John Tyndall was formally expelled from the BNP. An internal tribunal, held in Chigwell, Essex, heard seven charges against the former leader but the result was never really in any doubt. While four of the charges were dropped during the hearing, and he was found not guilty on another, he was still convicted on two others. Tony Lecomber, the key instigator behind the expulsion, was prosecuting. The four-man jury was led by Tony MacDonnell, a Leeds activist and hooligan, who would go on to be imprisoned for manslaughter.

Most of the charges revolved around the claim that Tyndall was deliberately undermining the party through his continuing attacks on the leadership in his publication *Spearhead*. Tyndall's defence that his articles reflected a political attack on the policies and the leadership, rather than the BNP as a whole, fell on deaf ears. A few days later he was informed in writing that he was no longer a member of the party.

Surprisingly, reaction to Tyndall's expulsion was muted, even in the London region, where support for the party founder was strong. During yet another all-London BNP meeting in early August, designed to relaunch the GLA campaign after the debacle of the earlier effort, feelings were high but few seemed prepared to raise Tyndall's expulsion publicly (probably because Lecomber and his close supporters were present and taking notes). The only comment that Arthur overheard was North West London organiser Ian Edward telling Lecomber that he feared some of the party's donors would refuse to give more money in protest.

"Well, fuck them!" was Lecomber's strong reply. He went on to say that "losers like that will drop away and the party would do quite well without them".

"We can do without [Tyndall's] disruptive influence and his poison."

Tyndall took the party to court and the leadership was forced to relent and readmit him back into the party, though this was to be a short-lived reprieve. The following year, Tyndall was secretly recorded making a speech at a BNP meeting in which he claimed that Asians and Africans had only produced "black magic, witchcraft, voodoo, cannibalism and Aids" and accusing Michael Howard, the Jewish leader of the Conservative Party, of being an "interloper, this immigrant or son of immigrants, who has no roots at all in Britain". This gave Griffin the excuse he needed to finally expel Tyndall from the party, and this time for good.

John Tyndall returned to his seaside home at Hove; he later died of a heart attack in July 2005.

A multicultural crowd celebrate the London being awarded the 2012 Olympics

CHAPTER FIFTEEN: END GAME

The launch of the Greater London Assembly (GLA) electoral campaign, which quickly descended into an anti-Griffin rally, was just a temporary setback to the party's plans in London. There was another 'launch' rally a few months later and, under Chris Roberts' stewardship, the party began to get itself into better shape. The combination of better organisation and an influx of new members in the aftermath of their electoral successes in the north of England saw several new branches spring up across the capital. Roberts was optimistic about the BNP's chances of getting the 5% required to secure a seat on the GLA, so we encouraged Arthur to learn as much as he could about their plans. Fortunately he was well-placed to do this, especially after he was asked to attend the regular London Organisers meetings, established to help coordinate the campaign.

The first such meeting he went to was in June 2003, held in the upstairs room of the Morpeth Arms, just 10 minutes walk from Parliament. The 25 people in attendance included local branch organisers, key party officials and a handful of seasoned activists. Croydon activist Bob Gertner chaired the meeting and there was a buzz of excitement to the idea, raised by several speakers, that the party could actually get two to three people elected. The meeting was generally good natured, except for obvious tensions between Eddy Butler and Tony Lecomber.

While much of the groundwork for the party's revival in London was down to Roberts, a new activist was emerging who was to play an ever more significant role: south London-based Richard Barnbrook. Barnbrook was not the typical BNP Arthur had got to know over the preceding 10 years. There was no obvious far right or antisemitic baggage: as a teacher and having a background in the arts, Barnbrook was culturally on a different level. That didn't mean he was without faults or annoying behaviour, of course.

At another London Organisers meeting held in December 2003, Barnbrook seemed in full control of the campaign. Chris Roberts had fallen out with Nick Griffin and was no longer fulfilling the role of London Organiser, and so Barnbrook, who was the London Development Officer, seamlessly moved into the role. However his dictatorial style, which included having a clock on the table in front of him to ensure they stuck to the allotted time for each item discussion, irritated everyone, including Tony Lecomber. If that wasn't bad enough, Barnbrook had brought with him an anti-bugging device, which had cost him £12.99. He switched it on and waved it around the room, and it proceeded to buzz incessantly. Everyone laughed. Either the room was bugged, the device was useless or Barnbrook simply did not know how to use it. Everyone had their own thoughts, and none were complimentary.

***

The British National Party gained 90,365 votes in the London Assembly elections of 2004, but with a 4.8% share of the vote it was just short of the 5% required to get elected onto the Assembly. While this was up from the 2.9% the party obtained in 2000, it was well short of what it had hoped or where it expected to be. Julian Leppert, the party's London Mayoral candidate, received 58,407 votes, a 3.1% share. Again, this was less than expected. In the European elections held on the same day, the BNP polled 76,152 votes, a 4% share.

It was quite a turnaround in fortunes for the BNP. When Arthur first joined, in the summer of 1994, the party was still basking in the success of its Millwall council victory nine months before and east London appeared to offer the BNP its best electoral prospects. Now, London was one of its weakest areas. Of the nine European election regions, only the South West and South East delivered smaller shares of the vote for the BNP than London.

***

The BNP had only just missed out on a seat on the GLA, but to us that was a massive success. Four months previously, we had agreed with Arthur that keeping the BNP off the GLA was going to be his last mission for us. He had been inside the far right for 10 years now and it was time to move on. Amid the huge successes over the years, such as identifying Copeland and causing havoc inside London BNP, there had been times when he doubted what he was doing and wanted to call it a day. And who could blame him. He had gone in as an anti-fascist in 1994 to expose and damage the BNP, which he had done brilliantly, but it was now time for him to get on with his life.

The BNP of 2004 was also quite different to the one he had joined in 1994. Back then, virtually everyone was a hardline national socialist and antisemite, racism was widespread and violence was woven into BNP members' DNA. Ten years on, the BNP had a degree of respectability. Whatever they now privately thought, publicly the party had withdrawn its policy of compulsory repatriation and was simply refusing to answer questions on the Holocaust, claiming it was ancient history. While many, like Griffin and Collett, were still clearly fascists, many of the newer recruits - especially those who joined after 2001 - were not. Racial nationalism had been replaced with concern over Muslims and in the post-9/11 world, the far right didn't seem so extreme or separated from the mainstream right. The BNP did not now seem as much as a threat in Arthur's eyes, and the excitement of infiltrating it had gone. Compounding that, many of the people who he had been close to over the course of his infiltration, including some he considered his friends, had long departed the party, so his outings amid new and